STOLEN DESIRE

The Desire Series book 7

BARBARA DONLON BRADLEY

ONE

Heather sighed as she opened her eyes and stretched. Before she could move, she felt a warm hand on her breast. It thrilled her that Storm always wanted her.

"I see you're awake." Storm's breath brushed against her cheek. His fingers traced the edge of her jaw.

She looked up at her mate, who had a knowing smile on his face. Heather smiled back. "And I see you are awake too." She was referring to the erection pressed against her hip.

"True, but I can't help it when I have such a wonderful partner lying beside me." Storm nibbled against her throat. "We still have time before we need to be anywhere."

"Why didn't you wake me earlier?" She shifted to accommodate him as he settled himself between her thighs. "You could have had all the time you want if you had."

"Because the twins aren't allowing you to sleep enough yet. I don't mind watching you sleep when I know you need it. It gives me time to appreciate having you in my life." He dipped his head to her mark. "And waking you up this way is an anticipation I look forward to. I don't mind stretching that moment out a little."

"Because you know what will happen when I wake." She tilted her head so he could have access to her mark.

"That is the best part."

She felt him smile against her neck as he pulled the soft tissue of her mark into his mouth before he worked his way down her body.

"You are incorrigible."

"And that is why I'm your heart." His tongue lathed her nipple before drawing the tip into his mouth. She arched up against him and he slipped his hands under her.

A growl escaped him when they were interrupted by the computer system. "Heather, you have a communiqué from Admiral Barrister."

She sighed again. This time in frustration. What did he want now?

"The last time he contacted us you ended up being whipped." Storm blew against the tip before he climbed back up her body. "I'm inclined to not let you answer him."

"Storm, I'm still part of Earth's security." She looked up at him, his face only inches above hers. "I can't ignore him."

"Fine, but you're not getting out of this bed until I say so." He rolled off her and helped her sit up and settle herself against him. "Put him on, Cim."

"Sir." She adjusted the cover to make sure she didn't expose herself.

"Commander, sorry if I interrupted something, but we need to talk, in person."

"Sir?" What was so important that he wanted them to make a trip to Earth. "You know it's not that easy for me to step away from my duties here."

"I know, but I have something to show you that you need to see." Bear pressed a key and changed the image they were looking at. The new picture was a holding cell. Inside was a woman who looked a whole lot like Heather. "Before you ask, I ran DNA tests against the data you gave me. She is you."

"That isn't possible." She suddenly felt cold.

"Tell that to her." Bear switched the image back to him. "Needless to say, this was something I didn't want Earth security to investigate too deeply so I pretended she was you. I'm on my way to Vespia and will need clearance in about fifteen minutes."

"We'll meet you at the landing port." Storm closed the communiqué and was the first one up. "I don't like this at all."

"We need to contact Bert as well. Perhaps he could shed a little light on what is going on." Heather stood as well. With a thought, they were both dressed. She loved that they found the underground ancient computer a while ago. It allowed her and Storm to remove or add their clothes with a thought.

Heather stepped into the twins' bedroom to find them still asleep. She touched their heads softly before she walked back into the main room where Storm waited. "They're sound asleep."

"Then let's go." He placed his hand against the small of her back as they headed out the doors. "I have given Bear clearance to land and contacted Bert to join us. Your brother has been made aware as well, so he'll be here when the twins wake up."

"Thank you." She kept her thoughts to herself.

"You okay?"

"Yes, my heart." Heather wrapped an arm around his waist and gave him a quick hug. "Just want to know what is going on."

"So do I, my heart."

They walked onto the tarmac and waited as Bear's ship touched down.

Storm looked down at her upturned face as he pulled her close. She knew he picked up on the fact that she was tense and far too quiet. "I know this bothers you. Your silence tells me more than any words. I want to know why there is a woman in Bear's ship who looks like you, too. Together we will get to the truth."

"I wish Bear had told us more. Why is she, me here? What happened to force me to travel back in time?"

"My question as well." They had come to the same conclusion. The woman in question was probably from the future which didn't bode well. She knew he could smell her fear and wrapped his arms around her in support. "I'm sure he will explain everything he knows, and your brother and Bert will explain the rest."

———

"I don't know what to tell you," said Bear. They stood outside the room where Heather's look-a-like paced the floor. "She came to me, claiming to be you, but from our near future with a message. Then she refused to speak after that."

"Who is the message for?" asked Storm.

"You." He looked at Heather. "Look, I tried to get her to talk to me, but she refused. She promised to explain everything once she saw Heather, which is why I brought her here. I didn't know what else to do."

"You did the right thing, Bear. I'll talk to her and see what is going on."

"I don't think so." Storm shook his head. After all they had been through, he didn't trust anyone, and that included an exact copy of his mate.

"Then how are we to know why she is here?" Heather looked at him.

"Storm, that woman has been quite adamant about talking to your mate. Heather number two has also promised to go through any tests you might want her to go through as long as you allow her to speak to herself." Bear shook his head. "It's all a little strange to me."

Kuarto walked into the medlab. "Really wish you would stay put when you call me. I went to the landing area as you requested and was told you had come here. This is where I was in the first place."

"Sorry," said Heather. "We needed to move indoors rather quickly."

"What is so important that you..." He spotted the other Heather. "Never mind. I'm assuming you want me to check out your guest?"

"Please?" Heather rubbed her hands on her skirt, her nerves taking control. "We need to get to the bottom of this."

Kuarto walked into the room where his sister's look-a-like waited. Heather watched as he ran his tests. Where did this woman come from? Why was she here? He was frowning when he came back out.

"She is you. The DNA proves it, but she is also older than you. About six weeks." He kept looking at his readings. "I don't know how this is possible."

"Thank you." Heather knew. This version of her had time-traveled. She didn't like the rock that was forming in the pit of her stomach. Something must have gone horribly wrong for her to come back in time. "Let's find out what I have to say."

Storm wrapped his arm around her waist to keep her at his side. "Wait for Bert. If that really is you then you know the consequences of getting too close to yourself."

———

Bert walked in and slowed his step when he spotted the second Heather. "Can I assume you called me because of her?"

"Yes." Storm looked at the other Heather for a moment. "She says she's Heather, but from the future."

"And the reason she's here?"

"We're not sure. I wanted my mate to wait until you had a chance to protect her before she spoke to herself."

Bert nodded and entered the room the other Heather occupied.

"Hello."

"How are you, Heather?" He had his back to her as he started working on the computer to create a shield to keep the women safe.

She looked out the window to where her counterpart stood. "I could be better. Who are you?"

Bert blinked. She didn't know who he was? He turned to look at her. "You don't know me?"

"Are you a visiting physician? I don't always meet them. My schedule keeps me quite busy."

"I am. I thought you would know me since I have been here for several months. I have seen you, her, several times since I've been here." He turned away from her to continue to work on the shield. So, *this* Heather didn't know him. Could she be from an alternate universe? A clone? Something wasn't right. "Kuarto asked me to try a new force field to protect you two from each other."

"That's probably a good idea. I wouldn't want to harm myself."

He pressed a button and covered her in the force field. "How does that feel?"

"I don't feel anything."

"Good. I'll let Heather and Storm know that." He stepped out of the room and walked up to Heather. "She doesn't know who I am."

"Not at all?" Heather looked at the other her.

"She thought I was a visiting physician working with your brother and she didn't question the fact that I was building a force field to protect you two from each other."

"That doesn't make sense, Bert. According to the readings, she's me from the future. She should know who you are." Heather rubbed her forehead. "Instead of getting answers, we're getting more questions."

"I'll take your brother's data and let you know what I find."

———

Bert sealed the second Heather in a force field then followed Heather in when she went to talk to herself.

"This is very strange." Heather watched the woman who looked just like her. She hated not knowing what was going on. Hopefully, she'd get answers now.

"I know, but I didn't know what else to do." The second Heather looked at Bert for a moment then switched the language so they were speaking ancient. It was obvious she didn't want Storm picking up on the conversation and had no clue Bert could speak it. "Our future is at stake."

"Why are you here?"

"To stop something horrible." She looked around before focusing back on Heather. "I know I have to prove myself first. You don't trust me, and I don't blame you, but our future is at stake."

"You said that before. What are you trying to stop?" She hadn't gotten any visions yet. What could be so bad she would travel back in time? And how did she do it if she didn't know Bert? "Why aren't you just telling me?"

"Because you won't believe me. I still can't believe it." She gave Heather a sad smile. "I know your mate as well as you do, and he won't believe any of this without proof. Run your tests. Once you're happy with your readings I'll explain everything."

———

"Why did she speak to you in ancient? I couldn't understand her," Storm asked Heather when they made it back to their room. He wasn't a happy man. He paced in front of her, his frustration radiating off him.

"Because she knew you'd eavesdrop in on our conversation. She also did it to help prove she is me. If that was an imposter, she never would have been able to talk to me in a language so few know. But she doesn't know Bert and that worries me." She stood and pressed her hand against his heart, stopping him in his tracks. "She told me she came back to right a wrong, but she wants to prove she is legitimate first. I want to give her the benefit of the doubt for now."

"I don't like this. There are only so many things that would cause you to go back and try to change the outcome." He touched her face, sliding his fingers along her jaw. "None of them make me happy."

"Then perhaps we should do something that will make you happy." She wanted to keep him from thinking about it too much. Trying to guess why she had traveled back in time could cause more havoc than the real reason she came back.

"I can think of a few things that make me very happy." He wrapped his arms around her waist. "They all include the two of us."

"And lack of clothing?"

"Depends on what you are wearing under your gown." He gave her a bone-melting smile. "Anything to take my mind off what your other self's presence probably means?"

"I didn't think ahead, but I can change that quickly." She smiled up at him as the computer added what she knew he liked. "I think it will help you get your mind off the current issue."

"Is it red?" he asked. He let go with one arm and slipped his hand inside the bodice of her dress. "It's definitely lace. That is always a good sign."

Heather laughed. She opened the seals of his uniform, sliding her hands over his chest as she exposed it. He needed to forget everything but the two of them. Maybe make him lose control for a moment or two. Those were moments she lived for.

"You are trying to distract me, aren't you?"

"You're my heart, and I love touching you." Her fingers skimmed across the contours of his muscles. "And I know how to distract you if that is what you want."

"Yes, you do." He opened the seams of her dress and grinned when he revealed the lingerie she had on. "You are very good at it."

She wore his favorite. The red lace of the bra and panty did little to cover her, but by the glow brightening in his eyes, he didn't care. It did what it was supposed to do, make him forget for a moment. His hands skimmed across her exposed skin, causing little goosebumps to rise.

"I love it when you dress like this for me." His fingers skirted along the edge of the waistband. She felt it to her toes. "It shows how much you care."

"You are my heart, and I want to keep you happy." She slid her hands up around his neck. "You know what makes me happy and you strive to achieve that every time you touch me. Why wouldn't I return the favor?"

He laughed as he dipped his head to her mark. "Right. And you're just doing it out of the goodness of your heart. You're as addicted to our intimacy as I am. Admit it."

The press of his lips to her mark had her sighing. She didn't need to say a thing. He knew the truth. His hands skimmed across the lace covering her, igniting her need. His touch had her wanting him inside her. "Storm."

"Soon, my heart. I wish to stimulate my playground first."

Heather felt his fingers at her core as he kissed his way down to her breast. Her head dropped back at the double attack. "Yes, but you're making my knees weak and I'm going to melt into a puddle at your feet in a moment."

"No, you won't." He wrapped one arm around her waist to help her keep her feet and he continued to pay homage to her, moving them slowly to the bed. He lifted her up and laid her on the bed as he slid two fingers inside her.

She moaned as her muscles tightened against him. The crotch-less panties allowed him complete access to her body without having to remove them.

"Oh, my heart." He nibbled his way back up to her lips, drinking from them as his hands skimmed over her, caressing the spots that pushed her closer to her release. He eased himself over her, then in one quick stroke, filled her.

She arched up against him. Her legs slid up his thighs to wrap around his hips. Heather's hands caressed his mark, making him shake a little.

"You aren't fighting fair." Storm touched her face as he set a pace for them. When her muscles contracted again, he shuddered.

"Can't help it. I was taught by a very good teacher." Her

words came out like a sigh. She shifted her hips and shuddered when he stroked just the right spot. "So close."

His lips latched onto her mark, and it started the beginning of her release. She felt it build as her blood raced through her veins. Then it unfurled inside, sending her flying out to the stars. She let go of her breath. "I never get tired of that."

"Hope not. I'm addicted too and you're the only one I want to share this with."

"That isn't very Vespian." But she loved hearing him say that. Vespian society allowed multiple partners.

"Don't care. I never had a partner that gives so openly the way you do." He pressed another kiss against her mark. "And that has spoiled me."

———

Heather stared at the other her. The woman from the future hadn't told her why she was here yet and that bothered her. Too many things weren't adding up. She wished she had Storm's strength with her, but he was with the twins at the moment, as per her request. He was going to drop them off with his mother then join her.

She didn't like the feeling she was having. One of impending doom. Not having any visions yet surprised her, but she bet they would start soon. Heather took a deep breath and walked into the lab her duplicate had been moved to. Bert stood in front of a monitor, watching the readings displayed there. He had been keeping his distance from the other Heather since they learned she didn't know him.

"Anything?"

"Only more questions." He turned toward Heather. "I've run a few more tests to get more detail. They take a little longer than a standard test so I'm still waiting. Something isn't quite right here, but I don't know enough to guide you one way or the other. Just be careful."

She nodded. Storm wanted to be there, but she had talked him into watching the twins because she wasn't sure if her other self would talk if he was around. Now she wasn't sure that was a smart move. Heather took a deep breath. She needed to focus. This would give her a few moments alone with herself. If she didn't take advantage of the time, then this Heather could suspect they were up to something. Since they hadn't had time to come up with a plan of any sort, she needed to act like nothing was wrong.

Heather entered the room and sat down. "You said you wanted to prove you are the real thing. How do you plan on doing that?"

"Has Kuarto run his tests?"

"Most of them, yes. We're still waiting for a few more."

"Then you have proof I'm you."

Heather nodded. The woman had to know that a simple DNA test told them that within an hour of her arrival. Why was she acting like she didn't know? "But you haven't explained why you're here."

She clasped her hands in front of her and rested them on the table she sat at. "In six days, there will be a ship approaching Vespia. Storm will greet them with guns blazing."

Heather couldn't help but smile at that. "Is that the problem? Is that why you came back?"

"Partially." She looked at Heather. "Understand that we've been through this several times. You don't remember, but I do."

"What are you saying?"

"There are several events we need to avoid. The first one is our new guests. They're not here to cause trouble. They need our help and that is why they're coming here. The first time Storm greeted them he started a war that would eventually destroy Vespia."

Heather sat back. A war? Why hadn't she had a vision showing her that? "What sort of help do they need?"

"They will explain it in time and I'm afraid to tell you too much. Dealing with timelines is hard to do. Once we make that first change to the future I come from I'll explain more."

"I hope so. You know my mate as well as I do, and he doesn't like being kept in the dark." She stood then and walked out. Heather stopped near Bert. "Figure it out fast, Bert. Please."

"I will."

———

Skye sat in a bar, watching Sam work as a waitress. He was undercover as a traveling purchaser looking for the rare and exotic. His boss was well-known, and money was no object. They were following a lead Bert had given them to track down one of the ancients. From what they had learned the man came into the bar frequently and would be looking for buyers such as himself.

He had been approached several times since arriving at the bar, and after receiving Bert's approval through the insert, he had acquired a few things to show he was for real.

The man they were waiting for walked in and Skye had to stare. He looked just like Storm with blonde hair. The resemblance was uncanny. Skye caught himself and looked away, hoping he hadn't been too obvious.

I need to call you back from your mission.

Skye had gotten used to the insert so Bert's voice in his head didn't startle him the way it did when he first got the stupid thing. *Our target just walked in. All we need is a few hours.*

Hurry, Skye. You're both needed here.

Sam came over to his table and picked up his empty glass. "Another?"

"Maybe in a minute."

"Boss says if you're not drinking, you're not staying. I'll bring you a new one." She looked over at the man who looked so much like her father. "The boss wants to know why you've been sitting here for so long. Most come in, drink, and leave."

"I'm meeting someone."

"Yeah. He's heard that too many times to believe it." Sam ran her fingers along the tray she held. "He wants proof."

"And how am I supposed to do that?" Skye frowned. This was a wrinkle he didn't want.

"He wants you to get something for him. That is your job, isn't it? To buy unique things?"

"I already have a boss." He looked up at her. "And if your boss wishes me to spend my credits somewhere else I can."

"It is only a bauble he wants and if you're good then this will be easy to do." She gave him an apologetic smile.

Skye stood. "I have heard this before. It will be easy, it's not a big thing. It will only take you a minute. That is a lie. If it was that easy your boss would have already gotten this little bauble of his."

"He has offered me as payment."

That stopped him. No one had the right to force his bondmate to have sex with anyone. "And how do you feel about that?"

"I'm not being forced into this, and I do find you attractive." She rested her hand against her hip. "Unless you don't like women of other species?"

"Oh, honey, you are something I could fantasize about." He sat back down. "But I must warn you. After being with me you won't want anything but more."

She laughed at that as she set a piece of paper on the table. "This is what he wants."

"I'll see what I can do." He flipped the paper open and wanted to laugh. The man wanted a small teddy bear. "This won't take very long. Does your boss have a small child?"

"Three, actually. Do what you can. I have other tables to take care of."

She walked to the man they were looking for. Skye could hear her speak to their target and had angled his chair so he could see most of her tables.

"Ready to order?" Sam asked the man.

"Who's the man you were just talking to?" He seemed nervous.

"Just a merchant. He says he's looking for the rare and exotic." Sam looked back at Skye. "He's a little cocky but nice enough."

"And you? You're new."

"Yeah. Just got here. Couldn't make a living at home and the owner was willing to give me a chance." She shifted her tray. "And he doesn't like it when I spend too much time with anyone if they don't order."

"The bartender knows what I want."

"Ah." She smiled. "Then I'll be right back."

After picking up the drinks, she dropped Skye's off. He grabbed her arm before she could bring the other man his drink. "Tell your boss what he wants is on its way to his home and I have included something for the other two children. Let him know the next time he does something like

15

this the person he makes such demands of might not be as forgiving as I am."

She nodded and continued to the other man's table. "Anything else?"

"Not right now."

Sam smiled and set his drink down. She passed by Skye and headed to her boss. Sam gave him his message. His face lost color as she relayed the threat. He looked over at Skye before speaking to her.

He wondered if the man told her she had to go with him when he left. It would work in their favor when they headed back, but it still bothered him that the owner had the audacity to offer Sam as a prize. Skye continued to sit there, ignoring everyone around him. This needed to end quickly, but how were they going to get their target to admit he was an ancient if they didn't even approach him?

———

"So you know nothing new?" The thunderous look on Storm's face would have frightened anyone else, but Heather knew him too well to let it bother her.

"Only that we will have visitors soon. I'm not any happier than you are, my heart, but until we have more information, I feel we need to pretend we believe my copy. Something tells me not to give her any reason to think she's failing her mission." Heather pressed her hand against his heart. "I would have thought I would be open about why I came back in time, and I don't know why my other self hasn't done it yet. She has a reason, but I don't like the lump that has settled in my stomach. Bert's tests are almost done. We will take the proper precautions once Bert tells us everything he has learned, but for now please do your normal growling but don't act like she is a threat."

"I want you safe."

"I know and I am. I haven't had any visions showing any of us in danger. What if she is for real? I might be hesitant about explaining my reason for being back here too if I was afraid that I could be the reason it happened. What if I revealed too much and changed the future to a point where it isn't recognizable?"

"That is all hearsay."

"Really? What about the butterfly effect?"

"Butterfly effect? Are you talking about the time travel theory from Earth?"

"Yes. There are several. The paradox where you go back in time to kill your grandfather so you never get born so how can you go back in time and kill your grandfather?"

"I don't like it. I would have come, told you what you needed to know, and gone back home. But she's stringing us along as if she has an agenda to keep. Have you asked her how she plans on going back to her own timeline?"

"No. And before you berate me for not asking her ten thousand questions, I want to see what she volunteers. If she is a plant, then the less we say the safer we are."

"So you are questioning if she is from our future too?"

"Yes." Heather touched his jaw. "Not knowing if she is from another timeline and reality or telling the truth about being from our future has me second-guessing everything. Bert is working on getting at the truth. For now, she has to believe we're taking her at face value. I don't want to tip our hand until we're sure she's a fake."

––––––

Skye sat and watched their target on the shiny surface opposite of him. He felt something the moment the man walked in. It reminded him of how he felt when he met

Bert. Looking back, he had noticed something when he met Sam and Heather. Could ancients spot each other?

The man got up out of his chair and came over to his table. "I hear you're looking for me."

"What makes you say that?" Skye looked at the man as he sat in a vacant chair at his table.

"Our waitress said you like to buy the exotic and that is what I sell." He rested his hands on the table as he settled in his chair. "But you really don't buy anything, do you?"

Skye wasn't sure what to say to that. "My boss sent me here because he heard this was the place to get some rare ancient artifacts."

"Ancient? Hmm, you're the same as me." He narrowed his eyes. "Or at least close. So is your girlfriend."

Skye watched as the man studied Sam. She started toward their table, but he gave her the look that told her to stay away.

"Your girlfriend can come over here. I won't harm either of you, but I would like to know why you're here and who sent you."

"Bert and Dian sent us to find you."

"Bert and Dian? She is alive?" He seemed hopeful for a moment before he shook his head. "Can't. Can't let her catch me."

"Her?" What was he talking about? "Bert wants you to come back. He's been searching for every ancient he can find."

"He won't find too many of us." He looked at his hands for a moment. "Tell Bert thank you, but I prefer to stay out here."

"He's going to want to know why. You were assigned to protect the royal family. What could have forced you to abandon your post?"

"You don't want to know."

"And what am I to tell Bert?" This wasn't going the way he wanted it.

"That our worst nightmares have become reality." With that the man got up and walked out of the bar.

Sam came over the moment he left. "What happened?"

"I'm not sure, but we need to get back."

"I want to stay."

"What?" He frowned. "Why?"

"Maybe he'll come back." She wiped down his table as she picked up his glass. "We need to know why he left."

"Bert wants us to get back to Vespia. Something has happened."

"I need a day. Let me talk to him and I'll be home."

He didn't want to leave her, she was his bond-mate and he needed to protect her, yet if he told her no, she'd think he didn't believe she could take care of herself. "I'll give you twenty-four hours, Earth time. If you aren't in my arms by that point, I'll be back here to get you."

"Promise."

———

Bert was working on a computer simulation when Skye walked in. "Glad to have you back. Where is Sam?"

"She's trying to convince your friend to come home. She should be here within the day." He looked at the screen. "Another experiment?"

"Sort of. We have a visitor that has sent up a bunch of red flags."

"A normal day with Heather and Storm." Skye studied the data.

Bert laughed. More information streamed across the screen.

"Is that temporal simulation?"

"Very good." He smiled as he turned to face Skye. "Yes. I'm running simulations on it to see why we have our guest."

"Why would your guest cause you to check timelines?" Skye leaned on the counter where Bert was working.

"Because our guest is Heather." He pointed to an image on one of the screens.

"I'm not sure I understand."

"It seems that something happened in the near future that caused Heather to come back in time to warn us."

"You mean there's two of them?" Skye looked at the image and shook his head. "You're trying to figure out how to avoid it?"

"Sort of." He continued to work on the data.

"Sort of?"

"There are some anomalies with the second Heather. Ones I know Ed would be able to work through very quickly where it is taking me longer. This Heather also hasn't told us why she is here, yet she did tell us about some visitors coming. I'm trying to see who they are and what they have to do with the other Heather coming back in time." He paused the screen on one piece of data that made him frown. "Oh dear."

"What?"

"I need you to do me a favor. Take one of my private ships and go see who is coming. If it is who I think it is, we could be in a lot of trouble."

TWO

Heather played with the twins in the playroom. Terrik had scaled the rock wall Storm added when they'd mastered walking so quickly and were tearing around at break-neck speed. She didn't like the idea, but her son and daughter climbed up and down it like they were born to it. Soon, they were going to have to find something harder to challenge their motor skills. They still wore their shields to keep them from getting hurt, but they didn't need it. They had their parents' agility. Kuarto had already tried to explain to Storm that the children needed to be children and that meant bumps and bruises.

"Terrik, please come down. Mommy needs to talk to you and your sister."

"Of course." He scrambled down quickly and curled up in her lap, his sister right behind him. "What, Mommy?"

"I want you two to go on a trip with a very good friend of mine. He's going to take care of you two for a few weeks."

"You and daddy not coming?" asked her daughter.

"No, sweetheart. We're expecting company soon and I

thought this would be a good time for you to see Earth. Admiral Barrington will take very good care of you."

"Bear!"

"Yes." She smiled. "But you will have to obey him. No excuses. He is the law with you two."

"We will listen to him and do what he says." Her daughter was always the one who listened to reason. Her son was a lot like his father and could be quite pigheaded when he wanted something, and she knew Bear wouldn't put up with it. "We love Bear."

"And he loves you." She hugged her children, knowing she was going to miss them. "Go on back and play while I speak to your father and Bear and I'll come back and help you pack."

Heather stood after giving each of them a kiss. She headed into the main area of their rooms and out into the hall, then down to Storm's office. Bear sat at Storm's desk. He looked up when she walked in.

"So you explained to your son he had to behave?"

"Yes. Zunni has promised to keep him in line." She sat in a chair in front of the desk. "Thank you for doing this."

"I'm surprised you're willing to send them away with me. You have been very protective of these two."

"I know and that overprotectiveness is telling me to send them with you." She clasped her hands in front of her.

"Had a nightmare?"

"Not yet, but I suspect they will start soon."

"I will protect them like they're my own."

"I know you will, Bear, and thank you."

———

Sam continued with her shift, hoping the ancient Bert sent them after would show up again. A soft smile filled her lips when he did. He took the same table he had before and signaled her over.

"Back for more?"

"My usual." He looked around. "Where's your boyfriend?"

"His boss called him home."

"And you?"

"I was hoping to talk to you, see if I can convince you to come back with me." She turned on her heel and went to the bar. After picking up the drinks people had ordered she dropped them off at different tables. It wasn't too busy right now, so it gave her time to talk to him when she dropped off his drink.

"I already said I couldn't go home. It was too dangerous."

"Why?"

"There are people who will know if I go back, and they will follow me. That would be disastrous."

"So you hide? What if the thing you fear the most is already happening?"

"No!" He looked around after his outburst. "You don't know what you are talking about."

"My mother was created by Ialog and my father is the catalyst. I think that qualifies me."

"But it's too soon." Fear filled his eyes. "You are their child and full grown?"

"It's a bit complicated and I'll explain it if you come back with me."

"No."

"Then explain to me what is too soon?" Sam wiped his table. "Or have you been in hiding too long?"

He wrapped his hands around his glass and was quiet for a while before he finally spoke. "Tell me about your mom and why you think I could have been hiding too long."

"I don't know much, but I know my mother is frightened and she doesn't frighten easily."

He sighed. "Tell Bert I will talk to him."

"Excellent. I have a ship waiting."

"No ship. I won't go with you, but I will use your communication system."

Sam knew Bert wanted to see him in person. How was she going to convince him to go with her?

———

Heather and Storm stood on the tarmac as Bear's ship lifted off. Her children would be safe, but God was she going to miss them. She leaned into Storm for his strength.

"You okay?"

She nodded.

"On the verge of tears?"

She looked up at him, tears already spilling on her cheeks.

"My heart, you didn't need to send them away."

"Yes, I did. Something told me to do it, and this would be the only chance to get them to safety. If I'm wrong, then you can chastise me later."

"I trust you and your intuition." He wrapped his arms around her. "I've had you cleared from working with the elders today. Your team is doing an all-day exercise that might keep your mind on the task at hand instead of missing the twins."

"Thank you." She wiped the tears away. "Will you be with us?"

"Not right away."

"You didn't set this up just for me, did you?" She stepped back and looked up at him.

"It's been on the books for a couple of weeks." He smiled as he touched her face. "The time just seemed right."

She nodded again. "Guess I should be going."

"Fridon will meet you at our rooms so you'll know what you need."

"Thanks." She pressed her hand against his heart. He returned the gesture. "My heart."

"You'll be fine." He pulled her close and captured her lips with his. "They will be too."

"I know." She looked up at him with shining eyes. "I'm not worried about them. Bear is a different story."

Storm laughed. "Our children are a handful, but Bear will be fine with them."

———

Sam landed near Bert's complex. Her guest had been quiet on their trip to Vespia. When she tried to draw him into a conversation he gave her clipped answers. She wasn't sure what to do with him. Shutting down the engines, she went through her post-flight requirements. Once done she turned to her guest. "Ready?"

Without waiting for him she stood and headed to the doors. Bert stood at the end of the gangplank that descended when she opened them. "Good to have you home, Sam. I assume you were successful."

"I'm not sure if that is the right word but I have brought your friend home." She hooked a thumb behind her. "He's not happy about this at all."

"That isn't unusual. It's part of his personality, isn't it Edaranest."

"Bert! Why did you force me to come here?" He walked

down the gangplank. "You of all people know how dangerous this is."

"I left long before you did, Ed."

"But you came to me." He stopped. "Never mind."

"I see."

Sam wished she did. She headed to the main complex where she knew Skye should be waiting. The doors opened but she received no greeting. No warm arms wrapping around her, no deep passionate kiss.

"I'm sorry Sam, but Bert sent Skye on a mission. He should be back in a few days."

She turned toward the android. "Thanks, Cim."

The two men came into the main room behind her. She moved to the computer to make a few comments on her mission before she could go to her room.

"I see you were successful." Cim followed her to the computer.

She looked at Ed who didn't look too pleased to be there. "We shall see."

Dian sat in front of a computer but turned when she heard Ed's voice. "Ed..."

"Dian! I thought you were dead. You just disappeared."

"Just trapped." She hugged him. "Ialog sent me back in time on Earth and it wasn't until Heather showed up that I could escape that timeline."

"Heather?" He leaned back to look at her.

"The woman of Bert's visions." She turned to look at the man in question.

"So she is here? And that one is her daughter?" He pointed at Sam. "How long has this Heather been alive?"

"Sam's life was accelerated by Ialog." Bert stepped up to them.

"That man has caused more trouble." Ed shook his head. "I hope this prophesy of yours is worth it Bert."

"Oh, she is." He smiled. "Wait till you meet her."

"She is on Vespia?"

"Yes and mated to the catalyst."

"And you still think she will save the galaxy?"

Sam didn't want to eavesdrop on their conversation, but she had never heard anyone talk about her parents so analytically. It made her feel cold.

"I do."

"We shall see."

———

Heather stretched her muscles while she stood next to Fridon. She was happy to get out of listening to the complaints of the people as she sat on the council. The people of Vespia showed respect to the council and were always polite. It was so much better than having to use a security force to stop the bickering, but it was nice to take a break. "So how is Micali adjusting to the Vespian way of life?"

"Better than I expected. She loves working with your brother. Her knack for healing makes her perfect as his assistant and she's learning so much."

"I'm glad. Taking her from the life she knew could have devastated her, but I think she has blossomed here."

"I know and that makes me very happy." Fridon stood and slipped his carrier onto his back. "Time to move out!"

Everyone grabbed their gear and followed him to the ship. They didn't know anything about where they were going or what the exercise was going to be. They excelled at so much Storm stopped telling them so they couldn't prepare.

They landed near a wooded area. Airbikes were waiting for them.

"Heather, you take point."

She grinned as she completed her uniform by adding her helmet and gloves, but so did everyone else in their squad. They knew she'd push them to keep up. They loaded their packs onto the bikes and powered up, their destination loading onto the screen they used to navigate by.

Heather took off first, forcing everyone to catch up with her. They zipped through the trees, following her and the destination beacon. No one said a word about her silence when she took off. Each mission had special instructions for the mission commander and key members of the squad that were only told to them once they had their helmets on.

She loved the bike. The speed at which they flew by the trees was exhilarating. Weaving between the large trunks of the tall trees, she watched her readings to make sure no one got left behind. Once they cleared the trees, they went into a v formation and raced toward the camp they would use for the night.

Heather pulled in first and was the first one off her bike. Touching the pole in the center of the area, she was greeted with her mate's voice. "Very good time. You missed the record by two minutes."

She wasn't too upset since she was the one who broke the record in the first place, and she was always within five minutes of her record.

"You will now separate and find the camp set up for you. The directions are now loaded into your helmets. You must make it to the camp before the trackers assigned to this task catch you. Good luck." The system then went silent.

"Did everyone hear that?" ask Fridon.

Everyone nodded as they started for their next destination.

Heather checked her readings before heading off to the right. She had an unfair advantage with her special ability, so Storm found a way to even the field by assigning a special cloaked drone to her. Something she shouldn't be able to detect, so Bert had a hand in creating it, yet she was always one step in front of it. Storm couldn't figure out how she kept beating it.

She didn't either, but her mind kept growing. Connecting with a computer other than Cim was out of her reach right now but maybe something small like a drone wasn't. It wasn't something she could prove but had learned not to rule out anything.

Moving as fast as she could, she headed toward her next target. The camp was a good hike if she could cut through the middle of the open grasslands, but that would let the drone catch her in about fifteen minutes. She had to take a longer route that might confuse the drone. If she did something out of the ordinary, she could throw off its analytical mind.

Bert built it to challenge her, so she always had to think ahead. Something she enjoyed. A slight sound caught her attention, and she slid behind a group of smaller trees. The drone hummed by where she hid. She grinned. Now it was in front of her, and she could keep it in her sight.

You're cheating. Her mate's voice filled her mind.

Ha! Am not. I can't help the fact the robot is now in front of me. And you are trying to distract me.

How far are you from the camp?

Right, like you're not tracking that mechanical toy of yours. Oop!

Problem?

Nope, but now you're cheating. The drone wouldn't double back like that unless I did something to attract its attention which I know I haven't done. She snuck around the machine to the site and ran the last few meters to grab the pole before the drone caught her movement.

"Congratulations. You are the first to arrive."

She grinned. Dropping her pack to the ground she waited for the rest of her team.

———

They joked with each other as they ate their meal. Their temporary dwelling was up and there had been no other message from Storm.

"You get the commander's space."

"What?" Heather shook her head. "I don't think so."

"Why not? You always sleep with him when he's here."

"Sorry, but no." She shook her head. "Knowing you guys, you'll turn the white noise machine up so you can leave me behind."

They laughed.

"Only to get a short head start on you 'miss I have to be first every time,'" commented one of the other women on the squad.

"I can't help it if you're slow." She ducked when someone threw a roll at her. "See?"

Laughter filled the air again.

"Besides, Fridon is in charge he should get the space."

"And have your mate show up in the middle of the night like he has done in the past and find me in his bed instead of you? Don't think I want to deal with that shock again."

Heather laughed. Storm's bellow the one time it happened still rang in everyone's ears.

They enjoyed each other's company until Fridon gave the order for lights out.

Heather curled on her side near Fridon. Like a protective older brother, he was never too far when Storm wasn't around. Closing her eyes, she felt her mate's mind touch hers.

Is everyone asleep?

Not yet. Some are still settling down. Why?

Just making sure everyone gets rest. Tomorrow will be very rigorous.

Right. You've planned something for this evening, haven't you?

Go to sleep, my heart. I promise you won't be startled out of your sleep in the middle of the night.

She knew her mate too well. Closing her eyes, she fell into a light sleep. If he was going to do anything she was going to be ready.

Her sleep deepened as she started to dream.

Would you like to see your prodigy, Heather?

She found herself unable to move, she was wheeled to a window where she saw rows and rows of men and women standing at attention. A huge army of warriors stood there waiting for their orders. All of them with gold and violet eyes.

Heather's eyes snapped open. What the hell was that? That was a little strange. A dream or a vision? She knew she couldn't sleep for a while so got up to move around. If she stayed in a seated position, Fridon, the watchdog, would wake as well and ask her a bunch of questions she wasn't ready to answer and end up waking the rest of the squad.

She did have to move quietly so she didn't wake Fridon anyway. He had a sixth sense when it came to knowing when something was out of line. Sneaking out of the temporary dwelling, she took a deep breath once she stepped outside. The air had a nice crispness to it.

She became alert when she sensed something off. It wasn't like she saw any movement, but something caught her attention. Pulling out her weapon, she inched her way around the tent and into the group of trees nearby. She planned on using it to hide her as she searched the perimeter. Hopefully, she would find nothing and laugh at herself.

Then she felt strong arms wrap around her as one hand covered her mouth. "You're supposed to be sleeping." The voice was low and deep, and she recognized it instantly. She relaxed and the hand dropped from her mouth.

"Storm." She whispered his name.

"My heart." He eased his hold so she could turn and face him.

"Did you come to spy on us?"

"No. I came to see you. I don't like sleeping by myself, but since you came out here, I want you to see something." He turned her around so she could see the temporary building. Within a few seconds, she heard Fridon curse and say her name. He was outside a few seconds later.

He came to the edge of the woods with a small cylinder in his hand. A light bounced off her uniform. "Heather, why did you leave the building? You know protocol."

"I couldn't sleep."

The light from his handheld bounced off another uniform. "Oh, sir. Sorry. I should have known you were here."

"It took you thirty seconds, Fridon." Storm's voice held pride. "The record is twenty-eight. My record."

"Yes, sir. Thank you, sir. I shall strive for fifteen seconds." He turned on his heel and headed back to the tent.

"I guess I should be going back as well."

"I don't think so." He picked her up and started walking away from camp.

"But I'm on a mission. I'm supposed to stay with my group."

"True, but since I am your commanding officer as well

as your mate you will keep us both happy." The ship came into view. He headed straight for it. "And when we're happy your squad will be happy."

"You trying to blackmail me?"

"Is it working?" He walked up the gangplank of his ship and closed the door.

"How is this helping my squad? You took me away from them. What if they're attacked while you're having your way with me?" She knew now that he had sealed the door, she wouldn't be able to get out. She knew him too well. He probably set the controls to answer only to him.

"The only thing that could attack them is the bugs." If anything were to happen at night, he would never have approached her. He'd never compromise a mission. "But if you wish to go back, I will let you return. Just understand that I might be a little irritated from not being able to sleep which could make the mission a little harder than I originally planned."

"You are blackmailing me." She placed her hands on her hips.

"Let me ask you this, did everyone abstain this evening?" Storm crowded her backward toward the bridge.

"Of course not." She looked behind her to make sure she wasn't going to back into anything. What caught her eye when they entered the bridge was his favorite chair.

"And where would you have slept if I had been there with you?"

"With you." She touched his face.

"I have learned that not having you next to me at night makes it hard to sleep." He kept her moving backward.

"Is that why you were out there tonight?" She felt the chair stop her movement. "You planned on joining us for the evening?"

"I had thought about it, then you appeared in front of me, and I had a change of plans."

"So, this isn't part of the mission?"

"Think of it as a perk."

She grinned when he used an Earth word. "A perk, huh? Okay. I'd like to make a comment and I don't want you to get upset or think I'm questioning you, but it's not like you to take advantage of any mission. No matter how much you need me."

"There is a woman who claims to be you sitting in our medlab. That changes everything." He didn't need to say anything more.

Heather pressed her hand against his heart. "I'll need to be back before anyone wakes up."

"All under control, my heart." He wrapped his arms around her. "I do believe you are overdressed."

"So are you."

"That is something I can fix." With a thought, he removed their clothes.

"Maybe I should have Cim removed from this ship so you can't take advantage of it."

"And ruin my fun?" He ran a hand up her back. "I wish I could carry a portable unit so I can do something like this all the time."

"And I'd never be able to stay dressed."

"You make it sound like a bad thing." He maneuvered her onto the chair. "I have made a few new modifications to this."

"Like what?"

"You'll see. It should be something you like since it benefits you."

"Really?" She sat, then waited for him. The smile he gave her as he joined her on the chair filled her with excitement. What had he planned now?

His hands skimmed over her body. Brushing the tips of her breasts, caressing her hips, dipping down to her mound. A sigh escaped her as she relaxed against the chair. She felt the chair shift against her back pushing her breasts forward. The moment the chair stopped moving she felt the heat of Storm's mouth on one breast. His hands were never idle, still sliding over her skin, gentle fingers touching the places that heightened her need. The heat of his mouth moved from one breast to the other.

She went to reach for him and found her arms restricted. "Storm?"

"You know how you always try to take control and most of the time I let you because of those wicked hands of yours?" He blew against the tip of the breast he had been paying homage to and smiled as it pebbled. "I have found a way around that so now I can bring you to new heights with no interference."

"You like my wicked hands." She tried to pull free but couldn't move.

"That is true." He kissed her stomach as his hands covered her breasts. "But I love the taste of you and want to take my time with you. Would you deny your mate such a simple request?"

"Of course not." She stopped talking when his mouth closed over her mound. And he said she had wicked hands. He sucked on the soft tissue for a moment before lathing the same spot, then he started alternating between the two sensations. When he inserted two fingers inside her the first of many orgasms shook her to the core.

"That's my girl." He kissed his way back up her body. He focused on her mark as he slid in deep.

"Oh God!" A second powerful orgasm raced through her blood as she wrapped her legs around him.

"And to think we're just getting started." He pressed his

lips to her mark as he waited for her to return to him. Her releases were beautiful to witness and when they were powerful, she normally had an out-of-body experience.

"Oh, Storm." She flexed against him and moaned.

"Told you you'd like the changes I made to the chair."

"You're telling me the chair is responsible for those orgasms?" She tried to move but still couldn't.

"My secret, my heart." He brushed a few strains of hair out of her face. "Still feeling boneless or are you ready for another one?"

"I don't know if I can handle another one."

"Ha. I know better. By the way, your hands are now free."

"Yeah, if I could lift them."

———

Bert showed Ed what he was working on. The other Heather filled the screen as Bert explained everything that had gone on.

"So there are two of them? How is that possible?"

"The other Heather came back through time." Bert gave him an odd look. They had all time traveled at one point or another. They always made sure it was safe but there were always risks.

"Not what I meant." Ed shook his head. "I mean how can they occupy the same time without causing the timeline to fall apart?"

"I have the second Heather shielded." Burt grinned. Sometimes Ed had trouble explaining himself and this was a perfect example. "What I find odd is her memory doesn't seem to be intact and there is something strange about her DNA."

"Hmm." He looked at the data streaming on the screen.

"What is so strange about her DNA? It shows she's Vespian."

"Exactly. She should show some ancient blood. Our Heather has seventy percent ancient blood. The second Heather doesn't have that."

"This shows she doesn't have any ancient blood. That doesn't make sense. She can't be her if the DNA has been changed. This is my area of expertise, and I don't know of anything that will strip someone of DNA due to time travel so what could have caused that?" Ed looked at the data as well as the image of the second Heather. She sat in the room unmoving. "What tests have you run?"

"These." Bert loaded the data on the screen.

"And all of them have come back inconclusive?" Ed turned to look at him. "Your data says you didn't run all of them at the same time."

"At first, I took the scans that Kuarto did at face value. He is one of the best doctors I have met, and I didn't see a reason to question what he did. We all thought that was Heather. That was my first mistake." Bert leaned against the counter. "Once I spoke to the second Heather and learned she didn't know who I was I started running other tests. So far everything I've done shows Heather as Vespian, and six weeks older than our Heather. Other than the DNA change I can't find anything that shows she's not our Heather. She's not coming up as a clone by my scans."

"But that is what you think she is."

"It's the only thing that makes sense."

"What do you need me to do?"

Bert smiled.

———

Storm climbed out of the chair without waking Heather. He had planned on letting her go back to the group until she made a comment that she needed to get back to keep Fridon in line. The reason for this mission was to test the man. He had been absorbing everything Storm taught him and the elders felt it was time for him to show what he had learned.

He needed to do it on his own. Heather being there might cause an interference that could change the outcome of the test, so Storm decided to make her absence part of the test. She wasn't going to be happy about it but that was the way it had to be.

Using the three-dimensional imagery Fridon had adapted from Bert's technology, he stood at the edge of the camp and waited. Fridon was the first one out. One by one the squad members came out of the temporary dwelling. He heard one of them mumbling about where Heather had gotten off to.

"Good morning." His voice stopped them in their tracks.

"Sir?"

"Heather has been kidnapped and your mission is to retrieve her by sunsdown. Your mission information has been downloaded to your helmets."

"Who is our enemy?"

"I am." Storm smiled. They knew what he was capable of. He wouldn't make it easy for them. "That is all." He ended the transmission and turned to where his mate was still sleeping. He knelt beside her and touched her shoulder. Her eyelids fluttered open, and she sat up.

"I need to get going." She swung her legs over and moved to the edge of the chair.

"There's been a change of plans." He smiled at her, knowing she wasn't going to react in a positive manner.

"But I thought…you're testing Fridon."

"The elders want to see what he has learned. The man who is my second will be stepping down in a year and they need to be sure he can fill in for me when they send me on missions. I will be training him for years, but he will officially be my second when the man retires."

"And the reason I can't be with my team?"

"No matter how much we might think Fridon stands on his own, with either of us there, we won't be sure. This way we will. And you can help me come up with the scenario for your rescue."

"You haven't done that yet?"

"Only enough to get them started." It wouldn't take him long.

"Ooh, this could be fun." She looked at her state of undress. "Do I get to wear clothes?"

"Why?"

"Because sooner or later they will try to rescue me and although you don't mind having me walk around naked, I'd feel more comfortable if I had something on when that happens."

"You know nudity doesn't bother anyone. You could be naked all the time and no one would say a word."

"I know."

He knew she'd rather cover up even though she didn't want him to think she was prudish. "You can put your uniform on when they get close enough, but I would like to see you in something we'd both enjoy while we wait for them to find us."

"Any particular thing?" She gave him a smile that started the glow in his eyes.

"I do like the red one."

"Did you bring any of them or shall I take advantage of Cim like you do?"

He touched her cheek. "Cim will help you."

She stood and closed her eyes. In seconds she was incased in the red underwear she wore for him when they first moved to Vespia. "Better?"

"Much." He walked around her, his hands caressing her as he moved.

"We do have work to do." Each time he touched her he picked up the scent of her desire rising a little.

"I know and it is the only thing that is stopping me from taking advantage of this situation." He trailed his fingers up over her lace-covered breasts, gently brushing her mark before he bent to capture her lips with his. "You need to make sure you keep my mind off your body and on the task at hand. Once we're done then I will show you how happy I am you're wearing that outfit."

———

Fridon led the team away from the campsite after they packed up their gear. There was something strange about the way this mission was going. Storm was working on another assignment. That was what he told him yesterday when he started this mission. Now Heather was their target. "Well crap!"

"Fridon, you have been spending too much time with Heather," said one of the women. "That is her favorite word when she realizes something isn't right. What have you figured out?"

"They are testing me." He turned back to the squad. "What is the one thing Storm keeps saying to me?"

"My mate and I want some alone time?" One of the male squad members quipped.

"Haha. He keeps telling me to follow my instincts. I have a tendency to ask what they think. I do it to show respect, but I'm getting the impression that Storm thinks I'm afraid to make a decision on my own."

"You do turn to them a lot. Respect or not."

"Well, now I can show them I know what to do."

"So what do you want us to do?" asked the woman who spoke first.

"Think like the commander and his mate." They gave him an odd look. "The commander is the best tactician I know, but I know how he thinks and works. Right now, they are listening to us. But Heather has a unique way of thinking. Her mind grasps these scenarios differently. It's how she is able to defeat so many different ones. She's the one we must be wary of."

———

"He knows you well, my heart."

"We are very close. He knows how I think, and I know how he thinks." She grinned. "And I like the way he tried so hard to not insult me. I have a devious mind and he knows it."

"What shall we do to make this a good challenge?"

"You have them heading to the next site?"

"Yes. They are following the path I set."

"Then block it. Make them figure out another way to get there." She watched as he pulled up the map he gave them. "Ooh right here will make them backtrack and could make them separate into two groups, especially if you don't give them all the data on the two paths. We've taken both paths and I know some feel one way is faster than the other. This will show his leadership skills if he can convince them to follow him even though they might believe he is wrong."

"You are devious." Storm programmed the information

in and blocked the path they were on. "And Fridon is going to know you planned this."

"He should and if he's smart, and we know he is, he'll use it to his advantage."

———

Fridon frowned when they came up on the blockage. "This can't be right. The commander would never send us this way if we couldn't get through."

"There are other ways of getting there."

"I know that." Fridon went silent as he stared at the forcefield that covered the narrow passageway. "This is Heather's doing."

"Why would she do this?"

"How many of you think the path to the right is faster?" He saw a smattering of hands. "And how many think the one to the left is quicker?" He got about the same amount of hands. "That is what I thought. They want to see what happens when I choose."

"So, which one?"

"Both." Fridon smiled. "Either one could be another trick, and this is a timed exercise. With two teams we could still reach the site within the timed deadline. Whichever team makes it there first will backtrack to the other team and help them make it to the site."

"Yes, sir."

"Oh, and this is a race to see which way is faster if these paths aren't blocked as well." They broke into two groups and set off for their next location. "We will finally find out who is right."

———

"Hmm. He split the team up on purpose." Storm mused. "Not what you expected was it?"

"Actually, that is what he should have done. Knowing that half of the squad thought one way was faster than the other, this will give them a little incentive while keeping them on task." Heather turned her gaze from the screen to her mate. She was proud he had kept his hands to himself while they watched the group move to their next destination. This outfit was one of his favorites.

"It's going to take them at least three hours to get to the site." He gave her a sultry smile as he moved toward her.

Heather grinned as she backed up. "Didn't you tell me that you remained focused on the task at hand when on a mission?"

"I do, but we're not part of that mission this time." He kept stalking her, maneuvering her toward the chair. "And we have time before they get to their destination."

She skirted around the chair, putting it between them. "But we need to make sure what we planned will work."

"And we will." He herded her toward the only clear wall on the ship. "But first I need to relax you."

"You think I'm excited?" Her smile widened.

"It's an aphrodisiac coming off your skin. You need me and I am more than willing to accommodate you." The moment her back hit the wall he braced his hands on either side of her, blocking any escape she might have tried. "I love the scent you give off. It excites me. Fires my need."

"You don't need to have anything fire your need. It is already very high." She touched his face, brushing her fingers along his jaw.

"True." He pressed his lips against her mark as he inhaled deeply. "But it is a wonderful aroma. One I can't ignore, don't want to."

"You act like it calls to you." She tilted her head so he could have better access.

"It does." He nuzzled her throat. His breath sent tingles through her mark. "It tells me when you need me. I can pick it up anywhere. This wall could be fun, but I want to use the chair again." He lifted her up, lathing her mark before he covered it with his mouth as he carried her to it.

The way he focused on her mark took all the fight out of her. He was right, she was excited. Not knowing when he was going to pounce had her thinking about it constantly, arousing her in the process.

He straddled the chair with her in his arms. Gentle hands moved her until she was lying in front of him, legs on either side of the chair. His mouth moved from her throat to her lace-clad breast, sucking on the delicate peek as his fingers crawled down her body to her core. She felt him smile against her breast as he slid two fingers inside her. The crotch-less panties made it easier for him to have access to all of her. He then pressed a kiss to the valley between her breasts and latched onto the other nipple.

She arched against his hand. His touch always sent her flying. Her need to feel him inside her started to climb, but he could be very stubborn when it came to what she wanted, however, there were ways she could still get it. Her hands slid across his back to find he was still wearing his uniform. When she tried to remove it with a thought nothing happened.

That's not going to work this time.

What did you do?

Asked Cim to help me out when you decided to try to get the upper hand.

You think having the computer do your bidding will stop me? What are you plotting?

You'll see. She opened her mind, so he was with her. He

stood in front of her naked, just the way she wanted him. He went to reach for her and found he couldn't move.

What is this?

Since you have control on the physical level, I thought I'd try controlling the mental. She walked around him, her fingers leaving a warm trail across the small of his back.

Then you plan on trying to arouse me in your mind while I do the same to you physically?

I have thought about trying this for a long time, but it never happened. Guess you had me only feeling too quickly.

Are you saying I'm not doing my job? He kissed his way down her stomach.

Never! She paused as his wet kisses caused goosebumps to rise. *But you did say we had some time.*

I did, didn't I.

She pressed a kiss against his mark as she continued to walk around him, her hands continuing to roam his torso. *I love touching you. The way you respond to my fingers on your body.*

I feel the same way, my heart. You are so pure in the way you react to my touch. That is why I want to bring you to such heights every time.

She felt a wave of desire flow over her, stopping her in her tracks for a moment.

You liked that. He did the same thing again, making her suck in her breath.

If you keep that up, I won't get my fantasy.

If I can make you scream is that a bad thing?

No, my heart. She touched his heart in her mind. *You know that. But if you don't enter me soon, I might scream in frustration.*

We can't have that.

The mental image she was holding shattered when she felt his penetration. Next time she might complete that

45

fantasy, but he always knew where to touch her to make her need escalate. Her body accepted him again and again as he set a pace to bring them to their climax. It was just out of her reach. She met him thrust for thrust, trying to grasp her release. Heat pooled in her core. Tendrils of euphoria filled her as she finally caught what she was after. She floated along, feeling boneless once again.

Storm touched her face. "My heart."

"You have this way with me that amazes me every time." She touched his face as well. "I am so grateful you are mine."

"I wouldn't want it any other way."

THREE

Fridon was the first to the next site, which was the way it should have been. He was the leader. Heather looked at Storm with pride in her eyes.

"I knew he was your favorite."

"You are my favorite." She wrapped her arms around her mate. "But Fridon's like a brother to me. I want him to do well."

"He will. I have trained him."

"We have trained him," she corrected.

"Be glad no one is here to hear you, or I might have to punish you." He wrapped his arms around her and pulled her against him.

"Really?" She looked up at him with a sparkle in her eyes. "I could turn the mike on, so the squad hears you."

"You like my punishments a little too much." He dipped his head to her mark.

"You do, too."

"Heather? You there?" She heard Fridon's voice.

Heather touched Storm's heart as she tried to figure out where the voice was coming from.

47

"Your helmet, my heart."

"Right." She smiled at him as she reached for it. Placing it on her head, she connected with Fridon.

"So, are you still the prize or part of the plot to test me?" He didn't waste any time.

"I'm still the prize."

"Then why did you help?"

"This is no ordinary kidnapper. It is my mate. Look Fridon, you need to remember that I am still the prize, but my kidnapper didn't take me to harm me or gain some boon, he wanted time alone with me."

"And he's going to do everything in his power to keep you with him, including use your training if he needs to."

"Exactly."

"Got it."

———

Bert waited for the simulation to run again. He had gotten the data from the tests and wasn't happy with what he found. With Heather and Storm away on a training mission he decided to work on what could happen. If he could figure it out, they could prepare.

Each time he ran it something changed. Too many variables to pinpoint the real future, he needed more data, but they all had the same theme. Their new visitors were after Heather.

"Bert, Skye is back from his mission," Cim informed him.

"Good." He went to the landing site and entered the ship. Turning on the security system he sat down and smiled. "Thank you for following my instructions and remaining undetected."

"I'm not sure why you wanted me to be so careful. Who

are these people?" Skye pulled up the data he recorded as he floated by the ship in question.

"They are from my people's past. I thought they had been destroyed." He looked at the markings on the image. "But it looks like I was wrong."

"You going to fill me in?"

"This ship is ancient. Ialog was the captain of it, but he lost it in a battle with our enemy. I heard they had captured it and pressed its crew into their military."

"So, you think it is your enemy in the guise of your people?"

"That is what I'm afraid of, but I won't know for sure until I see the captain."

———

"They're very close." Heather looked away from the screen to smile at Storm. "And in the time I expected."

"Don't be smug. You'll have to go with them and won't be here where you have all this." He gestured to himself.

"And I love having all of this." She brushed her hands across his chest. "But they are my team and the best. We knew they'd be here long before you wanted them to be."

"And you want to get dressed."

"I don't think this outfit will fare well when we're hiking in the woods." Heather touched the strap of her bra. "But no one needs to know that I have this on under my uniform. Only you."

"Just for me? I might have to kidnap you again."

Heather closed her eyes and her uniform appeared. "Thank you for letting me wear this. You could have kept me in my underwear, and it would have fit the scenario."

"I know, but you work hard to have them see you as a

member of the squad and not my mate and I respect that."
He crowded her backward.

"What are you doing?"

"Restraining you." He pressed her against the wall and
pinned her arms up against it. She heard a snap and
looked up.

"When did you install those?"

He did the same thing with her feet. She was now
spread eagle on the wall. "I thought about using them to
keep you still while I have my way with you, but also knew
if I used them for our intimacy then when I used them for
this mission, I wouldn't be able to keep my hands to myself.
Seeing you like this has me wanting to keep them away just
a little longer so I could peel off that uniform and taste the
passion I know lies underneath."

"You are cruel." She pulled against the cuffs her hands
and feet were caught in, but they didn't budge.

"Be glad I'm not taking advantage of this."

———

Fridon heard Storm's last comment. It sounded safe for the
moment. He sure didn't want to interrupt them. Perhaps
Heather would assume he was listening in and was trying
to get her mate to talk about the security around the ship.

"My heart, you have a one-track mind." Heather
laughed. "My team is the best. They will rescue me."

Fridon grinned. They would. He squeezed the small
device he had created, glad he brought it with him. There
had been times in the past where he wished he had something like this so went to work making a prototype. Having
access to the ancient computer helped. Now he could open
any locked door, hack into any computer, and override
security systems. He knew it would be good for other

things, but he had started with those basic programs and would add what he needed as time went on. Like the ancient system, it was a learning tool.

Storm walked around. He had to be very close to the helmet for it to pick up his footfalls. The floor was reinforced with a special element to keep sound down. Fridon wondered if Storm figured he was listening in.

"So did you change your passcode to enter the ship?" asked Heather.

"You trying to give Fridon information?"

Heather laughed. "What makes you say that?"

"Because that is what I'd do if I were in the same situation." Storm was quiet for a moment. "Helmet off."

"Crap." He lost the feed so there was now no help from Heather. Then he saw it. Heather had been busy when she was helping Storm set everything up. She had downloaded all the new security information to make it easy for Fridon to break in if Storm hadn't anticipated that. He pulled his helmet off and looked at the crew waiting for instructions. "They are on the commander's ship."

"How do you plan on approaching him when his sensors will pick us up long before we can see the ship?"

"True." He pulled the device out of his uniform and held it up in the palm of his hand.

"Another toy?" One of the other team members pulled out one similar. Each time they went on missions they always wished they had brought a particular tool or item. At night they would talk about having the perfect tool. One to answer their every need and he had created it. Therefore, he went to work, a special device created for each member and their particular talents. Everyone was very happy with the way they worked when they got in a tight spot. It had taken him a little longer to figure out what he needed in the field, but he loved the challenge.

"Yes." He grinned. "Since I always end up dealing with the electronics my gadget is made for that. We know the commander has changed our passcodes, but this will override anything he has done and get us in."

"How are we going to get close enough to get in?"

"You leave that up to me." Sometimes it was best not to give out all your secrets.

———

Storm watched the screen as the team surrounded the ship. "Looks like your friends are ready to try to get you back."

"They're not trying, Storm. Whatever you have plotted will not stop them." She pulled on the cuffs that had her pinned on the wall. "I'm not real thrilled about how they will find me, but they will win this mission, just like we always do."

"I could take your uniform off and enjoy the view until they get here."

"You already told me you couldn't keep your hands to yourself if you did. It is much safer this way and you know it, unless you wish the rest of the squad to see just how you make me scream."

"I wish I could make you scream every time, but those are my rare gifts from you." He gave her a smile filled with promises. "And I always try to get those screams as often as I can. Having you like that is very tempting, but I think you're trying to distract me from the task at hand." He turned back to the screen. "It looks like they are splitting up and surrounding us. I count four. Four? Ah, there's two more. So where is Fridon?"

There were eight people in the squad including her. "Are you asking me?"

"Thinking out loud, my heart. I know how he thinks

and he's trying to distract me by having the rest of the team attack from different angles."

"He also knows how you think."

"Oh, I have taken that into consideration." Storm turned to look at her with a knowing smile. "And I know he has too."

"So, what devious plan have you devised?"

"You sure are nosy. Perhaps I should distract you." He moved the images to the wall he had his mate pinned to and approached her. With a flick of his wrist, he opened her suit to reveal her throat and a bit of red lace. He pressed his lips to her mark.

"Storm, you sure this is wise?" Her voice softened as his lips worked their magic on her.

"When it comes to arousing you, it is always a beautiful thing. How can that be wrong?"

"But you're supposed to be watching the team, not focusing on me."

"I have the computer telling me everything that is going on so I can do both." He opened the seal further to allow his hand to snake down her body to her core. His caresses had her sucking in her breath. "My heart. You fill me with such joy with the way you react to my touch. You never hold back."

"Storm." She pulled against the cuffs, wanting to touch him as need consumed her.

He pulled the delicate tissue of her mark into his mouth. Her scent changed as she got closer to her orgasm. A tremor raced through her body. Another sign she was getting close. Storm changed his stroke, making her impending orgasm back off. He wanted to extend this a little more. The fact that she couldn't stop him made him want to torture her a little bit. If she had been free, by this point she would be riding him, not submitting to his hand.

The computer made him aware someone had breached the door to the ship. He pressed another kiss to her mark as he withdrew his hand and resealed her uniform. "I'm sorry my heart, but we'll have to finish this later."

"What?" She sounded annoyed. He would be too.

"It seems I have found Fridon. He has gotten the hatch to the ship open and is allowing the rest of your team to enter." He still had his weight pressed against her. "Unless you don't care how they find you."

He let the comment hang between them. Heather had always been a bit shy about sex and he understood why. She was so honest in her reaction, a part of her that she fought to keep just between the two of them.

"That is so mean." Heather gave him one of her best glares. "I will get even with you."

"I know, and I'm looking forward to that." He turned as the first member entered and leveled his weapon at them. "So, who wishes to be shot first?"

No one answered, which didn't surprise him. They had been trained by him. Although they all wore their helmets which made them all look alike, he knew who was who by their stances and mannerisms. Fridon was still missing. It would be totally against his character for him to be hiding or lagging behind, so he had to be up to something. "So where is Fridon?"

"Behind you."

Storm felt the blaster between his shoulder blades. He grinned. "Very good."

"Yield, sir."

Storm turned to disarm him, but there was no one there. He laughed. "Alright, Fridon. I will yield, but you must show me how you did this."

"Drop your weapon and release our crewman."

Storm placed his weapon on the ground and hit a

button to release Heather. At the same time the computer called an end to the exercise. He wasn't sure what to expect but having Fridon just appear in front of him shocked him. He kept it to himself, giving the man a smile and a raised eyebrow.

"I created another gadget. This one for me since I am the one who is the tech of the group."

"Show me." Storm wanted to know what he used to keep him invisible. It would be something everyone could benefit from.

He held the small device out to Storm, who picked it up to study it. "It has basic functions in it right now, but as we face different challenges, I'll be adding different things."

"I like the cloaking device. Can I assume you have an electronic lockpick in this?"

"It's a little more complicated than that but essentially that is what it is."

"You need to put that cloak in each of the devices you have created so far." He tossed it back to Fridon. "Good job. Everyone has the rest of the day off."

———

Storm landed the ship on the tarmac. He released everyone but Fridon and Heather.

"That cloak of yours was ingenious," commented Heather. "I know Earth has been trying to perfect something like that for a while but hasn't been successful."

"We have something close to this on our ships, but no one has been able to make it work for personal use. I gave it a tweak here and there and came up with a working prototype." He grinned, proud of his little invention.

"It didn't hurt having access to an ancient computer, did it?" Heather poked him in the ribs.

"No, access to Cim allowed me to create it quicker. I could test it without building it with his help. That allowed me to work out the bugs before I made it. Without the computer, I would still be working on the prototype."

"Send the specs to me, Fridon, and let's see what else you have on it. I can see this as a very important piece of a soldier's protection." He looked at his mate for a moment before turning his attention back to Fridon. "And if you don't mind, I'd like to hang on to this for a few hours. I'd like to try a few things with it."

"Yes, sir."

"You're dismissed."

Fridon and Heather turned to leave.

"I haven't released you, Heather. We have some unfinished business."

She didn't look happy but stayed put. The moment Fridon was off the ship Storm sealed the hatch and the ship lifted off again.

"If you think I'm going to allow you to put me in those cuffs again you're mistaken." She frowned at him, but he could hear her heartbeat pick up speed. The thought excited her.

"My heart, you were so close before we were interrupted. Don't you want me to finish what I started?" He stepped closer, knowing she would step back, maneuvering her right where he wanted her. Her back hit the wall and he pounced. "I promise to be gentle."

"You are always gentle." Heather shifted, trying to escape, but he had her pinned once again. Linking his fingers with hers, he lifted her arm until the cuff closed around it. "But you know I don't like this trapped feeling."

"Even though you know the pleasure you'll experience?" His fingers made short work of her uniform, leaving her in the wonderful red lace he loved so much. He knew he needed to arouse her, make her forget about the restraints. Storm pressed his lips against her mark, sucking on the delicate skin as he lifted the other arm, only letting go after he heard the soft snap of the closure.

She was tense and could have fought him if she really wanted to, but she remained still, turning her head so he could have better access to her mark. Her trust humbled him, and he wanted her to enjoy this. His excitement over this was a palpable thing.

Storm still had to restrain her legs. He smiled against her throat as he planned on how to get her to open her legs for him. Nibbling his way down her body he paused at her breasts, He drew a lace-clad nipple into his mouth, receiving a sigh from his mate. She started to relax a little. Her fear being replaced with desire.

Using feather-light touches he worked his way across her stomach then down to her mound. His fingers slid into her folds, caressing her, pushing her to forget her fear. He dropped down and laved her core before nipping at her thigh. Heather still wore the boots from her uniform, and he needed to remove those before placing her ankles in the restraints.

"Storm."

"Just removing your boots, my heart." He kissed the inside of her thigh then the back of her knee before he caressed her calf, easing his hands down to her foot. The boot came off easily and he slipped her ankle into the cuff. Pressing kisses against the arch of her other foot after he removed the second boot, he eased it over to the other cuff. He stood and smiled at her.

She looked back at him. The passion he had filled her with fading, but he wasn't worried. It wouldn't take him too long to bring it back. He placed a hand on either side of her head. Leaning in enough to feel the heat radiating off her body, he put his lips close to her ear. "Now I get to see how much my playground can take."

"You already know what I can take."

"I know the point when you don't want to take anymore." He pressed a kiss to her mark. "But now I can take my time."

"Storm."

"Trust me, my heart."

"I do, but it's just not fair that I can't touch you." She pulled against the restraints.

He rested a hand on her thigh. The heat of her skin penetrated deep, making him want to touch more. "I promise to make it worth your while."

Having her at his mercy like this was a fantasy come true. Her honest reaction to everything he did made him giddy with excitement and now he wouldn't have to worry about her taking control. The desire to touch her drove him to place his second hand on her stomach. The hand on her thigh started to climb up, brushing the lace that covered her curls before continuing up her midsection. He wanted to arouse her slowly. Build the fire inside her so hot it would consume her.

He thought about keeping his uniform on then changed his mind. If he pressed his weight into her he wanted to feel her flesh against his. This was just as arousing for him as he hoped it would be for her. He pulled his uniform off. Knowing Heather watched his every move, he did it slowly. A striptease just for her. Her breathing changed. She liked what she saw.

How would she feel when she couldn't see him at all? He held Fridon's creation in his hands. Storm grinned at her before he pressed the button.

"What are you doing?"

He laughed. "Arousing my mate."

"By being invisible?"

"This way you can't assume anything." He brushed his hand against her stomach again. "You won't know where I am or where I am going as I travel your body."

"I thought you saw Fridon's device as an asset for all soldiers?"

"Oh, I do. This is my way of testing hand-to-hand combat." He skimmed his hand up and palmed one of her breasts. "You have to admit that the close physical contact you are about to experience qualifies."

"Storm."

His mouth closed around the nipple of the other breast causing Heather to suck in her breath. He pulled the tip into his mouth, circling it with his tongue. Her heart beat faster as he lathed her nipple. His hand worked the other nipple, plucking at it gently while his mouth sucked then his tongue lathed the one he had been focusing on. Heather whimpered.

Storm pressed a kiss in the valley between her breasts before he did the same thing to her other breast. His free hand working on the first puckered tip as well. Then he worked his way down her body. His hand skimmed along her waist and hips as his mouth blazed a trail to her belly button. He stopped long enough to dip his tongue in and make her laugh. It was still a ticklish spot for her. It also gave him the time he needed to drop to his knees.

The need to taste her was overpowering him. He also wanted to hear her moan. She was close and it wouldn't take much to push her over. He pressed his lips to her hip then nibbled on the inside of her thigh. Heather shifted in the cuffs. Storm brushed his mouth on the skin just above her mound. Moving around her body like this kept her from figuring out where he was going to touch her next. Frustration radiated off her. Time to end that.

He wrapped his hands around her thighs and gave her a quick lick. Her breath hitched. The muscles under his hands tensed. Storm nipped at the inside of her thigh then he nibbled on the other, building her need higher. When he latched on to her core she cried out.

Need surrounded him. The scent of hers floated off her skin. Heather was ready and so was he, but he wasn't done yet. The exquisite torture he was putting them through would be well worth it in the end. One of his hands inched its way up to rest at the apex of her thighs. His fingers ached to feel her muscles tighten against them as they drove inside her, heightening her want and pushing her closer to a release. She thrust her hips toward him, sending silent signals of what she wanted.

His tongue brushed against her as he inserted one then two fingers inside her. Stroking her, reaching for the spot that made her lose control. One finger brushed it then another before he pulled out to do it all over again. Muscles tightened against his fingers, wanting to keep them inside so they could continue their assault. Storm obliged her. His fingers slid against her walls, one at a time so she was constantly feeling the stimulation. He lathed and sucked her until he knew she was on the brink. The moment she was ready to lose control he stood and drove deep into her.

She moaned her joy.

The clamps restraining her opened and she wrapped herself around him.

Storm had her pinned against the wall, struggling to keep his control while she lost hers. His lips closed around her mark, and she screamed as her world shattered. Her climax exploded around them. Like white hot lava, it burst out of her, consuming them both in the flames of her release.

Her heart beat so fast he had to give her time to calm down. He touched her face. "My heart."

"Wow." He knew that was the only word she could breathe. Her body still quaked from the aftershocks.

"That was so beautiful." He pressed a kiss against her mark and received a tight squeeze from the muscles still surrounding him.

"Oh, Storm, that was, wow."

He slid his hands around her derriere to carry her to the chair and changed the angle of her hips to make it easier for him to walk. He was greeted with another vise-like clamp from her muscles. "I want to move us to the chair but if you keep gripping me the way you are we might not make it."

"Can't help it. Every time you move the angle changes, and it feels so good." She clung to him; her voice soft.

Storm knew the chair to be perfect to heighten her next release, so he wrapped his arms around her and carried her to it. Each step was excruciating and wonderful. The simple movement of walking had her sliding up and down his shaft. Even though the movement was slight it sent a ripple through her each time. A part of him wanted to return to the wall but the chair was much closer now. Two steps and he was able to lower them to the cushions with a sigh.

Heather sighed with him. "Supernova?"

"I believe so. Do you have another scream in there for me?" He slid out and plunged back in.

"Storm." She arched up against him. Her legs tightened around his waist. "Please."

He hit a button on the chair to adjust the angle before he set the pace. His mate's heart pounded in her chest as she met him thrust for thrust. Her breath caught in her throat. She was getting close again. "Not yet, my heart."

She moaned when he changed the tempo, not happy when she was so close, but he planned on making it up to her. Her neck beckoned to him. The soft tissue begged for his kiss. Heather stopped breathing for a second when he pulled her mark into his mouth. "You need to breathe, my heart."

"I know." Her voice came out like a whisper. "Please don't stop."

Her excitement spurred him. He started to pump into her, feeling her need escalate. Her muscles tightened against him, giving him an exquisite vise to slide through. Everything felt so good.

Heather's breath hitched. "So close."

"I know." He picked up the pace, the scent of her release beginning to fill his nose. Her mind shared the climax beginning to take her over. His orgasm was imminent too. He held her close as he drove into her. His desire to make her scream once more drove him to hit the spot he knew would give him what he wanted. Each time he went in deep, brushing against the spot, then pulled back out. Heather shook with each penetration. Her body hugged him. They were going to go up in flames.

Heather started to keen, her mind focused only on the climax inching up her body. He used his hand to fuel that climax. If she had another scream in her he wanted to hear it. Her body clenched around his shaft.

Storm started to lose control. "My heart, I can't hold on."

"Storm, I—" The scream he hoped to hear started low and built with intensity as she hit her climax. It flung her out to the stars. He let go, following her along the wave that brought the scream out of her.

Their breathing labored, they clung to each other. He knew Heather wouldn't be able to move any time soon. He wondered how long it would take for her to speak.

She pointed to the wall that held the cuffs.

"Yes, my heart?" He found it hard to string thoughts together himself.

"Love."

He chuckled as he held her close. "I know. I do too."

———

Heather walked across the tarmac in her uniform like nothing had happened. She knew better. So did her mate, but unless the ship started talking, no one would know. Damn handcuffs. They were her undoing. Two screams. Normally Storm was lucky if he got a moan out of her.

He wrapped his arm around her waist and pulled her close. "I told you, you would enjoy those cuffs. Two screams. My, my. I believe that is a record."

A blush spread across her cheeks. She could feel the heat. "You don't have to act like the conquering hero."

"Can't help it. I pleased my mate today. It was a joyous thing to see." He grinned down at her.

"I think your head—" Heather stopped when she saw Bert standing there waiting for them. He never came into the city. "Is there something wrong?"

"I need to speak to the two of you and it is urgent." He fell into step with them.

"How long have you been waiting?" asked Storm.

"Not long. I was able to speak to Fridon and the council while I waited."

The council? Heather felt her heart drop.

"They are waiting for us now."

She looked up at her mate, not liking the odd feeling in the pit of her stomach. They went to the council's hall and then passed through to their private chambers.

Fridon stood there, looking out of his element until they walked in the room. He moved to Storm's side. Heather took her spot on the council. She felt odd wearing her uniform instead of her council clothes.

"First I hope I have proven myself to you over the last few months." Bert addressed the council. "My goal has always been to find my people. I don't want anything else." He looked at each person there as he spoke. "But in my searching I have found something I wish I hadn't."

Heather looked at Storm. Did he draw danger to the planet while looking for his people? Sam had told her that Ed hadn't wanted to come back because of someone he was afraid of. Her daughter didn't know what, but with everything going on she wondered if he feared their new guests.

"My sweeps are untraceable, which works in my favor because I have found an old enemy of my race." Bert looked at Heather. "They will pretend to come in peace because that is what they did when we first learned about them, but please heed my words. They are out to conquer your planet."

"Why would they come here?"

"For Heather."

Storm growled.

"I know." He held his hands up as he continued. "I have run the data several times and she is always the focal point. I don't know why yet. I don't have enough information. Which is why I have come to ask permission to run some special tests on the other Heather. The DNA tests Kuarto ran on her do show she's Heather, but I took the samples and ran more tests. I'm finding anomalies I shouldn't but the samples he had left isn't enough for me to do what I need to get to the bottom of my questions."

"What sort of questions?" asked Heather.

Bert looked at her. "I would rather have the answers than to guess and worry you for no reason."

Heather nodded. Bert wasn't sure what he could say in

front of the elders and between Bear's visit and the training mission they hadn't had a chance to talk. "The council knows all my secrets. I trust them to keep them. Tell us your fears."

"From what I have found she has no ancient blood in her."

"Then she isn't my mate," said Storm.

"All the other readings say she is."

"How is that possible?"

"I don't know. That's why I want more samples, specific ones for tests that will explain this."

"Of course, Bert, but we would like you to run your tests here," said Anseri. "If we have a new enemy, we want to be sure they will not be successful. I will have space set aside for you near the medlab."

"Thank you. I have a few more requests if that is all right."

Anseri nodded.

"First, I was successful in finding one of my fellow ancients and he has offered his help with my research on the other Heather. The second is I would like to run those same tests on you, Heather."

"No." Storm was the first to answer. "She has been poked and prodded enough."

"Will it help you, Bert?" asked Anseri.

Heather knew Storm was just trying to protect her. So did his mother, which is why she asked the question. She wouldn't seem like she was countering his comment if it came from his mother.

"Yes, and I promise it will be quick and painless."

"Let's go." She knew Bert had brought all he needed in hopes the elders would allow him his request. Heather stood. To her surprise so did the rest of the council. Great. Looked like she was going to have an entourage. The council went first, followed by Bert. Storm took her hand and walked at her side with Fridon right behind them.

"You sure you want to go through with this?" Storm looked down at her, keeping his voice low. "I had hoped all these strange tests would stop now that you're my mate."

"I had hoped too, my heart." She rested her head on his chest for a moment. "But if it will help explain things I want to help."

He didn't like the idea but remained silent as he slipped an arm around her shoulders.

"Oh, and I didn't complain when you poked and prodded me earlier. Why the sudden change of heart?" She spoke the words softly, barely above a whisper. Heather knew Storm's sensitive ears would pick it up where no one else would hear her.

"That was different." Laughter danced in his eyes. "And you liked it too. Twice."

She felt the heat of another blush fill her cheeks. She looked him in the eyes. "And I'm not denying that."

"Good, because if you did, I would have to prove it to you again." He leaned down and captured her lips with his.

Her body melted against him. It took Fridon clearing his throat to remind them why they were following the council.

They entered an empty room. Bert pulled a small device out of his pocket and within seconds the room was filled with the equipment he needed. He gestured toward a table, and Heather sat herself down on it. Then he moved to his computer. After pressing a few keys, he smiled at Heather. "All done."

She hopped off the bed.

"The other Heather?" Storm asked.

"If you can have your brother bring her in it will be just as quick."

He stepped out long enough to talk to Kuarto who

brought the other Heather in. Bert kept out of sight as he did the same thing with her. When he was done, Kuarto took her back to the room she had been held in.

"Why did you hide?" asked Heather. "She has already seen you."

"I'll let you know in a moment." He smiled as Ed transported into the room. "This is Ed."

"He is the other man we saw in the videos." Storm looked at him in shock.

"You have seen the videos? Which ones?" asked Ed.

"The ones dealing with my creation," answered Heather. "Your resemblance to my mate is uncanny. Can I assume you are a relative somehow?"

"Yes." He looked at Bert. "She is the prophesy?"

Bert nodded.

"She doesn't seem overly bright."

Storm snorted.

"I believe she was trying to be polite," said Bert.

"And I see you have the social skills of a porcupine." Heather crossed her arms over her chest. "What did you want to show us, Bert?"

Bert grinned as he brought the two files up, side by side. Ed did rub some people the wrong way because of the way he saw things, but Bert needed him. They looked at the readings.

"These belong to your Heather?" Ed studied the first set of readings. He whistled when he saw her DNA strand. He then brought up the ones they had been working with before. The ones that wouldn't give them the data they wanted. None of the patterns were the same.

"Yes. Heather has a protective enzyme that shields her true identity. We normally have a small window before this sample will do the same thing." Bert pointed to the other two sets. "This is our time traveler. Can you see it?"

"Right here. The new set repeats. The second set is degrading. That's not supposed to happen even in a clone."

"Cloning hasn't been used in years," interrupted Heather. "They've been banned throughout the galaxy."

"Yet a clone is what she is, and the process wasn't completed properly. She's falling apart inside." Bert made sure he had Heather's attention. "That Heather did come from the future, her DNA proves that, but she's not you. This Heather was created just before she came back."

"She's falling apart? Can that be stopped?"

"My heart, are you sure that would be wise?" Storm touched her cheek.

"That woman could have all the answers." She turned toward Storm, realizing their audience had never seen her question him before. "I only wish to learn if it can be done so an informed decision can be made."

He remained silent and she feared she had overstepped her boundaries, then he gave her that heart-stopping smile of his and pulled her into his arms. "Can she be saved?"

"Yes, we can stop the degradation easily."

"And why did you hide?" Storm asked after a mental prompting from Heather.

"I hid because she only knew me as a visiting doctor, and I didn't want to change that. We haven't detected any insert that might transmit information, but we're not done with those scans yet. They are a little more intricate so take more time."

"You think she does have something?"

"No," said Ed. "It's more of a precaution."

"So the question is did she come back to warn us or distract us." Heather had questioned this whole situation but never figured out the truth. She sure hoped she didn't find out too late.

FOUR

Heather remained quiet as she and Storm headed back to their rooms.

"My heart?" He didn't want to intrude in on her thoughts, but he was worried about how she was handling it.

"I'm fine." She looked up at him. "I'm just trying to figure out what is going on. I had a dream a few nights ago that I thought was odd, but until now I didn't think much of it."

"What did you dream?"

"I heard a voice wanting to show me my progeny." She leaned into his strength as they came to the corridor that led to their quarters.

"That's it?" The doors opened and they entered their rooms.

"Yeah." She wandered around and traced the top of the couch in front of her. "It was short and pretty clear. Normally my visions are convoluted and take me a few days to figure out. I wasn't sure what it was."

"Until now."

"I'm still not sure." She looked at her mate. "I need more dreams or visions to give me more to work with. I do know I don't like the feeling I'm having in the pit of my stomach. It tells me trouble is coming."

———

She woke up screaming. Storm held her as she regained control.

"Shh, my heart, it's okay. You're safe. I've got you." He caressed her back, hoping it would help calm her down.

"Oh, God, Storm. It was awful and centered around you. You were in a ship, circling a much larger one. The ship you were in blew up. I was standing on some sort of observation deck and watched. I felt our link sever. It was horrible." Tears streamed out of her eyes. "Promise me you won't fly that ship. Promise me!"

"You can't get rid of me that easily, my heart." He held her close. "What did you see?"

"I wasn't in a ship I recognized, but I was able to see the ship you were in." She buried her face in his chest.

"You saw me inside the ship?"

"That wasn't part of the vision." She looked up at him. "But I was positive you were in it. For some reason, you were the one who took a scout ship out instead of someone else. I'm not sure why. You were swinging around the other ship, passing an array and then yours blew up. I felt our connection break, screamed, and woke up here with you." She clung to him like she wanted to crawl inside his skin. "There are other snippets, but that is all I remember right now."

"I know more information will come to you as you work through this vision. I just don't like the fact that you didn't get them until now. And the other ship. Can you describe it to me?"

"I might be able to create an image of it. I'm sure Cim can help." She sat up.

"And where do you think you're going?" Storm didn't let go.

"To get you that image while it's still fresh in my mind?"

"It can wait." He pinned her to the bed. "My mate is upset, and I need to calm her down."

"You can do that." She touched his face. "But let me do this first."

"Are you telling me no?" He sounded shocked.

"Never." She grinned up at him. "Not when you make my body sing the way you do, but you also know this will drive me crazy until I get it done."

"And how many times will you have this vision?" He brushed a few strands of her hair out of her face.

"I don't know." She relaxed in his hold. "But enough to get a very clear image."

"Right." He pressed a quick kiss to her lips. "And when do you do your best in trying to explain these crazy dreams?" He pressed a kiss to her right collarbone then pressed one to her left.

"When I'm relaxed." She melted a little more.

"Very good." He pressed his lips to the valley between her breasts. "And when are you relaxed?"

"Right after you make me boneless."

"Exactly." He captured one of her nipples with his lips, using the gentle sucking motion with his mouth to make her forget everything but what he was doing to her. A soft sigh escaped her. He loved the challenge of arousing her. Her honest response to him always took his breath away.

The heat of his mouth wiped the fear from her dream away. He always knew what to do to make everything melt away. It was just the two of them. Feather-like touches in all the right places. Their hearts beat in unison, waiting, antici-pating the joy that was to come. His mouth then hands caressed their way down her torso. Drawing a laugh when he nipped just above her hip.

"Sorry, that tickles."

"I know in the beginning I took your laughter to mean you weren't being aroused, my heart, but now I know better. The sound of your laughter is so beautiful. Like you. Don't be sorry for something so pure."

The heat of his tongue against her core made her forget about the laughter that had just erupted from her. Once again, he brought her focus where he wanted it. Need started to build in the pit of her stomach then flowed through her veins.

It overpowered her as it took control. She moaned as she arched up, wanting more. Storm knew what she wanted and worked his way back up to her mouth. He captured her lips with his as he entered her. She felt a wonderful thrill run through her. The way he filled her always did that.

He set a slow pace. At first, she wanted to take over, but he created such a wonderful sensation she didn't want him to stop. Each time he drove in deep and pulled out almost all the way. He hit just the right spot, and her body shook with delight.

"Storm." Her voice sounded so faint. Heather was finding it hard to keep her thoughts together. He started moving faster, increasing the friction between them. Her breath hitched. Her need for her release tightened everything inside. She sucked in her breath as her muscles clamped down on him.

"My heart." He touched her face as he changed the tempo once again, frustrating her for a few seconds.

What he did she felt to her toes. Her body started to hum. She felt like she was standing on the edge, waiting for that little push to send her freefalling. It came when Storm stroked that one spot. The moment she felt him slide against her she started to vibrate in his arms. Everything splintered around her. All that was left was the wonderful cloud she floated on with her mate.

———

Heather stared at the woman who was her clone. What memories did she have? Did she know about the twins? Sam? "Will she remain in a force field when I talk to her?"

"No," said Bert.

"Yes," said Storm at the same time. "We don't know why she is here. Why would you want to talk to her unprotected?"

"My heart, I understand your concern, but the only way I can really see why she is here is to touch her. She is my clone. If I was aware of her creation, then I would have made sure I would have touched her at one point or another. What if I left us a message?"

"Heather."

"You know we need to get to the bottom of this." She touched his face. "I have to take the chance. Bert will make sure nothing goes wrong."

"No." He held her close like he wasn't about to let go.

Storm was serious. This was the only way, but she couldn't go against his wishes in front of other people. He would never forgive her. She also knew he was trying to protect her. What if he was right and her clone caused her harm?

She rested her head against his chest. "Then let's go back to our rooms."

Why do you feel it is necessary to touch her? He ran his hands over her hair.

I'm not sure, but after that vision I have to wonder if she is here to create the future she is from, not save us from it. If something went wrong and I had a chance I would have placed a message in her in the hope that I would figure it out and retrieve it.

What do you think the odds are of that happening?

I don't know and won't know until I try.

I want to be there with you.

Of course. I think your presence will help distract her.

"Bert, can you keep her protected?" Storm kept his arms around her as he focused on the ancient.

"I wouldn't let anything happen to Heather." Bert moved about the room. "She is the future. I do have a few questions to make sure that protection is the best it can be."

"Alright," Storm growled. He wasn't happy about any of this and the fact he was letting her do it anyway showed how much he trusted her visions.

"How long do you think you need to make contact?" Bert looked at her.

"Seconds?" Heather wasn't sure. She hoped the information, if it was there, would transmit the moment she touched her counterpart.

"Before, when you went to see her, I had the force field around her and so strong you wouldn't be able to accidentally touch her. This time I will put it around you. It will be just strong enough to keep her from transmitting anything but thin enough you should be able to pick up anything you might have planted without picking up anything you shouldn't."

"Thank you, Bert." Heather went into the room with Storm right behind her. The other Heather stood when she saw him.

She took a step toward him, hope in her eyes.

"Don't shoot. Whatever you do, Storm, don't shoot that ship," she said, her words frantic.

"I had a nightmare." Heather sat down. Those four words caught her doppelganger's attention.

"What did you see?"

"Storm's ship exploding." Heather found it interesting that her double didn't correct her and called it a vision. Didn't she know she had them?

"Yes." Her shoulders slumped. "That is what happened. He shot at the ship he was outside of and it retaliated. The image was horrible."

"Then all I need to do is keep him from flying that ship." Why did she use the word image? Even if she was her clone, she would have the memory unless she was created after all this happened. That made Heather think. Where did their memories separate?

"No." She touched Heather's hand then backed off. "No, he needs to fly the ship. We've tried that before."

"So, we're caught in a loop?" She felt information unfurl in her mind, but she had to ignore it until she was alone and could focus on it.

"In a way, but we have access to time travel so hope to break it." She emphasized the 'we' like she meant someone other than their group of friends.

Heather sat back. Why didn't she know that they had already time traveled? That should be part of her memory. Why didn't she remember that Bert had access to all this? Time to get some answers. "We? We who?"

"The people who are coming. They are trying to help us get Storm back."

"Who are they?"

"I can't say." She looked at her hands at that point.

Heather watched herself, knowing she couldn't trust the woman. Too many inconsistencies. "Why does Storm go into the ship?"

"I don't have an answer to that either."

"Why not?" She had said Storm shot at the ship but now she was saying she didn't know why he was in the ship. It didn't make sense.

"I must have blocked it out."

Heather fought the frown that wanted to spread across her face and schooled her features. Her mind wouldn't block something like that unless the block was forced. This Heather didn't know about her abilities. It was obvious she didn't have the same ability, or she would know they were suspicious. The whole thing made her head hurt. She needed to speak to Bert. "Thank you."

She stood and headed out of the room.

Storm had been quiet through the few moments they were with the other Heather. She could feel the questions in her head but kept her thoughts to herself. Instead, she just rested her hand against his arm. She planned on answering him as soon as she could.

She stopped in front of Bert. "Something isn't right. I know you've been running more tests. Have you gotten the data back yet?"

"They are ready. Ed and I were working through them when you wanted to speak to yourself."

"What have you found?"

Bert looked at Ed. "Several things."

"Can I see the tests you have run on the other me?"

"Sure." He pulled everything up. "What are you looking for?"

"She acted like she didn't know about my mental ability. I want to know if you detected anything on your tests. She also didn't know the details of the explosion. Could her mind be blocked?"

"I didn't detect any block." He pulled up details to show Heather. "There is one thing we found earlier that worries me."

"And you didn't think to tell us?" growled Storm.

"I mentioned it before, but now I have all the data to explain everything." He centered the information he wanted them to see on the screen. "Remember earlier I mentioned that she showed Vespian where I didn't detect any ancient blood?"

Heather nodded.

"This happened during the cloning process."

"Why?" Heather felt the beginnings of a headache. The data she absorbed wanted to take over.

"That was what we were trying to figure out."

"Then she isn't my clone."

"I didn't say that." He turned from the screen to look at Heather. "Cloning depends on your technology. Some clone to increase their population. Some clone to replace. If you have the proper equipment, you can clone an exact replica, with the memories and desires of the person you are cloning. When you clone for population, you might not want that and can make alterations to what you copy."

"So, if someone wanted to clone me, but still control me, they could alter my DNA?"

"Yes, but most don't. When you alter DNA, you run the risk of degradation." He looked at Ed.

"Then that is why she's degrading."

"Yes, but knowing they have an ancient ship, that

shouldn't have happened. Unless it was done on purpose. It's the why we can't answer." Ed took over. "Whoever cloned her should have wanted her to pass any tests done on her. Now our tests are more advanced than anything here on Vespia so we caught it quickly, but most technologies would have figured it out as well."

"But maybe not fast enough to stop whatever she came here to do." Heather didn't like this at all.

"We'll know more when your guests arrive."

"Thank you, Bert, Ed." She placed her hand on Bert's arm. "You two have given me a lot to think about." Heather looked up at her mate. Her head felt like it was going to explode. "I think I need to rest now."

Storm watched her with a frown on his face. "Are you okay?"

"I'm fine, my heart. Just need to meditate for a little while. I'll be good after that."

———

Bert looked at Ed once they left. "Why didn't you tell her your other theories about the lack of ancient blood?"

"Because I'm not sure if I'm right. Why worry her until we have to."

"We know the ship and we know who captured it. We also know she's been hunting every ancient she can get her hands on. One of the reasons I went into hiding."

"If that is Reasta we will tell her. Until then we wait."

———

Heather curled up on the bed. Her mind was already starting to decipher the information she had gotten from her clone and there was a lot. It overpowered her with the speed it filled her head. Storm had gone back to the security center but had planned on coming back as quickly as he could. She had hoped her mind would wait for him, but everything was unraveling too fast.

Her head hurt from all the data. Closing her eyes, she hoped it would give her a little relief. More and more information flooded her, forcing her deeper and deeper into her mind. She felt like she was spinning down a drain. When she finally landed, she was in a white room. Heather stood up, trying to figure out where she was. Using the word room didn't describe where she was. It was more like an area.

"Where am I?"

"I was going to ask the same thing," came another voice.

Heather turned to find Storm walking up to her. "My heart?"

"Heather?" a new voice asked.

She turned again and found Bert with them. "Are you two as confused as I am?"

"Yes," said Bert. "I was in the lab, reviewing the tests I had Ed run then I was here. Where are we anyway?"

"I'm not sure," Heather replied. "I was meditating. The images I picked up from my clone began to fill my mind and did it so quickly I retreated. Then I found myself here."

"We must be in your mind then."

"But this isn't what it looks like."

"Perhaps we're deeper than you normally go. Can you show us some of the images you have received?"

Images started flashing nearby.

"I didn't see that wall before," commented Storm. He walked up and touched it. Heather laughed.

"That tickled." She looked at him. That proved they were inside her mind. "Okay, so what now?"

"Do you feel comfortable sharing those images with us?

Let's see what information you sent back?" Storm wrapped his arm around her shoulders.

"That had to be my goal if you are here before I have had a chance to go through any of them." One image caught her attention. "Stop."

The picture froze on the screen. The image was a row of windows embedded in a section of a ship. "That is what I saw in my vision."

"You sure?" Bert didn't sound happy with her statement.

"Yes, why?"

"Because that is Ialog's ancient ship."

"Then what you suspect is true." Heather turned to look at him.

"Until we see the ship in person I don't want to make any guesses." He crossed his arms over his chest. "Did you see a face in your vision?"

Heather shook her head.

"Why, Bert?" asked Storm.

"What if the ship had been taken over again and my people are on their way home? We need to wait and see."

She allowed the images to continue. The three of them watched the screen, not sure what they were looking at.

"Wait." Bert pointed to the screen. "Can you back that up?"

"I think so." Heather focused on the images and got them to go backward. They went slower, making it easier for them to see the details.

"There." On the screen was the face of a woman. "Does she look familiar to you, Heather?"

"Haven't seen her face yet in any of my visions. Who is she?"

"Her name is Reasta. She was the one who came to us

asking for help and the same one who has been hunting us ever since."

"Hunting you? Why?" asked Storm.

"When we first met her, she told us her people needed help." Bert didn't answer his question directly and that worried Heather. "We took her at face value, but then my people started disappearing. In the beginning, we weren't sure what was going on, but it didn't take us long to figure out she was at the center of it. When we confronted her, she fought back. It wasn't pretty. Reasta was a lot more powerful than we realized. She's the reason the ancients left Vespia. She is dangerous. Never forget that."

"And how are we to protect ourselves against her?" asked Storm.

"I think that is why we're in Heather's head instead of sitting in one of the labs discussing this."

———

Storm opened his eyes to find Kuarto only inches from his face. "Do you mind?"

"What happened?" Kuarto straightened. He ran his scanner over Storm.

Storm looked around and found himself in the medlab. Bert was just sitting up in the bed next to his. How did he get here? "Why am I in the medlab?"

"Because you were talking to the security guard on duty when your eyes rolled up into the back of your head and you slid to the floor. Bert is here because I found him on the floor as well when I walked into his lab." He crossed his arms over his chest. "You going to explain what happened?"

Heather walked into the room at that point. Crossing to

her brother, she rested a hand on his arm. "I'll explain everything later. But everything is okay."

Her voice was smooth, calming. He blinked a few times. "All right, but I would like to run a few more tests."

"No more tests." Storm sat up. "I need to get back to security."

"I'd like to get back to my work as well." Bert swung his legs off the bed and got to his feet. "If that is okay with you, doctor."

"I guess, but I'd like to find out what caused the two of you to pass out like that." He looked at his sister. "Can I assume you had something to do with this?"

"You know I can't control my mind when it expands." She smiled at him. "Come by our rooms this evening and I'll explain everything. Bert, you are invited as well."

———

Storm escorted her out of the medlab. "Why did you invite your brother to our rooms this evening?"

"What?" She looked up at him. "I didn't do that, did I?"

"You did. I think." He rubbed his head against his head. "Now I can't remember. Something strange is going on, my heart."

"I know." Heather wasn't sure what they were talking about anymore. "Did you really pass out?"

"I don't remember, but you came in like you knew what was going on. Don't you remember?" He slid his arm up and down her back.

"No. I remember being in our rooms then felt a strong urge to go to the medlab, but most of it is a bit of a fog." She looked up at her mate. "I'm almost afraid to ask what happened. What if my lack of memory is self-imposed to protect me?"

"Come with me to security. I'd feel better if you weren't left alone right now."

"You don't need to babysit me, my heart." She walked with him as he headed to the main office.

"I know, but this way nothing will distract me but you."

———

Heather sat on the couch next to her mate. Kuarto sat across from her while Bert sat to Storm's right.

"So?" Kuarto looked at the other three. They were acting a little strange and he didn't know why, but hopefully he would in a minute.

She smiled at her brother. Taking Storm's hand, she nodded to the other two. "Join hands."

"Really?" Kuarto's voice held a note of annoyance. "What are we doing? A séance?"

Heather didn't answer, just kept that smile on her face and closed her eyes. The white area reappeared. Storm, Bert and Kuarto appeared nearby.

"Where are we?" asked Kuarto. He looked around in awe.

"Someplace safe." Heather looked at each of them before focusing back on her brother. "I know we have been acting a little strangely, Kuarto, but I don't know who to trust when we're awake. This is the one place we can work openly. I trust each of you to help me with what is coming. The images I downloaded from my clone tell a different story than what she is painting, but we can't show that we know. All I ask is that each night, after we've gone to sleep you join me here for an hour so we can prepare for our visitor. When we're conscious we won't remember any of this. It is for our protection. Whatever decision we make here we will do while we're conscious even though we might not remember doing it."

"Why?"

"Because of the woman who is commander of the ship that is coming." Her image appeared next to Heather. "Although she can't read minds, she can tell who lies. It is her gift. If we try to hide something from her on a conscious level, she'll know."

"So, you want to work on the unconscious level?"

"Yes. We'll be seen doing some strange things, but it will be worth it."

———

Skye Latimer was glad to be back. Bert had sent him on several errands over the last few days, keeping him away from Sam. He couldn't wait to see her. He had worried that the bonding would cause trouble between them, but it had only brought them closer. Every moment he was away from her made him miss her that much more.

Her training had gone well, and she had excelled at it, but knowing who her parents were he wasn't surprised. He found her lying on her stomach on the couch, reading, with that stupid cat curled up on the small of her back. The first thing he did was pick up Pumpkin.

"Sam, this cat of yours is too huge for you to still treat it like a kitten."

"Pumpkin is a standard tabby, and my baby." She rolled over and took the cat from him. After petting her a few times, she sat Pumpkin on the floor and stood. "She keeps me company when you're not here."

He wrapped his arms around her. "And when we're both gone?"

"Mom takes care of her."

"How about we forget about the cat and take care of each other?"

"The last time we did that she parked herself on your chest at the most inopportune moment."

Skye laughed at the memory. Sam had been riding him, close to her orgasm when Pumpkin climbed up onto his chest and stared at him. The cat wouldn't budge either.

"Let me put her up so she won't interfere." Sam picked Pumpkin back up and walked to the bathroom. "Oh, by the way, my mother would like to talk to you."

"What? Another wonderful dinner with your father glaring at me the whole time?"

"He has gotten better."

"Yeah, at least he doesn't growl at me anymore." He wrapped his hand around her wrist when she closed the door after locking Pumpkin in. "What time does she want us?"

"That's just it." She leaned against the door as he closed the distance between them. "We don't need to go to her. She'd like to come here, through me."

"Oh." He nipped at her ear. "Wait! What?"

"She wants to use my mind to talk to you."

"No."

"Skye." She touched his cheek. "I know her abilities bother you, but she has always respected my wishes. I just know she's quite insistent. And your distrust will make you wonder if she's lurking inside somewhere to take over while we're having sex and that will distract you. Just let her have her say so we can relax."

He frowned. Sam knew him too well because that would distract him until he was sure Heather would leave them alone. "I'd rather talk to her in person."

"She knows that, but what she has to say to you she doesn't want on any camera on Vespia. Bert's ship is the safest place to have this conversation and she can't come here right now."

"She's not going to climb into my head, is she?"

"Don't be silly. She hates doing this, but feels it is the only way." Sam hesitated for a moment. "She sent the twins away to keep them safe."

"What is she afraid of?"

"I don't know. She said she'd explain everything to you."

"And the two of you have already discussed this haven't you." His words came out a little bit like a growl which made Sam smile. He was a lot like her father.

"Yes, and I'd recommend you back off before she takes over."

Skye did step back. Crossed his arms over his chest and glared.

"Did I interrupt something?"

"Close. Your daughter let me know of your desire to talk to me, so we waited."

"You were afraid I'd watch, weren't you?" She smiled. "You still don't trust my abilities."

"I have been around too many with powers like yours where that type of power went to their heads as time went on."

"Then you're not going to like what is going to happen next." Heather touched his temple before he could stop her. "There is a darkness coming and everything we love is being threatened. I have been having visions and received information from a reliable source to reinforce my visions. Skye, the people coming don't know about you. They know about Sam, but not that she has found her mate. I'm not sure how this woman knows what she does, but I'm assuming it is from other timelines. She has tried this before. I need you to spearhead this. You're the only one I can trust."

"Why me?"

"Because you are the wild card. That woman can't know that we have an ancient among us and Storm, well, he gets killed. I need you to stop that. Everything I know I have given to you. I have also created a link so as I have other visions you will see them too when you sleep." Heather touched his arm. "I know you don't like this and feel invaded, but I don't know any other way to save everyone. And Skye you can be as mad as you want, but I won't remember doing this. It is for everyone's protection. If you try to confront me, I won't know what you're talking about and if you push you could jeopardize everything."

———

Storm came into their rooms to find Heather sitting on the couch meditating. He grinned. He knew just the thing to break her meditation. Kneeling in front of her, he pressed a kiss to her lips, then each cheek before he focused on her mark.

A soft sigh escaped her as she tilted her head so he could have better access.

"Done meditating?" he murmured against her throat.

"Yes." She smiled as she slid her hands through his hair. "I have better things to do than meditate when my mate is with me."

"You do, don't you." He pulled her to her feet. "And it's just the two of us. Nothing to interrupt us. Our guards will keep everyone away for as long as we want."

"What do you have in mind, my heart?" She pressed her hands against his chest which was blocked by his uniform. "Any particular color outfit or would you prefer using the hot tub?"

"Hmm, both sound wonderful. We could combine them." He ran his hand down her back. "What would you like?"

She gave him a knowing smile. Heather closed her eyes. The dress she wore disappeared and she was now standing in a beautiful dark blue corset with a garter and hose. Blue high heels covered her feet. Her breasts came close to spilling out of the top. Her hips were covered with a very short skirt that just covered part of his favorite playground.

"This is new." He trailed his hands across her exposed stomach then along the edges of the top of the corset.

"Have to keep you interested." She stood proud in front of him. He always loved what she wore for him.

"My heart, you know I don't care what you wear." He walked around her.

"I know." She touched his face. "But I love to see that little jolt you get each time I come up with something new. It's like pretty wrapping paper over a present you have begged for every day, and you have finally gotten it."

"You know me well." He spoke against her ear from behind her, causing goosebumps to rise on her arms.

"Like I know myself." She leaned back against him. "It also melts in water."

"Really?" He grinned as he came around the front again. "So, shower or hot tub?"

"That is up to you since I chose the outfit."

"That wall looks really good." He started backing her toward it. Once he had her pinned his lips went right for her mark. The scent of her arousal floated around his head as he sucked the tender issue of her neck into his mouth. His need for her never wavered.

"This wall won't disintegrate this corset, and neither will your drool."

He laughed as he released her. "You think highly of yourself."

"My heart." She grinned at him as she danced out of his embrace. "You look at me as a tasty morsel all the time. Why wouldn't I think you drool?"

"Have I ever drooled on you?"

"Well, you do make me wet. That counts, doesn't it?" She walked slowly backward toward their bathing area.

"Oh, my heart." He followed her. "Saying things like that just makes me want you more."

She laughed as she entered the bathroom. Moving past the shower she headed toward the outer area where their hot tub was.

"I thought I could pick the spot?"

"Your brain has been screaming hot tub since I told you this outfit melted with water."

He grinned. "You should make it edible."

"It is." She smiled back. "But this is a lot of material for you to try to consume."

"Is that a challenge?" He followed her into the small garden where they had built the hot tub. With a thought, he removed his clothes. The perks of having an ancient computer being able to read his mind.

"I know better than to challenge you." He stood only a breath away. Heather reached out and ran her hand along his jaw. "I also thought we'd try the edible underwear another time."

She slipped out of her heels and unhooked one of the nylons she wore.

"Wait. I wish to do that." His warm hand glided across the silk texture. "This doesn't melt?"

"I thought about it but then decided the corset would be enough." The heat of his hand on her inner thigh sent a shiver of delight through her.

"And the skirt?" He crouched down in front of her.

"Unties at the hip." She sounded a little breathless. Her desire for Storm always amazed her.

He smiled when he found the string that kept it on, gave it a quick tug, and let it flutter to the ground. His hands snaked around to her derrière to hold her still as he took a deep breath. Her need spiraled up when she felt his tongue lathe her. Heather opened her stance so she could brace herself as he spiked her desire higher. As his tongue worked its magic on her, his hands moved around her thighs, releasing the stockings, and helping them slide down to her ankles.

Heather didn't think she could keep her feet much longer. "Storm."

"I know my heart." He stood and touched her face. "Let's move to the tub."

He wrapped an arm around her waist, lifted her, and carried her to the edge of the tub. She thought he'd put her down so she could climb in, but he held onto her as he slid into the tub. Storm eased her onto the lip of the tub, careful to keep the corset dry. His fingers skimmed along the edge of the top. Excitement came off him in waves. "So how does this work?"

She scooped up a little water in her hands and drizzled it against her hip. Where most of the water dropped the material faded away, revealing skin. Other areas lightened and became transparent.

"Okay, let me." Like a child with a beautifully wrapped gift, he took his time removing sections of the outfit until the only parts of her body still covered was what he loved to focus on. Now she knew what to design when she created the edible outfit.

"You missed a couple of spots."

"I did, didn't I." He brushed his fingers against the sections he had left. "I'll have to fix that. The real decision is where to start."

"Why did you leave something on my right hip?"

"Because that is a ticklish spot, and the sound of your laughter is a wonderful thing." He touched her face. "The question is should I start there?" He touched the spot where he left part of the corset. "Or here." His fingers brushed the soft flesh of her breasts. "Or here." His fingers slid into her heat.

She quivered in anticipation.

"Normally I start with your mark." He brushed his fingers against it. "But the corset didn't go that high. If I do start, there I run the risk of melting the rest of the outfit off your body before I have the chance to enjoy it."

"I'm about ready to melt and you have barely touched me." She sucked in her breath when she felt his lips against her mark. "I see you can't help yourself."

"You know me well." He gave her one of his heart-stopping smiles before he kissed his way down to the first part of her body where he left part of the corset. His mouth closed around one of her nipples. "Hmm."

"Thought you'd like the flavor." Heather braced her hands on either side of her hips. It would give her something to do with her hands since she was too well known for stopping him because of her needs instead of letting him have fun with his favorite playground. He taught her on the ship that she should let him do what he wanted to her. The screams proved it.

Her head dropped back as little flames of need licked

their way through her. It didn't take much for her to feel desire overpower her. Storm's touch did that to her. A sigh escaped her when he moved from one breast to the other. His fingers caressed her thigh, working their way into her folds. He stroked her, forcing her want for him higher. "Storm."

"I haven't removed all the pieces of your garment yet." He continued to stroke her as his mouth moved back up to her mark.

"I can jump into the water and fix that problem quickly." Desire made her breath hitch.

"That would be cheating and a good cause to tie you up again." He murmured against her neck.

The thought his words invoked sent little frissons of delight racing up her spine. "Storm."

"Shh, my heart, and enjoy." He pressed drugging kisses down her throat, across her collarbone, and down to the other breast. Heather found it hard to sit still. Her mate knew it too because he wrapped an arm around her waist to keep her where he wanted her. Between the draw of his mouth on her breast and the wonderful caresses he continued to use she felt her orgasm begin to blossom.

Her breath came out in little pants. Storm switched his rhythm when he picked up the scent of her impending release.

"Lie down for me, my heart." The glow in his eyes could have lit the room.

"But your need…"

"Can wait a little longer." He came up out of the water enough to lath her belly button and press her back to the cool tile before he blazed a trail of hot open mouth kisses to her core. His caresses had her opening for him before she felt the warmth of his mouth against her.

She wanted to feel him inside her so bad. The anticipation of the depth of his penetration sent excitement racing through her veins. "Please, Storm."

"Soon." He inserted two fingers inside her and her muscles clamped down on him. The combination of his tongue lathing her and the in and out motion of his fingers had her shaking.

"So close." Then she felt the orgasm bubble up, from the pit of her stomach to roar through her, filling her with euphoria and sending her out to the stars. Just as she reached the height of her release Storm picked her up and slid her down his length. Her breath caught in her throat as the release grew again, causing the wonderful out-of-body experience she always felt in his arms.

When she could finally feel again it was his fingers on her jaw. "Wow."

"That was beautiful." He pulsed inside. "Ready for more?"

"Always, my heart. Although I still feel a little bit like jelly."

"You feel exquisite to me." He pressed his lips to her mark. "But you always have."

"You're biased." She tightened her muscles against him as she started to move up and down his shaft.

"Only because you're mine." He tilted her away from him, wanting to hit the spot that made her scream.

"What? Two screams weren't enough for one day?" She reached for the rim of the tub, so he didn't have to hold her the whole time.

"Going for the record, my heart." He rocked into her. Setting a pace that would have them breathless quickly.

"Isn't two a record already?" She closed her eyes as little fissions of heat filled her blood.

"Yes, but it's not going to stop me from trying to make

you scream again. It is a beautiful sound." He sucked in his breath when her muscles clamped around him.

"So, you will always try to make me scream while I will always try to make you lose control." Heather was proud she could still string two words together. Her desire pushing to take control. "Sounds like a deal."

Storm drew little circles against her skin when he found he didn't need to support her anymore. First around her hip, then up her torso until he reached her breasts. The feather-like touches made her sigh.

Each time he filled her she felt need lick at her insides. Muscles tightened and relaxed with every stroke. Storm quickened the pace, making her breath catch. A tremor raced through him, and she knew he was close.

Making sure her grip was strong, Heather slid her legs up higher on Storm's waist, changing the angle of his penetration. They both moaned at the same time.

"My heart." Storm's voice was deep, much deeper than normal. His hands roamed over her, touching all the spots that aroused her. She wished she could do the same thing. Watching him lose control was wonderful to see.

As her orgasm raced toward her again his did the same. Her body vibrated with the power of it as it swept over her. She floated in the water, feeling boneless. Storm lifted her and cradled her close.

"Wow." She rested her head on his shoulder, unable to move at the moment. Their intimacy couldn't get any better.

———

The ship coming toward Vespia was now close enough for the council to pick up a transmission from their impending guests. Heather felt her heart pounding in her chest. Last night she had dreamed of the face of the woman who killed her mate. The odd thing was that the face seemed familiar, but she couldn't figure out why. Heather prayed it wasn't the one she would see when they answered the hail.

Storm stood beside her, his arm around her shoulders, holding her close.

"They are responding, sir."

"Put it on."

The image shimmered onto the screen. A tremor raced through her when she recognized the face. The woman in her dreams. A small voice inside her told her it was time to put everything into action.

"This is Reasta, commander of the spacecraft Veisom. Am I speaking to the Vespian council?"

"You are," replied Storm's mother. "Your ship hasn't been cleared to enter Vespian space."

"Yes, ma'am, and I apologize for that. I would like to request permission now."

"And why do you wish to approach Vespia?"

"We have ancients among us who wish to return to the planet they called home."

"Ancients?" She looked at the other council members for a moment. "You have proof?"

"I am sending you the data right now." The smile on her face was too fake. She looked around. Her gaze settling on Heather.

"Thank you." Anseri looked at Heather as well, then she turned back to the screen and gave her own plastic smile. "You may not pass into our space until we have cleared your information."

The screen went black. She turned to Heather and Storm. "You will need to go through what they sent Storm. We never learned what happened to the ancients. Perhaps this will help us understand why they disappeared the way they did."

He nodded to his mother before escorting Heather out of the main hall. "So did you recognize her?"

Heather nodded. "I'm scared, Storm."

"Why, my heart?"

"If this doesn't work, she's going to ruin our lives."

"It will work. There is nothing that will keep us apart."

She looked up at her mate. Heather hoped he was right.

FIVE

Skye found himself in a white area. "What the hell is going on?"

"My heart, why him?" He heard Storm growl his comment and headed toward the sound. Heather, Storm, and Bert stood there waiting for him.

"Because he is the only one Reasta doesn't know about." She touched Storm's chest. "My visions have been filling in the gaps from what I got from my clone. There are things she isn't aware of, and we need to make sure she never learns about them, like the twins or the fact that Sam and Skye found each other. I'm not sure yet, but I don't think she knows about my visions. The things she doesn't know about are going to be the ones to help us win."

"And Skye?" Storm looked at him.

"I have given him my visions so he can know what needs to be done to defeat them. He will be the only one who remembers anything. We will still meet like this and continue with our plans until necessity stops us. Skye will make sure they are implemented."

"How much time do we have?" asked Storm.

"I'm not sure. That ship is what? Three days away?" Heather tried to give her mate her best smile. "Plus, the time we have while the council decides on this."

"We could tell the elders about your visions and send them away." Storm touched her face.

"And I thought about that, but I fear it would give us the wrong outcome. My visions have always shown me that if I try to change them things escalate. Telling the elders what I see might keep these people away but could make the situation worse." She looked at Bert. "Have you finished your computations?"

"Yes, I've run several timeline scenarios. Each one says the same thing, sending them away is not the answer. That tells them we know what they are plotting. We need to get through this without arousing their suspicion and causing a war that will devastate the planet."

"Can someone explain to me what is going on?" Skye didn't want to listen to twenty minutes of them acting like he wasn't there.

"You have been getting my visions?" Heather turned her attention to him.

"Yes, but I can't make heads or tails out of them."

Heather nodded. "That doesn't surprise me. It took me time to figure them out."

"Can you make them stop?"

"I can, but I don't want to." She brushed a strand of hair out of her face. "But I can help you understand them better, but it means a stronger tie to my mind."

"Heather." Storm's voice showed his dislike over the idea. Skye wasn't real thrilled either.

"My heart, I have to do this. The fate of our planet is at stake." She didn't move from Storm's side, but Skye felt a slight brush in his head. "That should do it."

"Now what? I'm going to hear your thoughts all the time?"

"No, but as my mind works its way through the images, figuring out what they mean you will be part of that process. Now understand the dreams, or my visions always come while I sleep so you'll get them that way as well, but the thought process I use to figure them out will be while you're awake. You should be able to push them into the back of your mind and ignore the process, but in the beginning, it will be a bit overwhelming."

He didn't like this. "What do you want from me?"

"The people coming are here for me and Sam. That is what I got out of the visions so far. You are going to stop them."

"How am I supposed to do that?"

"That's why we're meeting like this until they take me. We're going to come up with a plan that will save us all."

———

Skye helped Bert and Ed pack up all of their equipment from his complex on Vespia. Everything had to go so no one would know he had ever been there. Skye was amazed that everything fit in the two ships Bert had.

"So you're just going to go into hiding?" Skye asked.

"It might seem like that but that woman coming tried very hard to destroy my race. If she were to know we're here helping you she would do her best to remove us from the equation. In order to help all of you we must disappear. Heather plans on removing me from their records. Luckily, I haven't interacted with that many people here and no one knows about Ed or Dian. It should be easy for her to purge me."

"The power of her mind frightens me." Skye knew he needed to trust her, but trust came hard for him.

"Because you don't understand it." Bert transported the last of his items to one of the ships. "You have trusted me, why?"

"There is something about you that I connect with."

"There should be," said Ed.

Bert shot him a look that kept him from saying anything else. Skye wondered what Ed was hinting at. He went back to their conversation. "And Heather?"

"She acts like this meek woman around Storm, but I know better. I have seen her files."

Bert started laughing.

"What?"

"It's not Heather that bothers you, it is her mate. She is from Earth and was trained in security, yet she allows Storm to dominate."

Skye glared at Bert but didn't argue with him. The stories he heard about Heather didn't fit the demure woman he knew. She had a backbone, he had seen hints of it from time to time, but she allowed Storm to control her and that was what didn't fit to him.

"You have not spent enough time with the two of them. The woman you see is for the rest of society. She is under constant scrutiny so must behave as expected for a woman of her station. She can't be herself when she is in public. I think having that connection you will get to know the real Heather."

"I don't like the fact that she's connected to me. What if she tries to manipulate my mind?"

"How? Are you afraid she'll change your feelings for Sam? Or Sam's for you?" Bert shook his head. "Sam is her daughter she's had a mental connection with her since she met her while captured by Ialog. If she wanted to meddle, she would have done so a long time ago."

"Yet she's getting ready to do that." Skye didn't want to talk about this anymore. "So why two ships?"

"You and Ed are going to help me merge them into a space complex for us while Heather changes the memories of anyone who knew about me, the twins, you, and Sam. Since we can't be on the surface when she does that or our memories will be altered as well this would be a good time for me to give you everything I can to help the plan Heather is implementing." He approached his ship. Once he opened the gangplank he turned back to Skye, who hadn't moved. "We need to get out of here before she gets started."

————

Heather sat opposite Toki.

"You sure this is what you want?" she asked as she leaned over and covered Heather's hand with her own.

"No, but I can't think of anything else that will do what I need." Heather didn't like the idea of what she was about to do, but it was the only way.

"If this woman is as dangerous as you say, why are we letting her come here?" Toki watched her. "Because your visions say we should?"

"You have visions, don't you follow yours?" Heather worried that she could mess up everything and reveal just what she was capable of. She had been able to keep her ability within the tight circle of family up until now, but this threat was too big for her to hide what she could do.

"Point taken." Toki got up and started placing crystals in a circle. "I need you to sit in the center, Heather, before I seal this. It will help amplify your reach. I need to know how many minds you have tried to reach at the same time, so I know how many to use."

"Four." Heather stepped into the circle.

"Four? That's all? Are you sure you can do this?" Toki had most of the crystals in place. Even though she knew Heather's mental abilities were very strong, she couldn't help but make a joke. "Maybe I should get more crystals."

"Funny. It's not the question of if I can do this, because I have to. It's more of if it will work."

———

Skye stood outside Heather and Storm's quarters. He was now her personal security guard. To Heather and Storm, he had been with her since she had been kidnapped by Ialog almost two years ago.

The doors opened and Storm stepped out. He nodded to the Vespian guard before he turned to Skye. "You have her itinerary?"

"Yes, sir."

"She's speaking to your admiral."

Skye nodded and headed into their quarters. It felt strange to be in there, but to Heather and Storm he had been doing this for a while. Admiral Barrington's face filled the screen.

"I'm not sure if the government will allow you to do radio silence for such a long period of time."

"Sir, the people coming here could start a war. I am only trying to keep Earth out of it for as long as possible."

"Heather, we're supposed to be allies."

"Do you want to go to the president and tell him that the treaty with Vespia has drawn our planet into a war you didn't ask for?"

"Of course not, but two of our best security agents are on Vespia. You need to be protected."

"Fine Bear, I'll resign and send Latimer back to you. No ties. You can live your lives without repercussions."

"You know I can't accept that. How many times have you tried to resign?" He paused for a moment. "What is going on, Heather?"

She sighed. "Nightmares."

"Got it." He ran his fingers through his hair. "Which is why you sent the twins with me."

"Twins? Bear, the children you have are from a niece who needed to go into deep space. You will take care of them until she comes back. Key word is desire. When I say that you will remember everything as it should be."

Bear nodded slowly.

Skye couldn't believe what she just did. Her voice dropped a few octaves, going across to Bear velvet smooth. Hypnotic and aimed only at him. How did she do that over a comlink? Other people he knew with such an ability had to be in person to alter other people's thoughts.

"I'll send your message to the President, but I don't know if he's going to go along with your request." The admiral didn't seem fazed by what happened.

"Then if I don't hear from you in the next five days, I'm going to assume he went along with my request. It isn't forever. Just long enough to see what their real purpose is."

"Keep her safe, Latimer."

"Yes, sir."

The comlink ended and Heather turned toward him. "Ready?"

He nodded. Skye was glad her power wasn't currently aimed at him. He didn't know what she did to him, but he didn't feel like he had lost any of his memories. Sam was his bondmate. She still had that stupid cat. Now he had to see what Heather had altered around him.

Heather headed out of their rooms and into the hall. "Storm has moved our training to the field."

Okay. He had never trained with them. What did that mean?

"He's left our uniforms at the gym. We need to hurry to catch up."

———

Skye found being Heather's bodyguard a bit of a challenge. The mornings were filled with her working out with her squad, which he was able to join. The afternoons consisted of Heather sitting in the main hall of the elders listening to people complain. He didn't know how she could sit there and do nothing.

When the elders adjourned for the evening Heather went to the gardens and talked to the people. This was when he found himself working the most. She trusted everyone and let them near her without caring for her welfare.

"Heather, we need to keep you safe." He spoke softly in her ear when a group of youngsters ran toward her. "Allowing anyone and everyone come up to you isn't safe."

"They're children, Skye."

"Not all of them. How do you know that the people who are coming haven't sent people here to spy on you?"

"He's right, you know." Storm's voice came from Skye's left. He felt the warmth of Storm's hand on his shoulder as the man passed him and wrapped his arms around his mate. "Your heart is too giving. What happened to that tough little security guard I mated with who didn't trust anyone?"

"She's still here, but your people have never given me any reason to feel threatened and I don't want to insult them by suddenly changing that." She touched his face. "I also know how to protect myself if I need to."

"Mother says we have another communiqué coming in from the ship and she wishes us to attend."

Heather nodded.

Skye wasn't sure if he should accompany them. She was with Storm, and he was her guard when her mate was working. It took Storm looking at him and asking him if he was coming for him to follow. The main council chambers had a huge screen he had never noticed before. The elders stood in the forefront around the screen. Heather and Storm stood in the back. He tried to stay out of sight of the screen by standing against the wall with the other Vespian guards.

He waited with the rest of them, wondering what to expect. The moment the woman appeared on the screen he felt something strange happen in his head. It felt like one of the many images Heather had shoved into his head snapped together with two others and hung in the middle of his mind. He tried to shake it, but he couldn't stop thinking about the image burning in his mind. All he could see was this woman gloating over Heather. What she was gloating over he wasn't sure of yet, but it didn't have a good feeling.

Was this what she went through when she had her visions? It would drive him crazy. Looking over at Heather he noticed the smile she had pasted on her face. That military one everyone used when they knew something was wrong but couldn't let on.

Skye turned his focus to the woman. She had the dark hair that Vespians sported, but fair skin like Heather. Her eyes were an ice blue with elongated pupils. They reminded him of a snake and gave him the creeps. She spoke to Anseri but he noticed her gaze would flick to Heather and Storm every once in a while.

"I hope you have had time to go through our data and give us permission to land on Vespia."

"We have checked everything you sent us." She looked at the other council members before she turned back to the screen. "You are welcomed on our world."

"Thank you so much." She closed communication.

Anseri gave the ship's information to the head of their landing bay to give them clearance. Once she made sure they could land she walked up to her son and his mate. "I hope you know what you are doing."

"Me too, Anseri," said Heather.

———

Heather sat on the bed. She had the weird sensation that someone was in her head when she recognized part of her vision. The way things connected caught her off guard from time to time but that was the first time she had the sensation that she wasn't the only one seeing what she saw.

"My heart?" Storm brushed his hand through her hair.

"Nothing. Just getting weird sensations with these visions."

"Do you know what she wants yet?"

"No." Heather sighed. "It's not making sense, yet I just have this awful feeling in the pit of my stomach."

"Then maybe you should go back to Earth for now. I want you safe." He sat down beside her and pressed his hand to her heart.

"The safest place I can be is at your side." She returned the gesture. "You are my heart."

"And if your vision comes true and I explode inside a ship? How will I protect you then?"

"The reason I have those visions is to make sure they are altered in some way. You won't leave me. I won't let you."

He touched her face. "How much time?"

"I don't know. A day or two?"

"Then I don't want to waste it worrying about what might happen." He pulled her toward him and pressed his lips against hers for a quick kiss. "I want to hear you scream for me."

"And how do you plan on doing that?" She smiled at him.

"Well, first, we're going to get rid of these cumbersome outfits." With a thought they were gone. "Then I'm going to make you forget about everything but the two of us."

"You do know how to do that." She brushed her hand against his mark.

"I do." He smiled as he leaned toward her. "I know what it takes to make this body sing for me."

Heather closed her eyes as his lips found her mark. Tonight, she didn't want to think. She only wanted to feel. His mouth moved down to her breasts, and she lay down. Her fingers caressed his muscles on his chest then his stomach. They glided along his arms and across his back, wherever she could reach.

"My heart, you are distracting me." He pressed a kiss to her stomach.

"Just like you are doing to me," she said, her voice soft. "I want to forget about everything but us two, Storm. I need you now."

He kissed his way back up her body, pausing at her breasts long enough to make her squirm. "You are trying to rush me again."

"I can't help it." She wrapped her legs around him. "I need to feel you deep inside. Building me up as you fill me again and again. I need you to take my breath away."

He looked up at her, tracing her jawline as he studied her face. "Why are you so frightened?"

"What if this is our last time together?" A tear slid down the side of her face. "Storm, I don't want to be without you."

"Your visions happen so you can change the outcome. You just said so." He wiped away the tear. "But, for argument's sake let's say what you saw comes true, you really want your last memories of our time together to be of moments rushed? I don't think so. I want you to remember our intimacy the way you should. With the passion I feel for you every time I touch you. I refuse to skimp and will tie you down if I have to."

"Storm."

"We have tonight, my heart, and I promise I will take your breath away. Again and again."

She knew he would. How could she explain the wildness she felt inside? She knew how he felt when he had to dominate her. When the desire was so overpowering, he couldn't wait for foreplay. That was where she was. "I can't wait."

"Yes, you can. Have you forgotten the two screams already, my heart?" He lowered his mouth to hers. Desire swirled deep inside. As his tongue danced with hers, she felt the flames of her need lick at her insides. His kiss relaxed her, turning her to putty in his hands. When his mouth left hers, she felt bereft until she felt his warm lips on her mark.

She wanted more. Heather caressed his rock-hard muscles, dipping into the plains and valleys she loved to touch. It caused Storm to growl against her throat. He might pretend he wasn't affected but she knew better. The slightest touch from her had his blood boiling.

"My heart."

"You never said I had to be passive."

"I would never ask that either, but you know how I get when you try to arouse me. It only makes me want to excite you more."

"I know." She brushed her fingers through his hair when he looked up at her. "And I will strive to do the same."

"Is that a challenge?"

She gave him an innocent look. "What do you mean?"

"You wish to see which one of us arouses the other the most?" He pressed a kiss on the delicate tissue between her breasts. "Because you know I will win."

"You sure?"

"Oh, woman, you are in trouble."

She slipped her hands between them, wrapping her hands around his shaft. "I think you are the one in trouble."

He growled against her throat again. His fingers skimmed across her skin like silk to draw the response he wanted. "You think you can best me?"

"I can try." Her hands moved down to the inside of his thighs, then around to his buttocks. "I love the feel of your body. Your hard muscles encased in soft skin."

"There is nothing soft about me right now, my heart." He moved a little farther down her body so she couldn't touch some of his more sensitive spots.

Heather laughed, first at his comment then at his shifting his body. Like that was going to deter her. She knew other sensitive spots that would get the desired effect she wanted. He latched onto one of her breasts and all thought flew from her mind. Soft featherlike caresses had her need spiraling out. Storm used those wonderful fingers and worked his way down to her core. He brushed his fingers against her sensitive nub, heightening her desire. Her legs rubbed along his hips in response.

"Storm," she said, her voice soft. "Please."

He pressed his lips to her stomach, licking at her belly-button, then he worked his way down to her mound. The moment his mouth closed on her core she wanted to scream her frustration. She loved how he worked to arouse her even more, but that wasn't what she wanted. The only thing that would satisfy her right now was the feel of his length deep inside her. Knowing he could read her mind and knew what she wanted had her wanting to growl in frustration. Her needs were important too. "My heart."

"I know what you want, but I also know what you need." He pressed another kiss against her hip. "You forget I know you best."

"Have not." She felt restless. Her legs moved against him in frustration.

She felt his fingers invade her and a sigh escaped. *Better, but I need you.*

Just wait, my heart. He stroked that wonderfully sensitive spot that brought the screams. Her breath caught as her body vibrated with excitement. *You're getting closer.*

She couldn't answer him at the moment. Everything was focused on the sensations she felt. Storm didn't hesitate as he continued to make her body hum for him. Between the pressure of his fingers and the heat of his mouth she could feel her orgasm creeping closer.

He pressed a kiss against her mound then climbed up her body. He brushed his fingers along her jaw as he entered her. A moan escaped her as he filled her. This was what she wanted, what she needed. His lips sucked on the soft tissue of her mark as he set a deep but quick pace. Her hands followed the muscles on his back as she tried to pull him in deeper. Each stroke brought her closer. Her body started to vibrate again. Her release eminent.

"So close." Her voice came out like a whisper. Storm

changed the tempo, pounding into her at a faster pace. Each time filling her completely. Her legs tightened around his waist as she felt the beginning of her release. Muscles contracted around Storm's shaft, making him shake. It started in the pit of her stomach, flowing through her bloodstream, and filling her with the joy only Storm could give her.

He drove into her, his body quaking each time he penetrated deep. She knew he was close too. Heather shifted her hips and felt her breath catch in her throat. Heather wanted to scream but couldn't. Then her world exploded. Her being broke into a thousand little shards of euphoria. Colors danced behind her closed lids. Her muscles tightened against Storm one last time and he hit his release too. They floated together, wrapped in an intimate cocoon of their own making.

———

Skye lay in his bed, wishing for Sam. After being around Heather and Storm and seeing their relationship, he realized they truly cared for each other and it made him miss his bondmate more.

He needed to talk to Heather about this, but each time they were in her mind it was all business. What he wanted was some private time with her.

He also saw the Heather he had read about. She stood her ground when she knew she was right and although Storm showed his displeasure, he never held his anger for long. Her subtle ways of giving her opinion when they were in public amazed him. He wouldn't have ever noticed it if he hadn't spent so much time with them. He finally got to see the real Heather and that made him more comfortable around them.

Closing his eyes, he found himself in the white area once again. Was he the first to arrive?

"Heather?"

"I'm here, Skye."

"Are we alone? I wish to speak to you about Sam."

"I am here." He heard the deep growl of Storm. "What about my daughter?"

"She is my mate, Storm." He looked at Heather who had materialized in front of him when he asked for her. Storm stood behind her with his arms around his mate. "I know this is an assignment, but what if I see Sam?"

"Oh." Heather touched his arm. "I didn't think about that. Sam will know you as my guard. I didn't build anything else in. I can if you need me to, but I don't know how different it would be. She won't see you as her mate but as a casual partner. Is that what you want?"

"I don't know what I want."

"There is nothing in this scenario that says you can't seduce her. I'm sure her attraction to you is still there. I didn't tamper with that."

Bert and her brother appeared, and the conversation shifted to their final plans.

"I fear my vision will come true within the next few days. Once it happens, we won't be able to meet like this anymore. We need to be sure we have everything in place before Reasta steps foot on this planet."

"Everything is ready except for those last-minute changes we know will happen," said Skye. "I have been keeping track of everything that needs to be done and we're as close to ready as we can be."

"Good." Heather breathed a sigh of relief. "I hope everything goes according to plan. I do want to make one adjustment. If changes are needed, we need a command word for Skye to use so that each of us will do what is needed without question."

"It would have to be something no one will question." Kuarto looked at Skye. "Any suggestions?"

Skye looked around. "How about this white room of yours? If there is something that needs to be done, or I have a question that needs to be answered I'll just say I wish we were in the white room. No one should question a statement like that. They might think it a bit odd but could take it as a human expression."

"Perfect." Heather smiled.

———

Skye stood behind Heather and Storm as the gangplank opened. The woman Heather feared stepped off the ship first. She bowed to the council and introduced her small contingency. Anseri introduced the council members, saving Heather for last.

"Heather, it is a pleasure to meet you." She took Heather's hand in hers. The smile she gave Heather made Skye uneasy. It was predatory in nature. "You are the mate of the future ruler of this planet, correct? Storm?" She turned her unique snake eyes toward Storm.

"Yes." He tightened his hold on Heather.

"And very protective." She noted the way Storm kept Heather close. Reasta looked around at the guards in the room. Her gaze flicked to him for a moment before she turned it back on Heather. "I hope we get a chance to talk later."

Skye's instincts warned him of danger and his hand slipped to his weapon discreetly, but she seemed to ignore him as she turned her attention to the council and spoke to Anseri. She handed over a pad to the leader. "This is the list of ancients who are aboard ship. I hope you can find a place for them."

Anseri nodded. Storm came up behind her and took the pad. "Storm is head of security so will take care of that. Perhaps you would like to join us for a repast?"

"Thank you." She bowed again before she followed the council out of the large hanger.

Storm fell into step with Heather at his side. Skye walked behind them. Storm flipped through the pages to see how many ancients were listed.

"Why don't you let Skye hold that until you can focus on it? It will save you from having to keep an eye on it while your mother plays hostess."

Storm looked at her for a moment before he handed it to Skye. As discreetly as he could he also flipped through the images, knowing that his implant would transmit the information to Bert. He would be able to tell him if the people on the list were actually ancients.

Skye found the whole thing boring, but he wasn't the only one. Storm looked bored to tears. He hovered over Heather, keeping their guests away from her. Storm wasn't alone in protecting Heather from their guests. He noticed the council also kept them at bay. A warm hand on his shoulder broke through Skye's thoughts. He looked up to find Fridon standing beside him.

"Storm has relieved us from duty so I'm thinking a nice strong drink is in order."

Were they friends in Fridon's mind? How did Heather do all of this? "As long as we aren't called into his office tomorrow morning for one of his silent glare sessions, I'm game."

"He loves to intimidate, and he might seem unhappy, but once you've faced his real anger then you'll know when he's displeased." Fridon slapped him on the back. "Let's go."

He looked back at Heather and Storm for a moment before he left with his new friend. Skye wasn't sure what to talk to the man about and hoped he would start the conversation. They stepped out into the night and across the plaza. The rest of Heather's team was there. Was this where they always hung out?

Fridon walked up to the bar where the rest of the team sat and ordered drinks for him and Skye. Since he ordered their regular Skye didn't worry that he was trying to pull some sort of prank. Sitting down next to the rest of the group Skye waited for them to speak or act. Not knowing what they remembered had him second guessing what they expected from him.

"You are quiet tonight," said Fridon.

"So is everyone else." Skye took a sip from his drink.

"Why do you think they're here?"

What should he say? He knew Heather and Fridon had a close relationship. Did she change that when she added Skye to the equation? "What did Heather tell you?"

"She has been very quiet about this, which is unusual. All I know is she is afraid and the way she and Storm have been clinging to each other I wonder how bad her vision was."

"I don't like this," one of the men from the squad said as he sat his drink down. Skye recognized the man but couldn't remember his name. "There is something wrong in all of this, yet Heather and Storm are allowing it to happen."

"You know they have to have a plan," said Fridon. "They always do."

"Doesn't stop me from questioning everything. I

wouldn't be in this squad if I just followed orders." He looked in the direction of Skye and Fridon. "I think we need to make a few plans of our own, just in case."

SIX

"I agree," said Fridon. He turned in his chair to look at Skye. He sat something on the bar. "I made you a little present."

Skye picked it up and looked at it before he stuck it in his pocket. "What is it?"

"Something you might find handy in the coming days. I created one for everyone on the team but haven't really named it." He pulled his out of his pocket.

Skye wondered what he suspected.

Fridon turned his on and pulled up the screen. "It does all kinds of things. There is a list of applications I have programmed into yours. Go through it and pick the ones you want to use." He took a sip of his drink. "Storm's favorite is an invisibility cloak. I used it on our last mission, remember?"

Skye didn't, but he nodded. To them he had been part of their elite group for several years. He pulled the small device out of his pocket and opened the list. This little gadget would come in handy and after he added a few of his own programs it would be perfect for what he might need for this mission.

———

Anseri had given them permission to go back to their rooms and Storm recommended that they go through the gardens near the palace. He knew how much Heather enjoyed walking through there and thought it would help soothe her a little. "I know how much you like this area."

Heather walked beside him, leaning into him as they strolled along a pathway. "You worry too much, my heart."

"Isn't it my job to make sure you're happy?" His hand rested on the small of her back. "Wouldn't you do the same thing for me?"

She looked up at him and smiled. "You accuse me of having a soft heart but you're just as bad. Being with you is enough to soothe my nerves."

"Ah, but I want to be sure. This garden means a lot to me."

"The picture." She was referring to the image of her in mid-orgasm that he released to Vespia. It was considered her wedding picture and highly arousing.

"My favorite picture, but I like how we got the picture more than the picture itself. You were beautiful." He pulled her close. "I would love to see you the same way tonight."

"So, you did have an ulterior motive in bringing me here."

"My heart, watching your face light up with ecstasy is a glorious thing to observe. Why wouldn't I want to see that?" He touched her face with the tips of his fingers. "I also know this is where you enjoy a few quiet moments to yourself when you can get them. These visions have you so tense I want to do anything I can to relieve that."

"Including making me forget everything but us."

"Of course." He gave her one of his heart-stopping smiles. "Now our favorite grotto isn't too far from here. If you're up to it."

She laughed. Instead of answering him, she took off running, her long skirt flying behind her, knowing he would follow. It didn't take him long to catch up with her and pull her into his arms, spinning her around in the process. A shriek of laughter escaped her. Storm swept her up into his arms and ran to the grotto, only letting her feet touch the ground when they were tucked safely inside.

"You could've had the guards after us with that shriek." He held her close.

"They would never interrupt us." She touched his face with such tenderness. "They would come close enough to see who we were and back off. Besides, that new photographer assigned to follow us would warn them long before they could anger you."

"He is very good at his job." Her dress had a slit that went from the hem of her gown to up high on her thigh and Storm took advantage. His hand touched her thigh before caressing its way up to her core. "I want you to know that the little slits cut into this gown gave me enough glimpses of what lies beneath to make me hard. I especially like the slit in your top. It's discreet yet had me wanting to back you into an isolated corner and slip my hands inside."

"My heart, I could be wearing a sack, and you would get aroused." The intimate caress had her knees feeling wobbly.

"You spent most of your life on Earth overcoming your sexuality. I know how hard it is to be around our way of life when you were raised to suppress it. You could have worn one of your elder gowns and no one would have said a thing, yet you did this for me."

"It wasn't that much." Heather still didn't dress as risqué as other Vespian women, but she wasn't dressing as reserved as before and knew Storm enjoyed the change.

"The way you tease me fills me with joy. I kept wondering if those holes would show me something I wanted to see." He took a hold of her hand and brought her to the bench. He sat down and looked up at her.

"You know me better than I know myself at times." She climbed onto his lap then maneuvered herself, so she straddled him. "I know you would never say anything about what I wear, yet I have heard you defend everything I do that is non-Vespian. I never asked you to do that, but you do it anyway."

"You are my mate and the most important thing to me. I want to keep you happy." He helped her settle in his lap. "My heart, you are my life."

"Which is why I dress like this for you. I know how much you enjoy the little outfits and I love the glow only I can put in your eyes."

He laughed as he held her close. "We make quite a pair."

"Is that photographer still following us?" She looked over her shoulder into the dark garden.

"If he is good at his job he is, but he is also discreet." He brushed his finger under her chin, getting her to look at him. "I will make you forget everything but the two of us."

"I expect you to. You have a reputation to uphold."

"I do?" He moved his hands along the seams of her dress. "Which one is that?"

"I have to tell you?" She opened a few of his seals as well and sighed when she touched skin. "That doesn't sound like my mate. He knows exactly what I'm talking about. He did make me scream twice the other day."

"Is that a challenge?" He wrapped his hand around the

back of her neck and brought her close. "You know I enjoy a good challenge."

"I know." She smiled as she eased her hands down his chest. Heather leaned in toward him and was gifted with his lips meeting hers. His tongue swept in and pulled hers to dance with his. The heat of his hands as they moved up her back made her sigh into his mouth. He had opened the seals so he could touch her skin the way he liked. Each time his fingers brushed against her body she inched closer to him. It didn't take long before they were flesh to flesh. Her dress pooled at her waist. "You are quite good at this."

"Making your body sing?" he murmured against her throat.

"Making my clothes disappear without my knowledge." She dropped her head backwards when he sucked on the delicate tissue of her mark. "I didn't even feel you open the seals."

"I am good at my job." His hands slid up into her hair. "Especially when you are my focus."

She touched his face.

Once again, she felt his lips against her throat. Something she loved. Heather tilted her head to the side so Storm could have better access. The feel of his mouth on her skin sent her desire spiraling. Her hands worked on the rest of the seals of his uniform, opening more of his body to her touch. The heat of his skin penetrated her hands as she glided them across his muscled chest, down his abdomen to his erection.

"You are not fighting fair, my heart."

"Oh, are we supposed to be fighting fair? Since you haven't fought fair either I thought I could arouse you any way I want." Her hand closed around his erection. He would rather she didn't touch him because of how sensitive he was but she also knew he enjoyed it as much as she did. She just couldn't do too much.

"Woman, you keep that up and I will make it my goal to get a scream out of you before we leave this grotto." He sucked his breath in when she slid her hand up and down his shaft.

"Is that a promise?" She pressed a kiss against his chest. Heather sighed when she felt his fingers slip into her folds. He knew just how to touch her to get her to do what he wanted.

"Yes, my heart. You know I always fulfill my promises." His fingers worked their magic, slowly massaging and caressing the sensitive spots he knew so well.

She squeezed his hardened member and was gifted with a shudder.

"Keep that up and there will be no finesse in our intimacy."

"If I can make you lose control just a little bit, I have done my job as your mate." She shifted her hips and brought her core against his erection. He shook in her arms.

Heather felt his hands on her hips as he lifted her. Once he made sure he was centered properly he eased her down his length. They sighed in unison as he slid in deep. Her muscles rippled against him as she adjusted to his penetration.

"You are going to make me explode if you keep that up."

She laughed. That was her goal every time. With his help she started moving, rising up then pushing herself down his shaft. The angle was perfect for him to hit the sensitive spot that made her scream. Her breath became labored as she got closer to her release.

"Not yet, my heart." He slowed her pace down. "We need to prolong this, enjoy our time together."

"Please don't misunderstand me because you always put my desires first, but you have been overly attentive since I told you the details of my vision. It has you thinking."

"Yes." He touched her face. "Your visions have become a reality too many times for me to ignore this one. We know this is going to happen very soon and if we can't change the outcome, I want to be sure your memories of me are the best they can be."

"Storm." A single tear slid down her cheek. She settled against him, her desire dissipating. "I don't want to live without you."

"My heart, I didn't intend for our conversation to become so morbid." He kissed the tear away. "I have two goals right now. One is to make you as boneless as possible as often as possible before your vision happens and once we get by it unscathed I plan on celebrating by making you as boneless as possible as often as possible to show you how happy I am that nothing happened."

"I noticed there is a theme there." She touched his face. "You don't have to focus on the boneless that much. It seems to happen whenever you touch me."

"I only want to focus on you." He captured her lips with his while his hands touched some of his favorite places. Storm still kept her shielded from prying eyes while he aroused her again. Heather felt him pulse inside her as he reacted to her passion growing. His mouth moved down her throat to her mark, drawing a sigh from her as her muscles tightened around his length. He groaned against her throat. "You feel so good."

"And just think, we've just started."

"And we have all night."

Skye's heart pounded in his chest when he woke up from another one of Heather's visions. Her scream still echoed in his mind. How did she put up with these things? He hated them. A bunch of images he couldn't make sense of. Knowing he wouldn't sleep for a while he climbed out of bed and went into the bathroom. He leaned against the sink as he stared in the mirror at his reflection.

At least he knew that having this power had its drawbacks. It made him respect her a little more.

His mind felt overloaded. Sharing thoughts with Heather had him going a little mad. He walked into his main room and picked up his handheld. Unlike Heather, he was creating an image board in a file to help him cope with what he saw. Since the only computer that could pick up anything from his handheld was Bert's he felt comfortable putting this info in it. The way Heather dealt with things drove him crazy. He didn't want to wait for the vision to come true for him to understand what it meant. So far, he had figured out the woman prominent in Heather's visions was the reason Storm was killed. He needed to hear her private conversations to see what she really planned for Heather. The visions hinted but didn't give him enough to know what was going to happen.

He picked up the device Fridon gave him. Just how well did this thing work? Skye knew he wasn't going to get back to sleep for a few hours so he decided to see what it could do.

The first place he went was the bar he had accompanied Fridon to. The place was busy and a perfect place for him to test out his invisibility cloak. So far no one could see him, or at least didn't notice him. Now he had to see just how well it worked. He weaved his way in and out of the small clusters of people there. Trying hard not to bump anyone who might figure out what he was using.

He spotted the photographer who followed Heather and Storm around. He seemed disturbed by something and since he was always with Heather and Storm, Skye wanted to know what it was.

Working his way around a few more people Skye got close enough to overhear their conversation.

"How's the job?" asked the man next to him.

The photographer looked up from his glass. "What? Oh, great."

"You aren't acting like it is great."

"They're concerned about something, and I guess that has me worried too." He picked up his drink and took a sip.

"There is something in the air. Anyone who has dealt with the council, or anyone associated with Heather and Storm have all been a little distracted. Something is going on, but no one is talking." His buddy wrapped his hand around his glass. "And it all started when that ship arrived."

"All we've been told is they are dignitaries from another planet."

"I know. That's the official word, but I think I'm going to trust my instincts and prepare for the worst. Something isn't right and we all can feel it."

He nodded.

So, most of the Vespians knew something was up as well. Could that be from the mindwipe Heather did? Could she have inadvertently put her worries into their heads?

"How is it working with Heather? I understand she has been a bit difficult to work with."

"Heather? No. She is very open and sweet, just very shy by our standards. She wanted a photographer that kept that in mind when they dealt with her. Something that hasn't happened in the past." He took another sip.

"Believe me I did a lot of research on her before I applied for the job. I had thought she was difficult too, but it's more a culture difference. Once I figured that out and took her feelings into consideration, she has been very easy to work with."

"Get anything good?"

"You know I can't talk about that." He finished his drink and stood. "I think I have had enough for tonight."

"Did I upset you?"

"No." He clasped his friend on the shoulder. "Just need to get home."

Skye decided to stick with the photographer for a little while. The man went home and uploaded his photos to a special server designed just for Heather and Storm. He didn't know about this. Something else for him to investigate. Heather never mentioned this, but it could be because it wasn't something she thought was important to his mission.

He saw some of the images that flashed on the screen. The intimacy happening on the screen was hard to miss. She was beautiful, just like her daughter. Seeing those pictures made him miss Sam more.

The invisibility worked well. Now he needed to see how far he could get with their alien guests.

———

Skye had a little trouble getting on the ship. He had to wait for someone to open the gangplank, but once that happened, he was able to move about the ship easily. They couldn't detect him. He made sure by following a guard to security to see if they had picked up anything that hinted to his presence. Fridon's little creation was working. The tour Heather and Storm had taken while he was with them helped as he moved about. A good look at the security grid helped too.

Voices floated from the main control room, so he followed it. There he found his target.

"I thought this man was eliminated." The woman in Heather's visions pointed to a picture of him.

"I wasn't aware that Latimer survived the attack until we saw him at the dinner this evening." One of the men, probably her second in command, spoke. "We know the blast hit him and considering the type of weapon we bought I don't know how he survived."

She was the one responsible for his wound when he worked with Mason? He had wondered who had hit him with the blast that would have eaten his body away if Sam hadn't brought her uncle in to take care of his wound.

"We need to know more about him."

"He's Heather's personal bodyguard. Heather's home planet wanted someone from their force with her after that last incident." The man froze a picture of him on a screen. "We were worried about him and Sam bonding, but it never happened. They were only together while they were working for Mason. The only time Skye wasn't guarding Heather. After that Sam went into the Earth Security force. If they have any relationship, it is only physical and only when she comes home which is rare."

"But he wasn't in the first timeline. I want to know why." She studied the image. "His presence could mean they know what we're up to. I have worked too hard to have this go wrong again. I want all his information."

"We have run all the computations the moment he was spotted. Nothing will go wrong. He is nothing but a guard. In the first timeline he was away on an assignment, but we made changes to make sure you get your outcome. We knew a few things would change and his presence is one of them." Her second in command stated. "And if Heather is aware of what you are trying to do then she is the one you have to deal with not a simple guard."

"You are right, but nothing can go wrong."

"We have checked and double checked. We have readied everything to remove Storm from the equation. Once he is gone the timeline will settle and everything will go as you planned."

"I know we have had this conversation many times, but each change we have made to this timeline hasn't given me the outcome I want, and we end up having to repeat the whole scenario." She pressed her hand against her chest. "You are sure killing Storm will allow us to be successful?"

"Everything we have run shows that, but you know this is our last try. We don't have the power to manipulate the timeline again if something else goes wrong."

"I know. That's why I'm questioning everything."

Skye wished they'd say more. Heather's visions were still too vague for him to make any plan of action, but at least he knew Heather had been right about Storm. He was pivotal in this and if he could keep the man from dying, they wouldn't be able to try again.

"Tomorrow I will work on manipulating them enough to get Storm out of the way. So far everything we have done keeps the timeline together for us. In the meantime, you continue to monitor the timeline and be sure it flows our way."

Skye wanted to absorb the data they had. He walked up to it, being careful not to brush against anyone or anything and watched as the timeline the computer was watching went through the different scenarios. Unfocusing his gaze, he took in as much as he could, hoping it would make sense when he went back and looked at it and give Bert enough data to update any schematics he might have on the ship.

———

Skye stood behind Fridon, waiting for him to go on his break. They were friends in this version, which Skye found a little amusing. It made sense since he was with Heather all the time and Fridon was with Storm. They spent a lot of time standing in the background.

"Crap, someone is trying to hack into the system."

"Crap? You sound just like Heather."

"I know." He turned and grinned at Skye for a moment. "Drives Storm crazy. Of course, he uses more human words now since he spent time in their past."

Skye shook his head. Fridon loved pushing Storm as much as Heather, just in different ways. The man allowed it too. He found Storm a little more likeable now. Not a lot but some. "So, what are they trying to access?"

"Your files."

"I wish we were in the white room." He watched as Fridon's face changed. Even though he hadn't been part of their meetings Heather put the command in his head so he would do whatever Skye needed him to do. How she did this he didn't know but right now he was glad she did. "You need to let them have access to my files. They need to know I'm no threat."

"But what if they get into files, we don't want them to?"

"They don't know how advanced the system here is and we don't want them to know. I know you can block them from anything you don't want them to see." Skye placed his hand on Fridon's shoulder. "Work your magic."

"Done."

"Then perhaps we should let them get their information while we have lunch?"

"You seem very confident in me." Fridon turned to look at him.

"You are the best."

"I know." He grinned.

They stepped out of the room and Skye whispered the code phrase again so Fridon would become himself again.

Now they had what they wanted. He knew what Bert and Heather created was perfect. They should see him as nothing more than a guard. Once they were sure he was no threat he could do his job.

———

Heather didn't want to leave her rooms. Something deep inside said today was the day they would take Storm from her, but she knew she couldn't hide forever.

Skye stood nearby waiting. "Ready?"

She nodded. Heather smoothed her skirt before she headed out into the hall. Her morning was filled with working out with her team. She pushed herself hard, hoping it would allow her to forget for a few hours, but everyone noticed.

"You, okay?" asked Fridon as he climbed a rock wall beside her. They wore no harness as they scrambled up the almost shear side.

"What makes you ask that?" She hoped to deflect his question rather than lie.

"Because I know you too well and when you get like this, you're worried about something."

"Our new guests have me on edge." She wanted to tell her best friend more but knew his open mind would put him at risk.

"Do I hear someone talking? Is this task a little too easy?" shouted Storm. "I can fix that."

Heather and Fridon looked at each other and grinned.

They finished climbing the wall in silence, knowing Storm would make them pay on the next exercise.

"Good." Storm waited until everyone had come back down and was around him in a semi-circle. "Since that wasn't hard enough for some of you. You're going to do this again. One at a time. No lights, no helmet and I'm going to change the holds on a particular interval that you'll have to figure out as you climb. Heather you're up first."

Heather walked up to the wall. None of them had put on their helmet up to this point while she waited for the room to go black. She turned to look at her mate who snapped on his helmet so he could see in the dark.

"I want the rest of you to put your helmets on so you can see this." He gave everyone time to attach their helmets. The room went dark. "Your time begins now, Heather."

She started scaling the wall, finding the finger and footholds without the light to guide her. She felt a few of those holds start to disappear, but she kept moving, taking the timing into count. It didn't take her long before she hit the top. She turned around and sat down, her feet dangling over the side. "Who's next?"

———

"Fridon, you're next." Storm turned the lights on so Fridon could take his place.

Skye watched Heather as she sat there with her feet swinging. Her agility amazed him. No wonder she was one of the admiral's best. It looked like she was climbing a tiny hill not a highly sophisticated apparatus. The lights went out, plunging them into darkness.

Thanks to the helmet he wore he was able to watch as

Fridon moved up quickly too. In fact, the whole team acted like they did this every day. Then Storm called his name.

Skye removed his helmet and approached the wall. He looked up at the rest of the team. His team now. What did they expect from him?

"Come on, Latimer. Show us what you got." Heather looked down at him, arms crossed over her chest and a knowing smile on her face.

"It's not a contest, Heather."

"Really? Gee, how many times have I heard 'can the little human keep up?' I know you were teasing me, and I get it, but Latimer helps me prove that we puny humans are worth our weight." She looked down at him. "Show them, Skye."

He wanted to laugh at the puny human comments since neither of them were actually human. But it also told him they expected his best. It sounded like Heather set it up to where they always tried to best their Vespian counterparts. He was grateful because he didn't have to pretend that he wasn't able to do something when he could.

He stood next to Heather once he finished his climb. His time was between Heather's, who was first, and Fridon, who had been second before Skye completed this exercise.

Storm grinned. "Our new guests want to see what we are capable of. I wish I could show them, but I don't feel we should show everything. They are aware of our team so most of you will participate. I am keeping three of you out of the exhibition. Heather and Fridon, since you two have other jobs that will keep you busy during the exhibition you will sit this one out, and Skye since you are Heather's personal guard."

Heather nodded, not showing any displeasure with Storm's decision. Skye followed her lead.

"We will use one of our better routines but not something we've pushed to excel at. I have loaded a list for everyone to look through. The one you pick as a group will be the one we will do. You have an hour to make this choice."

———

"You wish you were joining the team, don't you?" Storm came up behind her as she finished getting ready.

"Of course, but I also agree with you. The less they know about what I can do the better we might be. Until we know we can trust them I will be sweet, quiet, and demure."

Storm laughed as he stepped up behind her and placed his hands on her shoulders. "That might be when we're in public, but I know better when we're alone."

"You know me best." She turned to face him. "Do I fit the part of the mate of the next leader of Vespia?"

"You mean now? Or always?" He wrapped his arms around her and pulled her close. "You are the perfect mate for me. You look beautiful as always, and you wear a gown befitting the mate of the next leader of Vespia."

"My heart." She pressed her hand against his heart. "Ready?"

"I can think of better things for us to do, but mother will be very displeased if we're late." He put his hand against the small of her back and escorted her out of their rooms. Their guards, including Skye Latimer and Fridon, fell into place behind them. They entered the main hall where the meal was being served and were escorted to their table. Most of their guards went and stood with the rest of the guards lining the room while Skye and Fridon sat with them along with Kuarto and Toki.

"I see you have your entourage with you."

Storm glared at Kuarto.

"Gentlemen." It was all Heather had to say for Kuarto to flash her a smile then drop the conversation. She didn't want her brother to make a big deal of their guards. This woman needed to think their presence was normal. She also worried he'd make a comment about her not participating in the demonstration.

"I have been given the data on the people wanting to settle here." Kuarto looked at her when he said it. She noticed he didn't use the word ancient.

"Have you made your recommendations to the council?"

"Not yet, but I spoke to them about a few things that I did learn." He quieted down when a server placed a salad in front of him. "I find their readings very interesting."

"How?"

"Well, I have compared it to the records we have on the ancients and there is something odd about their DNA."

"Perhaps you shouldn't be discussing this here, doctor." Storm came close to growling his comment.

"I only bring it up because I have asked permission to discuss it here. The council thought Heather might be able to help me a little since she also has a strong background in the sciences." Kuarto set down his fork. "It is something Heather would be interested in. Come by the lab tomorrow and I'll show you."

"Thank you, Kuarto. I will." Heather smiled at her mate. She noticed Anseri looking in their direction. "Your mother is trying to catch your attention."

Storm glanced at the end of the table where his mother sat. Her slight nod was all it took for him to place his napkin on the table and stand. He smiled at Heather before he headed to his mother's side.

She watched as he bent down to hear her request, gave a quick nod, and headed back to his chair.

"Tomorrow."

Everyone at the table nodded.

Tomorrow she could lose her mate. Movement near the main doors caught Heather's attention. She stood when she recognized who had entered. "Sam?"

———

Skye tried not to react while he watched Storm turn in his chair then stand as well.

Sam came over and hugged her father before she walked around and hugged her mother. Skye noticed the sexy gown she wore. His heart beat harder as he took in the way it moved on her. It was low cut and form-fitting. The material was mixed with gauze that hid nothing from view. The see-through areas danced around her body as she moved.

He was already aroused from looking at the images he had seen on Heather and Storm's private server. The moment he had asked her about it she gave him permission to access it, warning him there wasn't much there. She was right, but he had to check anyway. What he found were photos of Heather and Storm, and some of them were highly arousing. Seeing Sam in that dress just made his situation worse.

"You look very Vespian." Heather held her at arm's length to look at the dress.

"Thank Anseri. She left me a note stating this might help me find a mate. I think she wants babies to play with." She smoothed her hands down the dress. "All it does is make me feel uncomfortable."

"That is because you have spent too much time with humans," said Storm. "But you do look beautiful."

"You have to say that because you're my dad."

Heather tapped Skye on the shoulder to get him to move over one chair. It took him a second to do as she asked. He was too busy trying to hide his anger over the reason for the dress. He was her mate. It didn't matter that no one remembered that or that they hadn't gone through the ceremony.

Sam thanked him and sat next to her mother. They talked quietly. Their heads close as they discussed something private.

What he didn't expect was to feel Sam's hand on his thigh. Perhaps she did it accidentally. When she squeezed it, he knew she knew what she was doing. Sam was flirting with him? Did she remember? Or was this part of the new scenario Heather wrote? He wanted to thank her either way. After seeing those pictures, being this close to Sam in that dress was arousing him and knowing he had to keep his hands to himself made it worse.

Sam turned to talk to the woman on his left and she slid her hand further up his leg. He grabbed her hand before she went any higher and caused him to draw attention to them. It seemed to make her happy. He saw a beautiful smile spread across her face as she finished her conversation and removed her hand.

Now what was he supposed to do?

Skye needed to talk to Heather. The meal was cleared, and they were allowed to mingle. Heather put a few things into play since they weren't meeting in her mind anymore and Skye needed to utilize it. He stood nearby, waiting for the moment when he could talk to her alone. Storm was called away by his mother and he made his move.

"I wish to speak to you."

"Of course." Heather turned to look at him.

"I miss the white room."

"It is very dangerous now."

"I only wish to ask a question. It's about Sam."

"Ah." She smiled at him. "I didn't take her passion for you away only the memory of your bonding."

So maybe they were lovers in her mind which is why she did what she did. "Thank you."

"You okay?" asked Storm as he came back to her side.

Skye quickly repeated the phrase so Heather would behave normally.

"Yes, Skye and I were talking about the upcoming exhibition and how we wish we could have participated." She pressed her hand against his chest.

"I only wish to protect you."

"I know." She leaned her head against his chest. "How is Fridon taking this? He's never been kept from any of the demonstrations before."

"He is my second so that takes priority over the team. Just like your position on the council and being my mate takes priority over the same thing."

"It will be strange being on this side, but I can't wait to see what you have planned." She took his arm, and they followed the crowd into the area where the exhibition was taking place.

Reasta joined them. "You aren't joining your group?"

"No." Heather shook her head. "There are times when I must be the diplomat instead of the security guard."

"Too bad. I was looking forward to seeing you work with them."

"Maybe next time."

Reasta moved off to take her spot.

Heather looked up at Storm. "Shall I join the council?"

"Mother did make a comment about where you would

be during this. Take Fridon with you. I won't be long." He pulled her into his embrace and gave her a quick but heated kiss. "Prepare to be impressed."

"You impress me every day."

Storm captured her lips again, drawing her against him and deepening the kiss.

"People are waiting," commented Skye. "Unless you want to become the center of attention."

Storm broke the kiss and touched her face. "He's right."

"My heart." She touched his heart for a moment before moving over to stand with his mother.

Sam joined her and all Skye could think of was how sexy she looked in that damn dress. It moved about her as she leaned or shifted her weight, exposing skin as it danced around her body. He couldn't keep his eyes off her.

At one point she softly whispered in his ear. "I am flattered that you like what I'm wearing, but if you keep staring at me the way you have been, people are going to know we're having an affair. I thought that was something you didn't want known because of your job?"

"I can't help it." He grinned. "You look amazing in that dress and I'm not the only one. Every man here is staring."

Sam smiled back and moved over to her grandmother who had signaled for her attention.

Skye shook his head. Heather's abilities were amazing. She had created an elaborate scheme in her head then transmitted it to the entire planet. He had always been leery of this little talent of hers, and he was right to be worried. If it hadn't been for Ed who had gotten tired of his mistrust. He glared at Skye and blurted. 'You know she was created, right? Do you honestly think that Ialog would have created something he couldn't control? Heather doesn't have a megalomaniac bone in her body.'

But Heather appealed to the one thing she knew would make him stay. Sam.

He watched her as she spoke to her grandmother and mother. He also watched Reasta as she observed her with her family. There was a glint in the woman's eye he didn't like. Instinctively he moved closer to Heather and Sam.

Heather noticed. "Problem?"

"Just doing my job." He looked at the woman. Heather followed his line of sight.

"I understand." Her posture changed. Her security training took over.

The routines Storm put together awed the audience, but Skye knew they were capable of so much more. He saw the one Earth and Vespia had done together. He'd worked with them for several days now. This didn't compare to what he knew they were capable of.

Storm walked straight to Heather. "What did you think?"

"Wonderful."

"Ha. You're biased." He took her hand in his and kissed the palm of her hand.

"Of course."

Storm laughed as he wrapped his arms around her. "And that is why you're my heart."

Skye felt a presence beside him which made him look. Reasta stood beside him.

"They are very much in love, aren't they?"

"Yes." Skye found it interesting that she used the word love. "Theirs is a happily ever after romance. No one thought two people from such different planets would be such a perfect pair, but they are."

"It sure looks like it."

"It is." Skye wasn't sure why she came up to him. Was it because she didn't trust him?

Storm signaled him to join them. "Excuse me."

He was happy to be away from her. Not knowing how to react around Storm had him standing at parade rest, waiting for the reason he called him over.

"You have the rest of the night off." He wrapped his arm around Heather. "I'll make sure my mate is safe."

Skye nodded. He looked around to find Sam, who was surrounded by several men. How was he going to separate her from them? He decided the best approach was to be obvious. Walking up to the small group he smiled. "Don't wear them out, Sam. I've been relieved of duty. Everyone have a good night."

Skye didn't look back as he left the ballroom. If she wanted him, she was going to have to follow.

———

Storm could feel Heather's stress over his comment earlier. She feared the dawn and he wanted to make her forget everything but them. He held her close when they stopped mingling for a moment. "So shall I tease you all night long or take you as often as the night allows?"

"I'd strive for the second but knowing your mother you'll only be able to do the first one." Those beautiful violet eyes held desire in them.

"I'll take that as a challenge." He gave her the smile she called bone-melting. She was right. His mother normally kept a close eye on them to make sure they didn't sneak off. It would be fun to see if he could get away before she could stop them.

Sam came over and said her goodnights.

"You're leaving a little early," Storm said after giving her a quick kiss on a cheek.

"You know I enjoy these things as much as you do, Dad,

and the crowd is thinning out. Anseri saw that I was bored so has given me permission to leave. I promise to spend some time with you tomorrow."

"I'll expect you for breakfast."

"Yes, sir." She gave him a quick hug before she hugged Heather then left.

"I do miss her." Heather wrapped her arm around his waist. "But I'm also so proud of her."

"Because she's following in your footsteps?"

"And yours. She is in security."

"Earth security. I would have been very happy if she had joined Vespian security instead."

"My heart, you know she needed to be away from us. We're both a bit overprotective when it comes to Sam. She would have wilted under our care. She looked beautiful tonight. Proud, confident."

"Desirable, just like her mother." Storm tightened his hold on her. "She had a lot of attention this evening."

"The gown your mother gave her helped."

"Yet she didn't seem interested in any of them."

"My heart, do you want her mated so soon? She's really not that old."

"I want her to be happy." He rubbed his hands up and down her back. "She seems to have an empty space in her now that I never noticed before."

"She'll find a mate when she's ready."

"Just like we did." He pulled her to him so he could capture her lips with his.

SEVEN

Skye stood near the hall, wondering what he should do. Sam was here, and she wanted him, but he didn't know how he contacted her in this world Heather created. Did she come to him? "Hell, we could have a special place we meet at."

"Expecting someone?" The soft sultry voice of Sam washed over him.

"You." He turned toward her voice.

"Then why were you talking about a special place? You planning something?"

"Maybe." She caught him talking out loud to himself. Great. Figuring out what was going on could make him stand out too much. He needed more information. How was he going to get that? "I'm surprised you got away so fast."

"Me too, but when Anseri gives you permission you take it." She linked her arm with his. "I have learned not to question her."

"Where to?" He hoped she wouldn't find his question odd.

"The gazebo is nearby."

"Not sure that is a good idea. Your parents used it recently and they might decide to use it again this evening. Unless you want them to catch us."

"Not really." She started walking, pulling him along with her. "Well, we have two choices, Dad's old apartment or your ship."

"Ship."

"Figured. You don't like the idea of being in Dad's place. Even though I explained to you he never took my mom there. That was his bachelor pad."

"You sound very human."

"I know. My last assignment had me working with a group that liked to use the ancient slang."

"Really?"

"Yeah." She looked at him and grinned. "If Dad heard the way I talked he would go ballistic."

Skye laughed. "That is a bit old."

"I found it fun and there are a lot of words I liked."

It didn't take them long to reach his ship. He did his best to keep them from being detected as they slipped inside, and he sealed the door. Sam just stood there for a moment, then blinked.

"Where am I?" She looked around before her gaze settled on him. "Skye?"

"Sam? You okay?"

"Yes." She smiled. "I had forgotten. That's all."

"Forgotten what?"

She looked at him oddly. "How long have you been working with my mother?"

"A while now." He didn't know the exact time he supposedly started guarding her. He only knew it was after she had returned from her encounter with Ialog. And that was almost two years ago.

"You don't know because none of this is real to you, right?"

Now that caught him off guard. "What do you mean?"

"Here, in this ship, I remember. I remember I marked you. That we're bonded. I remember I met you on that mission to trap Mason." She walked up to him and touched his arm. "Mom gave us this."

"Your mother's mind is very powerful to do all this."

"She had to. You know that. To save us all." Sam touched his face. "There's more."

"What?"

"While I'm here with you I'm her eyes and ears. I'm to answer any questions you have to help you during this."

"Has she taken over your body like she did before?"

"No." Sam smiled. "This is me, but I have access to her information. Like I can give you the details on what she has created for you, so you'll know how to react around everyone. If you have questions I should have answers. If I don't have them right away, I will be able to get those answers from her."

"She's not watching, is she?"

"No." She made a face. "You need to trust my mom right now. Everything she has done is to protect everything we hold dear. You know she made Dad like you."

"I did notice that." Skye did trust Heather. It might be grudgingly, but Ed was right, she didn't have an evil bone in her body. "He won't be happy when he finds out the truth."

"I don't know. To my dad, your job is to protect my mom. You do that right and he'll have to respect you."

"How much will you remember tomorrow?" That was part of the problem, Heather didn't want him to protect her. He had to protect Storm. Heather might be the focal point of these visions, but none of them showed her in any danger.

"Anything we discuss here will be locked away the moment I leave this ship. I'll only have access to it when I'm here, but Mom feels whatever you learn you should keep to yourself. Just to be safe."

He had to agree. She stood there in that beautiful dress. His heart started to beat faster as he imagined peeling the dress off her.

"You still with me?"

"I have missed you, Sam."

"And I have missed you." She brushed her hand against his mark and grinned when she heard him suck in his breath. "But I know you and you become hyper-focused on missions. I thought you'd want to learn everything you could before we focused on our needs."

"You're right, but I've been watching you move all night in that dress. My questions can wait." He pulled her into his arms. "My need for you can't."

"We have all night." She touched his cheek. "If you want to wait until later to get your answers that's fine with me. I don't have to be back until tomorrow morning."

"I know. Breakfast with your parents. It's already on my itinerary." Skye brushed his hand along her collarbone. He was looking for the seams. One ran along her right side and over her right shoulder. The moment he released them the dress fell to the floor. "So much better."

"You're a little overdressed now."

"That's something I can fix easily." He shed his clothes then wrapped his arms around Sam. "Being around your parents made me really miss you."

"They are a bit intense, aren't they?"

"Actually, I got a chance to see how much in love they are.

Your father is still very overbearing, but your mom doesn't let him control her the way I thought. When he pushes she pushes back." He inched her back toward the bed.

"You learned all that in just a few days?"

"I'm with them all the time." He eased her onto the bed. "Now I don't want to spend the rest of the night talking about your parents."

"You have other plans?" she teased him.

"I do. I want to kiss my way down one side of your body then kiss my way back up the other."

"Later." She flipped them over and slid down his hardened length. "Orgasm first, foreplay later."

He laughed. "God, Sam, I have missed you."

Her body hugged him intimately. He was glad she felt the same way he did. Foreplay was wonderful, but there were times when he was beyond it and this was one of those times. He placed his hands on her hips as she set a quick pace. The wonderful sensations he was feeling as she slid up and down his length had him shaking. If she kept this up he was going to explode a little too soon.

He flipped them over so he could control their pace better.

Sam laughed, knowing what he was doing.

———

"What's the matter, Skye?"

He gave her a frustrated look. "We have been apart for too long, and you want to race to the finish?"

"I have been without too," she replied. "We can take our time later, but not right now. Right now, I want to feel the joy I always do when I'm in your arms."

He pressed a kiss to her jawline, then to her cheek before capturing her mouth with his. He started to move. He took

146

his time at first then increased the pace as the wonderful sensations took him over. Sam met him stroke for stroke.

Each time he filled her he felt her muscles tighten against him. Each time he entered her it was long and deep and had her body quaking in no time. She was getting closer and closer. Her breath came out in short pants as her release started in the pit of her stomach.

"Oh God!" It grabbed her and dragged her into a wonderful euphoria.

"I love hearing you say that." Skye brushed a little hair out of her face.

"I love feeling you inside me." She smiled up at him. "Can we stay just like this while we talk about your mission? I sure don't want to move and don't want you going anywhere either."

"I don't mind as long as I can interrupt the conversation when the spirit moves me?"

"Are you kidding? If you don't, I might have to take control again."

———

"Come dance with me." Storm gave Heather the bone-melting smile that always had her doing what he wanted.

"Are you sure? The last time we almost caught the building on fire."

"I can't help we're so good together." He took her hand and urged her to the floor.

"Weren't we asked not to dance at functions because of that?"

"I believe the request came from Bear when we are at Earth functions. The humans were a little uncomfortable with the Vespian style of dance."

"We almost started an orgy, Storm, and you know it."

He just smiled. "She needs to know how it is between us. How the planet sees us. Perhaps she'll change her plans when she knows the truth."

He stopped once they were on the dance floor. Waiting for the next song to start. As music filled the hall once again Storm took her into his arms and led her through the intricate steps of their style of dance.

Heather found them beautiful, erotic. Their bodies touched from the knees up, moving across the floor. First, she was draped over his body as they worked the steps, then they'd switch, and he would be draped over hers. His hands, which helped her keep her balance as she followed his lead, also touched her in all her sensitive places. His touch was fleeting, nothing anyone would say was out of character for the dance, but she found it highly arousing. They never broke eye contact as they moved about the floor. The glow in his eyes brightened with every movement. His need was as great as hers.

Near the end of the song, Storm's lips started to play with hers, light feathery kisses, designed to make her sigh. The moment she did his tongue took advantage and slipped in, drawing her tongue to dance and swirl with his. He held her body against his. As the last note ended, she found he had maneuvered them near the large doors that led out into the garden.

"Where do you think you're going?"

Storm closed his eyes when he heard his mother's voice, but he couldn't hide his displeasure from Heather at being caught. He turned to face his mother with a smile on his face. "We were going out for a bit of fresh air."

"Oh, good, that can wait. I need you to meet someone." She gestured to a man standing nearby. "This is the general of Reasta's army."

Storm nodded. He offered his hand to the man who took it.

"You are the next leader of Vespia? Storm, correct?"

"Yes, and this is my mate, Heather."

"I am Doroni." He watched them intently, making Heather lean into her mate for support. "I notice you two constantly touch."

"Yes." Storm wrapped his arms around Heather.

"Curious."

"Don't you touch your mate?"

"We don't procreate the same way you do."

"How do you procreate?" Heather found his answer interesting and odd. Why would he think they touched only to procreate? It made her wonder how their society was set up. Did they shun physical contact unless involved in sex?

Unless they weren't humanoid they should be anatomically alike. Conceive and have children the same way. Touching should be a natural thing. All the races she had interacted with so far showed affection by physical contact.

"The females lay eggs which are later fertilized by a male."

"More reptilian than humanoid then."

He nodded, but the look on his face gave Heather the impression he said more than he should have.

"You are the General of war? Do you war a lot?" Storm steered the conversation back to a safer area.

"No." He laughed. "My position is very much like yours. I control the troublemakers."

"But you are also in charge of any aggressions against your people."

"Of course, but that hasn't happened in a long time." He waved off the comment. "I'm supposed to protect my people and keep them safe from anything that would threaten them. Is your job different?"

"Sometimes I have to protect my people from themselves." Storm saw his mother frowning. "Excuse us, will you?"

Heather saw him frown as well. "Is there a problem?"

"I haven't seen that look on my mother's face since my father came back. Something has upset her greatly." He didn't say anything when he reached his mother's side. He just touched her on the hand.

"Our guards have told me that your sister has gone missing."

"I thought she complained of a headache and went back to her rooms."

"She did, but I wanted to check in on her to see how she was feeling and there was no answer from her rooms. Fridon checked and there is no sign of her going back to her place. He's going through the surveillance recordings now."

"I'll go help him. Our law about not recording our religious leader could make it harder for him to find out where she went."

"It might be better if you stay here, for now. I don't want to alert the media that something is wrong." She looked up at him and smiled. "I'm sure it is nothing."

"Where is Kuarto?" asked Heather. She could search for him with her mind but knew it could give her abilities away.

"He went to the medlab with one of our guests. They weren't feeling well, and he offered to check them out."

Heather knew it would also give him a chance to run scans without raising eyebrows. "Perhaps he knows where she went?"

"I didn't want to worry him until he was finished with our guests." She looked at Heather. "It can wait."

"Let me contact my brother, Anseri. It will only take a moment. If she went somewhere else, he'll let us know and you can relax." Heather received a slight nod from Storm's mother and stepped to the side then pressed the small communication device implanted in her collar bone. "Kuarto?"

"What's up?"

"You by yourself?" Heather kept her voice down and looked around to make sure no one would overhear her.

"I'm just finishing up with one of our guests." She heard him dismiss his patient. "Do you need something?"

"Anseri is worried about your mate. She said she went back to your quarters, but she has tried to contact Toki and she's not responding."

"She was complaining of a headache." Heather could hear him putting things away. "Sometimes she goes to the Cave of the Crystals if it is caused by her work."

"The Cave of the Crystals?" Heather had never heard her talk about such a cave before and she and Toki were close.

"Don't tell her I told you about it. It is where the religious leaders keep their special relics. She has gone there before when she felt a little overwhelmed or needed to meditate." He hesitated. "She told me once it had healing powers. Our tracking systems don't penetrate that cave. Believe me, she gave me heart failure the first time she went there without telling me."

"Thanks, Kuarto. I'm sure that will ease Anseri's mind."

"Kuarto believes she's gone to the religious sanctuary," Heather spoke just above a whisper and touched Anseri's arm to make sure she heard her. Reasta had joined her, and

Heather knew it wouldn't be proper for her to know they were searching for their religious leader.

A slight incline of the head was the answer Heather received. At least that would relax Anseri until they were sure where Toki had gone.

———

Kuarto had returned to the party with a smile, but it was strained. He hadn't found his mate. "I don't know where she is. She's not in the caves. Although I'm not supposed to enter them, she normally answers when I go to the mouth of it. There's no evidence she has been there."

"Do you think our guests had something to do with her disappearance?" Heather asked in a soft voice. "Perhaps we should make them aware of what has happened? See what they do?"

"I'm not sure if that would be wise." Storm looked around to make sure no one would overhear their whispered conversation. "If they took her then they'd have to drop whatever façade they are using. That could force their hand before it is supposed to happen. If they didn't and she's on to something, then we're only going to put her in danger."

"Time to break it up, Anseri and her guest are coming our way," Heather murmured. "So, my mate still thinks that I need a guard, even though nothing has happened in what two and a half years?"

"How do you know nothing happened? Latimer could have kept you safe so nothing could happen," Storm countered.

"Oh, Heather." Kuarto laughed. "You're not going to win this one."

"I know." She jammed her hands on her hips to emphasize her frustration. "He's a little overprotective of me, but my heart."

"Children, you're not arguing, are you?"

"No, Anseri." Storm put his arm around Heather. "My mate was just expressing her opinion about her bodyguard."

"I like Latimer. He feels like family now." Anseri clasped her hands in front of her. Heather knew it to be a nervous habit.

"He's been here long enough to be family," said Kuarto. "I'm surprised you let him have the night off."

"With all these guards here, I felt he deserved it." Storm didn't volunteer any other information. "And it gives me an excuse to be close to my mate since it falls on me to keep a close eye on her."

"You don't need an excuse, my heart." Heather leaned into him as she pressed a hand against his heart. "I have always enjoyed your attention."

"I hope so because you will have all of it when we're back in our rooms." He pulled her to him and captured her lips with his.

"Don't make me hose you off." Kuarto always teased them like this and normally Storm would growl at him and continue his assault on Heather's senses. This time he broke the kiss, touched her face, then turned her in his embrace so he could talk to his mother and their guest.

"Perhaps it is time to retire." Anseri nodded at a guard who came to escort Reasta back to her people, then she smiled at Heather and Storm. "I can tell some of our guests are ready to go but wouldn't dare leave before we do."

"Shall we walk you back to your rooms, Mother?" asked Storm.

"I think I shall allow Kuarto the honor since his mate

has gone to lie down already. Their rooms are also closer to mine so he wouldn't be going out of his way."

"Yes, ma'am." Kuarto offered her his arm and escorted her out of the hall.

Storm waited the proper time before he led Heather out as well. That would allow the rest of the council to leave, then their guests. The guards would stay until the building was emptied.

"That was nice of your mother." She took a deep inhale of the fresh air.

"She looked a little tired, but perhaps she was just missing my father."

"I was a little surprised at his absence." Heather linked arms with him. When she met Storm, his father was thought dead. "He hasn't left her side that much since we rescued him from Ialog."

"The council sent him on a mission before our guests arrived."

As much as Heather wanted to ask what the mission was for, she knew better. "I know she'll be happy when he returns."

"So will I. I don't like seeing her sad. I had too many years of that." He looked down at her, desire glowed in his eyes. "Now. Let's not worry about anyone but us. The grotto is close."

"The grotto is great, but I think tonight we need our bedroom. The glow in your eyes says we're going to be busy for a while."

"We could stop by there to dampen the glow in my eyes." He gave her one of his bone-melting smiles.

"Hmm." Heather grasped her skirt and lifted it. "You have to catch me first."

She took off running, knowing Storm's long legs would have him catching up to her quickly, but her actions hopefully stunned him long enough to give her the head start she needed to make it to their wing. It depended on how much he wanted to go to the grotto.

She had just made it to the doors that would allow her inside when she found herself pinned to it.

"You know I could ravish you right here," Storm murmured against her throat. "It is dark, and no one is around."

"And you have done it before."

"I have, haven't I?" He released her and opened the door. "Now do you think you can outrun me?"

"No." She grinned. "But I can try. How much of a head start are you going to give me?"

"None." He gave her another one of his smiles. This one was more predatorial.

"Now how fair is that?" She gripped her skirt and lifted it.

"Never said I'd play fair. I could just throw you over my shoulder and carry you to our rooms." He leaned toward her like he planned on grabbing her before she could take off.

"You could, but then you wouldn't get the surprise I have planned."

"Surprise?" That stopped him. An excited glint entered his eyes.

"I just need to get into the room, my heart." She turned her body so she could take flight. "I promise to make it worth your while."

He touched her face with tenderness. "How much time do you need?"

"Count to fifteen and I'll be ready."

"I can count very fast."

"And I can run pretty fast."

"I have always outrun you."

"And I have always let you." She took off then, flying down the hall and through the doors of their room. The moment she entered she mentally told Cim to set up the scenario she had been working on. She turned to face the door and waited for her mate.

———

Excitement raced through his blood. He loved it when she did this. Wondering what she had prepared for him had his heart beating faster in his chest. He knew whatever she did he wouldn't be disappointed.

Storm walked into the room to find it darkened, lit only by candles. She had had their bed moved into the middle of their main room. There was something different about the bed then he realized she designed it like his favorite chair. Looking around he didn't see his mate right away. Where was she hiding? A slight movement caught his attention and he turned toward their bedroom door. She had some sort of wrap on, something she had started using recently to keep her outfits hidden from him until she came close enough for him to open the outer garment.

"Why are you way over there when our bed is right here, my heart?" He closed the distance between them.

"Because I wanted you to get the whole effect, and that wouldn't happen if I didn't make you look for me."

"You're the only thing I want to look at. The only thing I want to touch, to taste, to make shatter in my arms." He touched her face then took a hold of the ties that held her robe closed. "When can I open my gift?"

"Anytime you want."

He loosened the belt then let it drop to the ground. A flash of lace greeted him. Easing the robe off her shoulders he was able to see what she wore. The emerald green laced bra hugged her curves. The stretchy material was cut to where it barely contained her breasts, the edge of it just covered her nipples. The briefs cut high on her hips, but v-ed low on her abdomen. "Beautiful."

His hands skimmed along her exposed skin, edging along the lace. When he touched her outfit, the lace faded from sight. To test this, he placed one hand on one of her breasts. When he removed his hand, her breast was exposed. He grinned. "This is different."

"It dissolves with heat."

"Any physical contact?" He grinned more at her nod. "You know I'm going to have to test this."

"I was hoping you would."

The smolder in her eyes made him want to take his time with her. She was already aroused, and he wanted to build her desire to a roaring flame. He pulled her into his embrace and urged her to the bed.

"One more thing." She pressed her hand against his chest. Just as they reached the edge of the bed. Heather leaned down and lifted something.

"Really? I thought you didn't like being retrained." He touched the straps, made of a soft fur-like material.

"Who said they were for me?" She looked at him, a soft smile on her lips.

"Then let's see who uses them first." He knew better. When he used the ones on the ship, she saw firsthand how it enhanced their intimacy. He captured her lips with his, pulling her against him. Heather had already thought his clothes away. Her hands skimmed along his back. Storm eased her back onto the bed. As much as he wanted to drink from her lips longer her mark beckoned. Kissing his way down her throat, he drew the sensitive tissue into his mouth. Her desire spiked as she moved beneath him.

She lifted her legs and wrapped them around his hips,

pressing her core against his length. His erection pulsed against her, wanting to feel her heat accept him in. Heather felt it. He could tell by the quickening beat of her heart.

Storm wanted to go slowly, push her to the edge before he took her, push her need to the heights he knew she could reach but he wanted this as badly as she did. "My heart, I can't wait tonight."

"Good. I don't want to wait either." She touched his face. "Please, Storm, now."

He centered himself and slid in deep. Heather sucked in her breath when he filled her. Her legs moved up to his waist. He caught the scent of her desire spiking. "My heart."

"We both need this, Storm. A little wild before we can be tender."

"You sure?" He pulled her into a seated position. "I so enjoy making sure you reach your release."

"I have a feeling I will reach that release over and over before this night is through." She touched his face. "You will make sure of that."

"At least you know sleep is something that will be a while in coming."

"But I won't." She started a pace they liked.

Storm laughed as he helped her with the tempo. "You are my heart."

———

Heather didn't want to think about anything but the two of them. Tomorrow she could lose her mate so tonight she wanted to create memories that would last her a lifetime. She leaned back a little, giving Storm the angle that allowed him to hit the sensitive spot that brought her screams out. Each time he filled her she felt her need rise.

Closer and closer he brought her until she felt her orgasm uncoil from the pit of her stomach. Her body shook at the power of her release. She soared through the stars as it flung her out into the universe. Only her mate could do this to her.

———

"You are to be my connection to Heather?" Skye held her in his arms as he tried to digest the idea. "Why? I would think Heather would have wanted you somewhere safe."

"Her visions. Unfortunately, I show up in a lot of them. Never in danger." She looked up at him. "But enough for her to believe I am as integral a part as she is. She knew if she tried to hide me they would still go after me and bring me here. She didn't want to run the risk that they'd find out about the twins as well. It was safer to bring me here so you could protect the two of us."

"I don't like this. I need to rescue Storm and keep you two safe? And I can assume the word you is a basic term for anyone Heather considers needs protecting?"

"My mother has a big heart."

"In other words, I'll be saving half of Vespia." He saw how much she cared about her friends and family. Working with her the last few days proved that. The rough exterior he saw in her security files never showed the compassion she held deep inside.

"If this is more than you want to deal with I can make my mother aware so she can find someone else to do the job."

"I didn't say that." He had never worried about anyone but himself before. Now he had all these people depending on him and he wasn't sure he liked it. Doing what Heather wanted him to do wasn't the question. He was too good at his job to fail, and she knew it. "I'm just not happy about it."

"When you and I became bonded you promised to deal with my family." She took his hand in hers. "They're your family, too."

"Sam, I don't plan on backing out, but I was by myself for a long time." He linked fingers with her. "I'm just not used to it."

"But you have been in security for a long time, too. You've been responsible for so many people and have always done what needs to be done."

"Yes, but those people were strangers."

"So you're not liking this because you now care for the people you need to protect." She smiled. "I'm glad my family means so much to you and I have faith that you'll take very good care of them."

———

Skye entered Heather and Storm's quarters. He had gotten a missive from Storm asking him to arrive early. Storm sat at the table, while Heather remained in bed.

"I wish to speak to you before my mate gets up."

Skye nodded. Storm stood and headed out the doors. Skye followed, wondering what Storm wanted to talk about.

"You know about Heather's visions?"

Skye nodded again.

"She believes I'll die at the hands of our guests. If that happens you need to promise me that you will protect her. Get her away from those people."

"That is why I'm here. To keep her safe."

"Yes. Earth's reason for you to be here." Storm looked at him. "I know they also ask you to report back and have ignored your communiqués so you can keep your commander happy. I do the same for Heather. But now it is just the two of us. I fear she'll do something crazy if something happens to me. You have to stop her."

"Heather is a special person, and I won't let anything happen to her, but I also know she'd want me to keep you just as safe."

"My mate has a soft heart and would jeopardize herself to protect me. That can't happen. The visions my uncle had, that others have had, point to her being important to saving my race. That is more important than my life."

"She might not agree with you, but I will be sure that the future of your race is protected." Skye worded it so Storm would be happy with his response, and he wasn't giving away any information.

"Thank you. Now, we should get back before Heather comes out here looking for us."

———

Bert watched as the small ship he had lent Storm's father landed in the bay.

Iresna stepped down the gangplank. Ed met him at the bottom. Bert let him take lead since he was the one who sent the man off planet anyway.

"Was it hard to find?"

"No. Your directions were perfect." Iresna handed over a small pouch. "Most of the items you requested are in the cargo bay, but this I thought you would want right away."

Ed dropped the contents into his hand. There sat a small nondescript disc.

"That's it?" asked Bert.

"This will stop the clone from degrading. It has many

other functions, but I know saving her is our priority right now. Although I still don't know why."

"Heather feels for the woman. She was created, what happened to her wasn't her fault."

"And why did you go along with this?" Ed asked.

"Because I think she might come in handy later."

"Another vision?"

"Just a feeling." Bert slapped him on the back. "Let's go and make the correction to Heather's clone, then you can show me what else that does."

———

Skye stood beside Heather, watching the scout Storm was maneuvering outside the command ship of their guests. Other than a death grip on his hand, Heather showed no other form of stress. They were surrounded by the council, Anseri stood next to Heather on their right, the rest of the council was to their left.

Storm's ship tried to dislodge a piece of debris trapped in their engines. Why they were having Storm do it instead of one of their own people Skye didn't know, but this had to be the moment Heather's visions warned her about.

One of the technicians called Reasta to their station. They didn't say anything, just pointed to the screen in front of them.

"Cancel that." She spoke to the technician, saying it loud enough for everyone there to hear.

"I've tried, but I can't." He looked up at her. Fear coming off him in waves. What was he afraid of? Her?

"There has to be a way." She leaned down to work a few buttons. Everything that happened next felt like it moved in slow motion. A blast erupted from one of their guns seconds before the ship Storm was in went up in a blinding light. Once it faded the ship was gone.

"Storm!" Heather cried out and grabbed her head then slid boneless to the floor. Anseri cried out as well as tears slid down her cheek. The rest of the council surrounded her as he went to Heather.

"Heather." Skye tapped her face, but she didn't revive. Instinct had him shouting. "What the hell just happened? I saw one of your weapons discharge before his ship blew up."

"Something caused the weapon to heat up and fire. I don't know what to say. That never should have happened. We tried to stop it." She looked contrite as she looked at Heather's unconscious form. "Let's bring her to our medical center."

"I think you have done enough damage today." Skye scooped her up in his arms. "Her brother should look at her."

"Then have him come here."

Skye glared at the woman. Heather only fainted, why was she pushing to get her into their labs? "My job is to protect Heather and that is what I plan on doing. She needs her family when she wakes up."

"By the time you get her to your lab we could have already diagnosed her to see if she is in real danger. Do you want to take that type of chance with her?" She took a step toward him. "I'm sorry over what just happened. Let us make sure she's okay before it's too late. Once we're sure you can bring her back to Vespia."

Skye heard Fridon in his head, demanding to know what had happened. "Vespian Security wants to know what just happened. How am I supposed to explain to them that they just lost their future leader? If I don't go back with

163

Heather, they might take that as a sign of aggression and declare war on you. Is that what you want?"

"Of course not, I just want to be sure she is okay. What just happened was an accident. I wish we could turn back time and stop it, but I don't know how."

Skye knew that to be a lie.

"I know they must be worried on the planet. You can speak to them while we examine Heather. Try to explain things."

She sure didn't want him to take her back to Vespia. Would that ruin their timeline? Perhaps that was what he should do. Bringing her home and then traveling back in time to save Storm would be the easiest scenario.

Skye sure could use a little insight right now. Heather had shared her visions and plans so he knew what she wanted. What if he deviated? Would it fix the problem without following what she put in motion? Or make it worse?

Reasta looked like she wanted to snatch Heather out of his arms as he tried to figure out the right thing to do. Everyone trusted her visions. He had to as well. Now he had to play this right. If he pushed too hard, he could end up in one of their brigs. If he backed off too quickly, he might make them suspicious.

"Ma'am, Vespian Security is asking for answers. Shall I put them on?"

She turned to look at Skye with Heather in his arms. "Mr. Latimer I will leave this to you. If you wish to speak to them with her in your arms, I will turn on the screen now. If you will allow us to check her out while you speak to your people, then please let my guard take her."

He debated. The thought of letting them take her from his sight went against his training but he knew he had to do it. The visions Heather had shared with him showed he had to let her go. "Which way to your medical center."

The guard directed him to the lab and pointed to a table for him to lay her on.

"Where can I speak to security?"

"Here." The doctor turned on a screen and Fridon's face filled it.

"Latimer? What is going on?"

"There has been an incident." He turned to look at the group of people working on Heather.

"Where are you?"

"I'm in their medical center." He turned back to the screen. "Heather is unconscious."

"What happened?" Fridon looked pale for a Vespian. He had to know what their system said but didn't want to believe it.

"Storm was working on the debris stuck in the ship's engine."

"The council told me about it. They didn't have the right equipment, so we offered to help."

"One of their weapons fired and Storm's ship evaporated. He's gone, Fridon. There is nothing left. Heather crumpled at my feet right after. They are checking her out now." He could see Fridon's shock. Skye continued to give his version of what happened. "They have given us permission to allow Kuarto to come aboard to check out Heather with their doctor."

"I'll send him immediately. Bring her back as soon as you can."

"I will." He wasn't sure how easy that would be, but he would do his best.

EIGHT

Heather opened her eyes but didn't recognize where she was. She wasn't in her rooms. It didn't make sense, then everything that had happened came crashing down on her. Storm. Gone. Watching that ship evaporate. Her heart ached at the loss. Tears filled her eyes at the realization of what happened. A cool hand on her arm startled her. She turned her head.

"Oh good. You're awake." A doctor smiled at her. Not one she recognized.

She didn't say anything, just pushed herself so she could sit up. It took more energy than it should have. How long was she out? One tear spilled down her cheek before she locked her emotions deep inside. This wasn't Kuarto's lab. Where was she? As she looked around, she realized she was on Reasta's ship. They were supposed to stop her vision. What went wrong?

"We were worried. You've been unconscious for about two weeks." He must have alerted Reasta because she came into the room.

Two weeks? Well, crap. That couldn't be good. She

needed to know how everyone was taking the loss of Storm. Anseri must be beside herself with grief. Like in her vision, Reasta had found a way to keep her aboard her ship after the explosion. "Where's Latimer?"

"Your Earth commander called him back home." Reasta watched her.

Bear wouldn't have done that. Skye never would have left her either, so this was all Reasta's doing, but she knew better than to react. "Can I go home?"

"Soon, you did just wake up and we want to be sure there are no residual problems." The doctor moved around her, checking readings and making notations.

"Why did you kill him?" Heather looked at Reasta.

"It was an accident, Heather."

"I'm not stupid, Reasta. I saw the blast." She wasn't about to pretend everything was fine. Her visions showed her she fought this woman with every breath. "That little performance you gave us was just that. You wanted Storm out of the way, and I want to know why."

"Heather, you have it all wrong. I would never take your mate from you."

"Yet he is gone." Saying the words twisted at her guts, but she couldn't show her grief. Not until she was sure it was safe. She swung her legs off the bed. "I want to look at your records of the event. Let me see for myself that it was an accident."

"No need. I know Storm's ship exploded, and this might be a little hard to grasp at first, but we were able to fix that problem." She stepped to the side and in walked Storm.

Heather's heart started to race. Did Reasta save him? Everything they learned told them she wanted Storm out of the equation, why would she save him if that was true?

"My heart." He walked to her side and sat on the bed.

"Storm?" She touched his face, then his chest. Her

fingers brushed against his mark. The wonderful glow that normally blossomed in his eyes didn't happen. Something was wrong. She reached out with her mind. Nothing. This wasn't her mate. Heather pushed his hands away when he tried to take her in his arms.

"You deny me?"

"What is he?"

Reasta's eyes took on a hard glint. "What do you mean, Heather?"

"This is not Storm."

She sighed. "You picked that up pretty quickly, how?"

"I know my mate and this man might look like him, but my heart knows the truth." Storm sat on her bed, taking her hand after trying to wrap his arms around her a few times.

"He is Storm, with a few upgrades. A perfect copy, but my copy."

Upgrades? Her heart sank when she realized she was looking at a clone of her mate. "What do you want from me that you had to kill my mate and then try to fool me with this clone?"

"I want you to get to know this, Storm. He's now your companion." With that, she turned on her heels and left the room.

Heather was now alone with Storm's clone. She pulled her hand from his and climbed out the other side of the bed she had been in, wanting to put space between them.

"You are not happy to see me?" He stood.

"You are not my mate." Her Storm would be proving who he was by how he made her feel when he touched her. She'd be pinned to a wall by now with him buried deep inside. If this clone was a true copy why wasn't he trying the same thing?

"But I am." He walked toward her. "Every memory he had I have to a point. I remember us."

"How?" Just how much of Storm's memories did he have?

"It was done at my creation. There are several ways to clone. Some clone to repopulate their race and don't want the copies to have the memories. I was cloned to replace what you lost so I was made with the memories intact."

"What is the last thing you remember?" Did Reasta make him better than her clone or will he start to degrade too?

"Meeting Reasta."

"That is when she got a copy of your DNA." Heather found it hard to look at him. She wanted to wrap her arms around him. Have him hold her close. "Why does she want us to get close?"

"She hopes we will continue as we had before I died. She feels awful over what happened."

Heather wasn't sure that was true. "Reasta made a comment about wanting something from me. What does she want?"

"I don't know, but I can find out." He gave her his bone-melting smile. "In the meantime, I would like to prove to you I am the same man."

———

Skye stood with Bert, looking at the readings he was working through. The computations were intricate, but he was able to keep up as Bert went through the timeline.

"I think we have changed everything back to the way it should be, but I can't be sure until we bring Heather back."

"Let's get her now."

"We can't. Not yet." Bert looked at who was talking. "There are several things that I need to do before we can attempt a rescue and in order to do that, I need Kuarto and what we sent Iresna after."

"What did you send him after?" asked Skye, drawing his attention back to what they were talking about.

"Ed is our technician. He had made a device that was able to correct the errors in Heather's clone, but he didn't bring it with him when Sam brought him here."

Skye nodded. Storm's father had come back several weeks ago, "So you fixed the degradation."

"Yes." Bert grinned. "In order to rescue our Heather, we need to switch out the clone with the real one. Right now, Reasta can tell the difference between the two by the markers in their cells and I need to fix that. Ed's device can alter her clone to read as the real Heather. Once I do that, we can switch them out. It will take time but with Kuarto's help I can get it done faster." He looked at Skye. "Can you extract him without detection?"

"Of course, but he's in the center of the city at the lab in the palace. If I just walk in and take him people will notice." Skye pulled up the location of Kuarto on the screen. If he was in his quarters or away from the Medlab he might not be missed right away. "I'm not supposed to be here, remember?"

"True, but there are a few things in place to help isolate him for easy extraction." Bert smiled at the young woman on his bridge.

Skye looked at her for a moment before turning back to Bert. "You want to fill me in since I'm the one kidnapping him?"

"I'll let Toki do that." He nodded to the woman he had been looking at.

Skye turned to her and waited. She had been with Bert since the dinner the night before her brother was killed. Her headache turned into an escape route for her.

"I have left clues for my mate. I know he has seen them all but either hasn't made the connection between them yet or is waiting for the right time to follow them. They will get him to a safe place for you to bring him here."

"Are we to wait for him to figure it out or do you want me to go get him?"

"Like you said, if he were to just disappear people would take notice. You still have that invisibility device that Fridon gave you. Use it and tell him we need him to follow the clues now before it is too late."

"I'll leave now." Skye felt a wave of grief strike him hard. He gripped the counter nearby to keep his feet. "I think Heather is awake."

"You sure?"

"I've never felt such sadness before. She's awake."

———

Fridon sat in Storm's office, wondering how everything went so wrong. Losing Storm was like losing a big brother to him. Now he was the one in charge of Vespian security. He didn't feel worthy to take the man's place. The first thing he did was speak to Anseri about getting Heather home and she seemed to slough it off. She wasn't upset that Heather was still on their visitor's ship and he didn't understand that. There was something wrong with her, but he didn't question. Pushing right now might make the situation worse. He needed answers and knew he wouldn't get them from her.

He had been through all of Storm's files, finding in-depth information on their guests and the Heather clone. It was a start. The way Anseri was behaving had him wondering if she had been cloned and replaced. She hadn't grieved for the loss of her son. Didn't demand Heather be sent home. It didn't make sense. Kuarto would be the one to talk to if he wanted to get a few more answers.

Fridon walked to the medlab feeling paranoid. Was the doctor a clone too? Could he trust him with his theories? That was a gadget he could use for his little device. It sure would make it easier to know who to trust.

"Fridon? What brings you here?" Kuarto looked up from his work. Not one to sit in an office, he found the doctor working on the main medical computer. Micali was on a break so Kuarto was the only one there.

"Thought I'd ask if you have found your mate yet?"

"No, and I'm worried. She has never been gone longer than a day and it has been several weeks." He looked at the door before focusing back on Fridon. He kept his voice low. "Anseri told me she probably went on a soul walk, something she's never done before. I checked the records and there is no such thing on Vespia. Anseri isn't herself."

"So you have noticed it too."

"Yes, why hasn't she pushed to bring my sister home? Heather has been on that ship since Storm died when she should be here with family to help her cope." He shook his head. "It doesn't make sense."

"One of the reasons I came to see you."

"What do you need?"

"Perhaps we should talk outside?" Fridon didn't want to give anyone any more information if someone was listening in.

"It's time for my lunch anyway. Care to join me?" Kuarto walked out of the building with him, quiet until they were outside.

"Do you know what the hell is going on?" asked Kuarto.

"I wanted to ask you the same thing. Nothing seems right. Anseri acts like nothing is wrong. Storm is dead, which never should have happened, your mate is missing, and Heather is a prisoner." Fridon walked beside him. "I knew something was wrong before they arrived. It was the way Heather and Storm behaved."

"I notice it too, but they never said anything."

Fridon looked at him. They didn't say anything to him, but Heather knew how easy it would for someone to read his thoughts. Kuarto was always in the middle of their plans. Why didn't they use him? "I have a question for you. Do you have a way to tell if someone has been cloned?"

"As a matter of fact, I do." Kuarto lifted his right hand, revealing a small circular piece of metal. "I don't know who to trust and I tested it first on Anseri. She is a clone."

"Can I try that?" So, what he suspected was real.

"Sure, by the way, you're not one." He handed it over.

"And you?" He tested it on Kuarto and saw the readings. It showed he was clean. "How do I know this is right?"

Kuarto grinned. "Spoken like Security's leader. Keep it and use it. I can make another one."

"I have a better idea. Can you load it into this?" He pulled out the little device he had created.

"Yes." Kuarto grinned. "As soon as we're back in my lab."

———

Heather studied the clone of her mate with a lump in her throat. She wanted to grieve. Her heart was gone. Having this copy around her all the time just made it worse.

He tried so hard to fill in as her mate, but she couldn't, wouldn't let him. She wanted to go home and be with her family. Be with loved ones as she worked her way through her loss. Why wouldn't they let her go? They were treating her well, but she knew better. She was a prisoner. What did Reasta want from her anyway?

The Storm clone was so much like her mate she had to keep reminding herself that he wasn't the man she knew. Their mindlink was gone. His eyes didn't glow when he became aroused, and she knew that because this one kept pushing to be intimate with her.

"Please."

"Why do you keep telling me no? We belong together." He had her backed up against the wall. He kissed one cheek then the other, working his way down her throat.

"That might be true to you, but not to me." She looked up at him, hoping this Storm understood her fear. "I need time to get to know you. This version of you."

"You are willing to try?"

"Unless you're going to force me."

"I want you happy." He released her. "And I look forward to wooing you."

———

Heather sat in her room, grateful that Storm's clone understood how hard this was for her. It would give her a small reprieve before he started pushing again. The whole idea of having sex with him made her stomach lurch. She couldn't do it.

She looked around the calming space. They called it her room, but she knew the truth. No matter how nice they made it, it was a prison.

How was she going to get off the ship? That was what she had to work on next. They hadn't let her wander around very much so she had no idea if there were shuttles or pods she could steal. Heather also didn't know where the teleportation room was. All things she needed to learn about and right now she only had one source. The clone.

Storm's clone would be coming to get her soon. Reasta was working hard on getting them together so he spent a lot of time with her. Heather wished he would leave her alone. Allow her to grieve the way she wanted, but since he was being forced on her, she would take advantage and gather as much information as she could to find a way off the ship.

She looked at the door, knowing he'd be coming in any moment.

What did the woman want with her anyway? Her thoughts went back to her visions. Reasta showed her the progeny she created. Thousands and thousands of men and women. Is that what she wanted? What Ialog wanted? Were these the people Dian spoke about that Ialog had ties to? She said he wasn't working alone. Were they the ones who wanted one of her eggs?

Ialog had made a comment the last time they clashed about not wanting her but wanting one of her offspring. He wanted the one that carried the cure for the lack of births in all the races. At least that was what he told her. Was this race the reason why?

Heather rubbed her forehead in frustration. So many questions and no answers. She half wished she could talk to Ialog and learn the truth.

Her door opened and she locked her thoughts deep in her mind. Storm's clone walked in. Time to focus.

"Where would you like to go?" He gave her Storm's bone-melting smile. All it did was make her wish for something she couldn't have anymore.

"How about to Vespia?" She smiled back. "I'd love some fresh air."

"The air on this ship is fresh."

"Not what I mean." She looked at him. "I want to ride my airbike through the forest. Hear the animals scurry after their food. That kind of thing."

"But we can get that through the holographic center. I can see if it is free."

"Fine." Not what she wanted but it did give her some information. This Storm wouldn't break the rules to keep her happy. Something she hoped to use in the future.

———

Fridon followed the doctor down a path below the main compound where the elder's hall was. He never knew this cave was there and he had explored all over as a child. "This is the cave? It is something all religious leaders know about? I've been here many times. How did I miss this?"

"From what my mate said it is hidden unless you know what you're looking for." Kuarto worked his way down the rocky path. "Toki told me about it and how to find it because she would disappear for a day or two and I would get worried. I walked past it several times before she came out and showed me how to spot it."

"Have you ever been inside?"

"No. Toki said it was for the religious leader's eyes only. When I wanted to be sure if she was okay, I would come here and call to her. She normally came out to let me know she was okay, and she always answered, until now."

"Did you talk to her uncle?"

"Of course. I went to him right after I went to Anseri. He told me he was no longer allowed in the cave then told me to follow my heart." The cave came into view.

"And what does your heart tell you?"

"Find my mate."

"Then we need to find a way to enter the cave."

"I believe my mate has already given me the answer." Kuarto pulled out his medical scanner. "She's left me clues. All we have to do is figure them out."

———

Heather found it hard to stay upset with Storm's clone. So much like her mate, he was trying hard to please her. It reminded her of the man she fell in love with. The one who did sweet little things to win her heart. But instead of breaking down her defenses it just broke her heart a little more.

She kept her emotions deep inside. Her training taught her not to give Reasta anything to work with. She looked at her mate's clone's profile as they walked down a corridor. "Did you find out why Reasta wants us together?"

"She wishes for us to have a child together." He had taken her hand earlier and tucked it into the crook of his arm.

Heather nodded. That was what she thought. She wanted the child Ialog had mentioned. Why? "Does she know we haven't been intimate?"

"Of course, and she's not very happy about that."

"Did you explain to her why?"

"I did." He turned toward her. "She has demanded I be successful."

"Are you going to force me?" She watched his face, fearing his answer.

"No. I know you don't see me as your mate, but I want you to know that I remember every wonderful moment we shared. Trying to force you would destroy those memories. I can't do that but know it's hard being this close to you and not being intimate."

Heather started laughing. He might not understand the double entendre he just uttered, but she did.

"Why do you laugh?"

If they had their mental connection, he would know why and would probably take advantage of it. "It's the way the translator converts your words."

"I thought I was speaking human."

"You mean English. Humans have several native tongues. English is the one we use with offworlders." She looked at the clone. Storm knew that. Why didn't he?

"I understand." He stood there looking at her for a moment, unmoving. Then he smiled and patted her hand. "Reasta has made one request."

"A request or demand?" Heather saw the confusion on his face. "Can I say no?"

He didn't answer.

"What does she want?"

"For us to share a room. She has already set one up for us. That is where we're going now." He continued to lead her down the corridor.

Heather slowed her steps. "S.C. I don't think I can do that."

"S.C.?" He looked at her curiously.

"I can't call you Storm, but I have to call you something."

"Storm clone. Is that what it stands for?"

"Yes."

"I guess it is better than hey you." He gave her a heart-stopping smile. "Come, let me show you our new rooms."

She didn't want to go anywhere where she would have to be with the clone longer than she wanted, but she knew refusing would bring soldiers and restraints. As long as she pretended to go along with what they wanted, she would still have a little free movement, even if this clone was with her every time, and she needed that to find a way to escape. She walked with him, feeling the heat of his hand on top of hers. He stopped in front of a door.

"Here are our new quarters."

Heather took a deep breath. She wasn't sure she could share a bed with this man. He was so much like Storm it would be easy to ignore her heart and pretend he was the real thing.

The door opened and she felt her knees go weak. It was their room. Tears started flowing down her cheek as she slid to the floor. It was too much.

"My heart." S.C. lifted her and carried her to the couch as she continued to cry. "Reasta thought you'd feel more comfortable with familiar surroundings. I can have this changed if you wish."

Time to be a security officer on a mission. She kept falling back on that when she needed it, but now she had to remain that way the whole time. When she let it lapse she found herself in situations like this. Heather wiped the tears away. "I am fine. It was a bit of a shock. That's all."

"You sure?"

"Yes." She nodded. "I just need to meditate a little."

"I can find something to do while you do that."

"Thank you." She moved to the floor and sat cross-legged. Closing her eyes, she focused on the point she used to get into deep meditation. Here she could grieve the way she wanted without anyone to stop her.

Her mind cleared and she found herself in the wonderful little haven she built in her mind. Here she broke down. Let the grief she felt fill her then overflow. Thank goodness she and Storm had made the most of their last few hours being intimate and sharing the joy they had in each other's arms.

"My heart?" Her mate's voice flowed through her mind.

At first, she feared the clone had followed her, but she knew better. This was her mind creating what she missed.

Heather looked up and found Storm crouching beside her. He looked so real. Had her mind reached out to his soul? Was that possible? "Storm? Am I in heaven?"

He smiled. "I'm always in heaven when I'm with you." He looked around before he gazed back at her. "Where are we?"

"My meditation place." She wasn't sure anymore. Had she reached out further than she had ever done before and broken through the veil between the living and the dead?

"This is where you go to clear your mind?" He touched her face with tenderness, causing her to cry again.

"Yes, and I must have conjured you because I missed you so much." She got to her knees and wrapped her arms around him. The feel of his body against hers had a relaxing effect on her.

"I am here for you."

"You know what they have done, don't you? You now have a clone. One they want me to have sex with because they want a child." She looked up at him with tear-filled eyes. "That was why Reasta had you killed. She knew she couldn't control you, but she could control the clone."

"Have you been with him?" He brushed his fingers along her jaw as he spoke, but she knew he feared her answer.

"I can't." Another tear slid down her cheek. "I want you, not a copy."

"How did you know it wasn't me?"

"She made changes like our link doesn't work. His eyes don't glow when he is aroused. But she won't let me go until she gets what she wants. And she keeps pushing. Your clone and I have to share a bed now and she recreated our rooms."

He frowned as he wiped the tear off her cheek. "I wish I could be there with you, my heart."

"Me too. Seeing your face on that clone breaks my heart."

He pulled her close, his arms drawing her into a warm embrace. "Is he the only person you've seen? No Fridon? Kuarto? What about Sam? Or Skye?"

"She's kept me isolated." Heather shook her head. "I've spoken to Anseri via communiqués but that is it. I have been very lonely without you."

"I am here now, and I know how to make you think of nothing but us." He held her against him, his hands brushing along her spine. "I have missed being able to touch you."

"I have missed your touch." She brushed her fingers along his jaw, wishing for something she knew she couldn't have. If she thought it would be real she'd stay here with him forever. Heather looked behind herself for a moment. "I have to go. Will you come back?"

"Whenever you want me."

"Always. I want you always." She gave him a quick kiss then opened her eyes.

"I am sorry, Heather, but Reasta wishes to speak to you."

She dropped her head against the couch before she plastered a smile on her face. Knowing she could conjure her mate when she needed made her realize just how powerful her mind was. He felt so real. Perhaps this was her way of keeping the clone from confusing her. The man in her mind was the man she loved, not this copy.

S.C. offered her his hand and pulled her to her feet. They walked to Reasta's control center for the ship, their orbit stationary around Vespia. The council had allowed them to stay? That didn't make sense.

"Ah, Heather. Good to see you're settling in." She turned from the people she had been in a conversation with to focus on Heather.

"Why can't I go home?" She wasn't going to treat this woman any different than she had treated Ialog.

"You will in due time."

"Once I produce the offspring you want?"

She smiled at Heather.

"Why don't you just use artificial insemination?" The look Reasta gave her told her the truth. "You've already tried. That's why you kept me under for two weeks, but nothing you tried worked so now you're forced to do it the old-fashioned way."

"You are a very smart woman."

"And you're not happy because your creation doesn't thrill me." Heather crossed her arms over her chest. "You need me to go along with your plan or you will fail."

"Now, Heather."

"I want a few things." She dropped her hands to her sides.

"What?" Her eyes narrowed, not happy with Heather having demands.

"You want me to accept him as Storm and I'm sorry that won't happen, but I am willing to get to know your clone and give him a chance. He is almost Storm. There are times when he is my mate and times when he is your lap dog."

"And you don't like the lap dog." Reasta watched her.

"I want my mate back."

"Your concessions?"

"Time alone, off this ship. I'd like to go to the planet, but you keep saying no."

"How do you think people are going to react to seeing Storm after they know he died in the explosion?"

"I have a feeling the population doesn't know about his

death and I'm not asking you to send me to the center of the palace grounds." Heather looked around. "I just want to breathe the air and feel the earth beneath my feet."

"That is something I need to think about."

"Fine." Heather hesitated for a moment, making Reasta think she was done with her demands. The moment she turned away Heather spoke. "One more thing."

"What?"

"My daughter had a cat. Pumpkin. I was taking care of her while Sam was away. It would go a long way if she could join me."

"A cat?"

"A pet."

She watched Heather for a moment. Probably wondering why Heather asked for it. "I'll contact the council and see what can be done."

Heather nodded. She wanted more, and planned on demanding more, but would start with those two things.

———

Bert had his system keyed to any communications between the ship and Vespia. He wished they had more information, but he didn't want to give his location away. Reasta filled his screen as she contacted the council.

He smiled when he heard her request. "Skye, where is Pumpkin?"

"In my room. Why?"

"Because I just found a way to have eyes and ears on that ship. Heather has asked for the cat."

———

183

Heather cuddled with Pumpkin when the cat arrived; having something from home helped calm her. Pumpkin purred in her ear and preened at all the attention. "Bet you have missed this. I was afraid you'd be all skin and bones, but I see someone looked out for you."

Pumpkin meowed and climbed up on Heather's shoulder. She smiled and gave the cat a final stroke before she looked at Reasta. "Thank you."

"Does that animal do that all the time?" She watched the cat as it settled on Heather's shoulder, curiosity etched on her face.

"Yes." Heather pulled Pumpkin off her shoulder. She cuddled her for a few moments more before she perched herself back on Heather's shoulder. The soft purr rumbled next to her ear. "It's her favorite place."

"As long as it doesn't get underfoot."

"She'll stay in my room unless I decide to have her accompany me." Heather petted the cat. "Does this mean I won't get my other request?"

"I am concerned about your safety."

"Right." Heather knew what that meant. "So I'm trapped on this ship and only allowed to go to certain places and that is only with the company you have picked out."

"It is for your own good."

"Really? Or is it because it benefits you."

NINE

"It is working." Bert watched the scene unfold in front of them. "Now we'll know what is going on with Heather."

"It's about time." The deep male voice in his ear came across close to a growl.

"I know you want her with us, but it must be done just right."

"What do you think her other request is?" asked Fridon, who wanted to defuse the situation. He had transported up to the ship with Kuarto and Bert refused to send him back. He hoped he wouldn't be here too long, or someone was going to notice.

"Knowing Heather, she has asked to go home."

"Explain to me again why we can't just use the invisibility settings on the devices Fridon made and just take her?"

"Reasta needs to believe she is successful. Heather has set everything up so we can be. If we waiver we could destroy what she has done. We have to be patient. Wait for a sign from her to put the next step into motion."

"I don't like her being in danger like this. Especially since she doesn't remember."

"No one does, my friend."

———

Pumpkin's purr relaxed Heather. Something she desperately needed at this time. It also kept S.C. at bay. He wasn't quite sure what to do with the cat on her shoulder all the time. Pumpkin totally ignored him. The cat seemed to know that he wasn't worth her time.

The confused look S.C. would give Pumpkin made her want to laugh too. Her mate would have just growled at it and sent it running. Pumpkin could pick up the wolf in him and they didn't get along too well. It took Storm shifting and allowing the cat to check him out for the two of them to tolerate each other. Something Heather had begged him to do since they took care of the furry feline when Sam was out of town.

She remembered what she had to do to get him to go along with her desire and wished he was there with her. It was wonderful.

"You wish to go for a walk?"

S.C.'s words interrupted her thoughts. Heather looked up at her mate's clone. Knowing he wasn't her mate made her sigh at the memory of their intimacy before she slapped on a smile. "Where shall we walk?"

"We could walk through the hydroponics area. There's lots of vegetation and flowers there and I thought you would enjoy that. It might not be the garden at the palace, but I hope it will help relax you. You have been so tense."

"And you've gotten permission to go there." She stood.

"That bothers you, doesn't it?" He waited until she

walked in front of him to place his hand on the small of her back and usher her out of the doors of their room.

"Very much. I'm nothing more than a prisoner here." She moved so he wasn't touching her anymore.

"You don't have to be."

She looked up at him. "The price I have to pay is too steep."

"Is being intimate with me that bad?" he asked, clearly perplexed by her words. "I am a perfect copy of your mate."

"If you were a perfect copy, I wouldn't have been able to tell you weren't my Storm."

"You never did say what gave me away."

She couldn't tell him the truth. If he didn't know about the ability to shift, why give him the information? Why he didn't know made her wonder. Did Reasta leave the ancient gene out of his creation as well? Still, the memory should be there, but like with her clone he had holes in his memory. Reasta did say she made a few changes. Did she remove the memory when she removed the DNA? If so how? Her thoughts went back to her clone. She had no ancient blood in her, could that be why his eyes didn't glow? Because the ancient genes are missing? Maybe this copy couldn't shift like her mate could. "It doesn't really matter, so let's not worry about it."

"You don't trust me to tell me."

He knew her as well as her mate. "How can I? You don't make a move without being sure Reasta approves of it first. My mate would never let anyone tell him what to do."

"Even you?"

She had to laugh. Storm always put her first, but he was a very dominating man and was used to making all the decisions. "What do you think?"

They approached the doors that led to the hydroponics area. S.C. entered a password and the doors opened. "I think you can be as dominating as me."

The area was beautiful. Lots of plants crowded the walkway they moved down. A sigh escaped her as she felt herself relax. "This is nice."

"I thought you would like it. I have prepared a meal for us to enjoy." He took her to a small grassy area near some of the crops growing in the bay. On the ground was a blanket covered with a lot of her favorite foods.

"That was very thoughtful." She didn't want to spend more time alone with the clone. He was too much like Storm at times and Heather was finding it hard to keep him at bay. It would be so easy to just pretend he was her mate.

Pumpkin leaped off her shoulder.

"Where is she going?"

"To explore." Heather looked at him. "That isn't a problem, is it?"

"No." He watched the cat disappear.

"Good." She gave him her best smile. "Now what did you bring for us to eat?"

———

"Why are you staring at that screen like that?" Someone growled in Bert's ear. "That stupid cat is just exploring."

Bert turned toward the man speaking. He knew he hated having to wait, but Heather was the one who knew what needed to be done to make sure everything fell into place. They had to follow her lead.

"Because the cat might be able to find us a way in."

"Through the lab?"

"A lot of our old ships had a special bay door for direct deliveries of plants. Especially the more delicate ones, and if Reasta can't access the ancient technology she wouldn't have been able to maintain them as well as the main doors on the ship. She might not even know they are there. Depending on the sensors, we might be able to access it without being detected. Pumpkin will let us know if we can use that as an extraction point."

"Fine but know I won't wait very long before I go in there and rescue her myself."

———

Their meal had been nice. S.C. tried to seduce her, but she didn't want any part of him. His frustration with her was evident by the end of their visit to the hydroponics lab. The moment they returned to their room Reasta called him to the bridge, giving Heather a few moments to meditate.

Knowing Reasta called him to her made Heather wonder what they were going to try next. Short of tying her to a table and S.C. forcing himself on her it wasn't going to happen.

Heather sat on the floor of the living room and closed her eyes. Relaxing her mind, she slipped deeper and deeper inside herself until she found herself inside that white room again. Would she be able to call Storm's spirit to her side like she did before?

"Storm?"

"I'm here, my heart."

She smiled when he appeared in front of her. What she wanted to do was wrap her arms around him and feel his warmth, but would that be smart? All she was doing was postponing the inevitable. Heather knew she needed to accept his death and learn to move on. He'd never forgive her if she didn't.

"What is wrong? Have they harmed you?" He touched

her jawline, sending joy shooting through her. His touch destroyed any resolve she had to be strong. She loved to feel the heat of his hand.

"No." She hesitantly reached out and pressed her hand against his chest. A sigh escaped her when she made contact. Once more wouldn't hurt. Her grieving couldn't start until she was safely back on Vespia anyway. "They are pushing for me to be intimate with your clone, but I don't want to. No matter how hard he tries, he's not you. I've been doing my best to avoid it, but he's wearing down my defenses." She brushed her fingers through his hair. "I miss you so much."

"A rescue is in the works, my heart." He wrapped his arms around her and pulled her close. "Hold out as long as you can."

"How Storm? There is no way off this ship. Not that I can see." She leaned back to look up at him. "They keep me isolated and under constant surveillance."

"Wasn't Sam's cat looking around the hydroponics lab earlier? Perhaps she gave our friends something to use. A lot of ships have a bay door for direct deliveries."

"You know about Pumpkin?"

"Yes." He was quiet for a moment like he was hesitating.

"Storm?"

"I know you so well, my heart. You're trapped here and would want something from home. That cat made perfect sense to me."

"You're right, I did ask for her." Heather smiled. "You think they might have put something on Pumpkin to see where she goes on the ship?" Her desire to touch him grew and she brushed her fingers along his jaw.

"Yes. She is their little ace in the whole. If there is a way in, she will reveal it. We want you home, my heart. Safe and where you belong."

"And I want that too. I wish I could talk to them, tell them what I know. S.C. told me that there was no way they could have any security in the lab. The delicate environment wouldn't allow it." She rested her head against his chest. The sound of a heartbeat surprised her. Her imagination was making him too life-like. Maybe this wasn't a good idea. "He said it would be the one place where we could have some privacy. Storm, it's getting harder and harder to tell him no."

"Can you go back there?" He ran his hands up and down her back, relaxing her the way he always did. Maybe it wasn't such a bad idea after all.

"I think so, why?"

"The less you know the better you are." Storm's head dipped to her mark. She felt the heat of his mouth all the way to her toes.

"Storm, I won't be alone."

"My clone?" He lifted his head to look at her.

"And I have to assume he knows the same security techniques you do. I also don't trust him. Reasta has total control of him."

"Just try to get back there, my heart. As soon as you can."

"You're not going to leave me this soon, are you?" She touched his face again.

"I'll stay as long as you need me to."

"You don't know how badly I need you right now. If we could be intimate it might help me stave off that clone of yours a little while longer."

"This is your mind, my heart. We can do whatever we want here." His fingers traced the line of her jaw.

Heather pressed her hand to his chest and was greeted

with skin. She had forgotten that they could do this in her mind, but if she was intimate with her dead mate would she be able to move on? She knew every time her grief became too much to bear she would retreat here and just make it that much harder to accept what happened.

"You're not sure?" Storm could obviously sense her hesitancy.

"I want to, but what if this is wrong and just makes matters worse for me? I need to grieve, move on for our children." A tear slid down her cheek. "But I don't want this to end. I want you to be alive so much. I want as many memories as I can have of you and our love for each other. Even if I made it up."

"Our being together is never wrong. It is glorious and you know it." He ran his hand up her back, touching all the places he knew would ignite her desire. His lips pressed against her cheek where the tear fell. "I could break down your defenses. We know I'm very good at that, but I would never cause you any unwanted stress. It is your decision."

"My heart." She looked at him, gazing into his glowing eyes, and saw the need for her there. This could be her way of saying goodbye to him. Even if she was fabricating him it could give her the closure she needed to start to live without him. Maybe that was why she created him in the first place.

Touching his face, he felt so real. Her hands slid down his neck to trace the outlines of his muscled torso. His heart beat in his chest. The moment she felt it she rested her face against it to listen to the wonderful sound. She missed this.

"My heart?" His arms tightened around her. "Are you okay?"

"Yes." She smiled against his chest. "I missed the sound of your heart, the feel of your arms around me." She looked up at him. "The way you bring me to such wonderful heights when we're intimate."

"I missed you too." He lowered his mouth to hers, claiming her lips and begging entrance by tracing the seal of her lips. The moment she opened for him his tongue searched the recesses of her mouth to find his dancing mate.

His hands continued to touch all the places that ignited her need. A brush against the side of her breast, a quick dip into her belly button, a sensuous slide down her hip. It made her forget her hesitation. All she wanted to do was feel him inside her.

Her mind created their favorite chair and she found her back against it as Storm continued to kiss her. She wrapped her legs around him, sending the silent signals of what she wanted. Tears sprang into her eyes as she felt him slide in deep.

He kissed one tear then another away. "I don't want you to be sad, my heart."

"I'm never sad with your arms around me." She wiped her tears away and smiled at him. "Now I believe your job is to make me forget about everything but us."

He gave her his heart-stopping smile. "And I am very good at that."

He started to drive into her, making her forget her fears. She did want this. One last time with her mate. One stroke hit the right place and she moaned her delight. Heather tilted her hips, allowing him to hit the same spot over and over. Her body shook as her orgasm roared through her.

———

Heather opened her eyes to find S.C. kneeling in front of her. His smile made her heart flip. So much like Storm's.

"I didn't stop you from meditating, did I?"

"No." She wished she was still back in her mind with her mate, but he couldn't know what she had created there. "How long have you been there staring at me?"

"Not long. You seem so relaxed now. Like you just had an orgasm. I never noticed that before." He smiled and she felt it deep inside.

How could he know? Yet it wouldn't have surprised her if Storm had said that. He knew her best. This man had his memories. "So did Reasta give you an ultimatum?"

"She wishes us to stay together in this room until you conceive."

"No." There was no way she would go along with that. Especially after what just happened while she meditated.

"What?" He looked confused.

"As hard as it is for Vespians to conceive we could be trapped in here for years. I refuse to go along with it. Lock me up in a cell if you're going to do that. Strap me to a table and force me, but don't trap me in a room. I'll go crazy."

"We want you to be happy here, but time is growing short. She believes it won't take long."

"How can she say that?" What did she mean, time was growing short? Was there a time limit to her plan? Could her mate have died for no reason?

"I don't know." He watched her, making her wonder if he was communicating to Reasta as they spoke.

"If I go along with this unrealistic demand, and that is a big if, I want something in return for breaking my vows and sleeping with you."

"Heather, how are you breaking your vows? Your mate is dead. I'm not. I can be your mate, and no one need know the truth."

"The planet isn't aware of Storm's death?" The elders had kept it from the population? That didn't make sense.

How did they explain the explosion? She didn't know what to think.

"Reasta and the council decided to keep it quiet. They were hoping you would accept me as your mate."

"And no one would be the wiser?" Reasta was controlling the council and through them the planet. Her vision showed her she wanted an army from Heather's DNA and now she was controlling Vespia. What was her ultimate goal?

———

He opened his eyes and found Kuarto inches from his face. He pushed the doctor back. "Do you mind?"

"Don't collapse to the floor for no apparent reason and I'll stay out of your space." Kuarto checked his readings before he backed up enough to let him sit up.

"Damn it! Heather is working through her visions again." Skye Latimer stood nearby. "I hate it when her mind floods mine. I feel like I'm going crazy."

"What is she sharing with you?"

"The clone told her that no one knows about Storm's death."

"I'm not dead." Storm swung his legs off the medical bed he had been put on.

"And the only people who know that are on this ship," said Bert.

"I hate the fact that she doesn't know the truth. We need to get her back."

"And we will, but when the time is right."

"Anyway, she believes that Reasta has control of the council and the planet," Skye said, changing the subject back to Heather's vision. "She's working out how that blends with her vision of the massive army she saw of her progeny."

"That explains Reasta's desire for Heather to get pregnant, but not why? Why an army?"

"That is Heather's question."

"Heather has spoken to me, too." Everyone turned to look at Storm.

"How?"

"Through our mindmeld. It's the reason I found Kuarto too close to me earlier. She is reaching out to me when she meditates."

"You haven't told her the truth, have you?"

"As much as I want to, no. She believes she is speaking to my spirit, but it gives her a chance to give us information we're not getting from Skye or that cat."

"What have you heard?"

"The hydroponics lab doesn't have surveillance equipment in it. My clone let her know it was the one place where they could have some privacy. We need to get her out the next time she goes there."

"And you told her to go there soon, didn't you?"

"Of course. They are pushing her to sleep with my copy and she keeps refusing. Sooner or later, they will force her hand. We have the clone of my mate, and we're going to swap them out. Why not do it now? Reasta might figure out what was done, but not before we can get Heather somewhere safe."

"Heather is supposed to give us a signal."

"And exactly how is she supposed to do this? Who says this isn't it? I told her you were trying to rescue her, and she said she wished she could talk to you and let you know that the lab wasn't censored. Perhaps that is what you're looking for."

"The lab is our best bet, Bert. We need to make a decision now. Do you want to wait for Heather to say, 'hey here's your signal to come get me' or take advantage of what we have learned?" said Ed. "In order to do this, we need to watch their border ships movement, look to see when they switch them out. Find that hole in their security that will let us slip in undetected."

"And I need to get Heather's clone ready for the swap." Bert sighed. "You're right. Ed and I will work on masking the fact that she is a clone."

"How long do you think that will work? Reasta knows things she shouldn't," asked Skye.

"She shouldn't figure this out too quickly. Reasta might have ancient equipment, but from what Pumpkin has been revealing, nothing is up to date. She doesn't know how to improve any of the systems on that ship. It should give us enough time to get Heather home."

"And that is all we need."

———

Heather wanted to scream. She wanted to punch something too. Trapped in a room with her Storm clone had her going crazy. She needed a break. "Can we go somewhere?"

"Not until you are intimate with me."

"I'm not going to listen to you anymore." She sat on the couch, cross-legged, and put her hands over her ears. Time to act like she was losing it. Anything to get her way. She had been trapped there for three days and needed a break.

"Heather." Exasperation laced his voice.

She hummed to herself, keeping her gaze on the floor.

He grabbed her by the arms and dragged her to her feet. "You will do as you're told."

"You're hurting me."

He let go instantly. "I have been told to not be so lenient with you."

"So what are you going to do? Force me?"

"Reasta has threatened something far worse. She wants to drug you. Make you forget." He looked at her with sadness. "I have asked for a little more time to convince you this is the only way."

"Not here. Not where she can watch."

"You will be intimate with me if we go to the hydroponics lab?"

She wanted to back up time and keep her mate alive. "Yes."

"I will speak to Reasta."

———

Storm sat in the ship Skye was piloting with Kuarto as his co-pilot. They were going to bring Heather home. They couldn't do this fast enough. His mate's clone sat in a seat beside him. Kuarto had put her under so she didn't know what was going on. Bert had adjusted her DNA so she would read as the real Heather in any test Reasta's people could run. They shouldn't be able to see through the ruse before they got her to safety.

"You'll have about ten minutes to do this."

"I know, Skye. Bert explained everything to me. Knock out my copy and have Heather add her memories to her clone. Once that is done, I signal you to come back and pick us up." He stood as the ship docked. "I will make sure everything is done so no one will know I got my mate back. At least not right away."

Once he got the all-clear he stepped through the airlock into the hydroponic bay, sealed the door, and waited. Hopefully Heather would be there soon.

———

Heather didn't want to go through with this, but she had promised to be with Storm's clone to get out of the room she had been trapped in. At the time she just wanted out, but now she realized what was expected of her and she wished she had stopped herself. The memory of Storm during her meditation time asking her to go to the lab ran through her head. Why did she follow something not real? She felt like she was caught in a web and the more she struggled the tighter the ties binding her became. It wasn't fair.

S.C. brought her and Pumpkin into the hydroponics lab with a smile on his face. "You have made the right decision."

Did she? This felt like a betrayal to her. Even with the situation she was in, she wanted to honor the memory of her mate.

Pumpkin had perched on her shoulder once again. A little comfort before she had to do something that went against everything she believed in. She wasn't quite sure why she had come up with the scenario she had of Storm in her mind. How would his spirit know what anyone was planning? But it was a glimmer of hope and she needed that at this point. Perhaps against all odds they were really trying to rescue her, and her mind had picked up on that and it interpreted it in her creation of her mate in her mind.

Her heart flipped a little when the door opened, and they stepped inside. How was she going to get out of this?

———

Storm hid in the lab and waited for Heather to arrive. Not knowing if she would do as he asked had him worrying about being caught. He had the cloaking device on so he shouldn't be detected, but it didn't make him feel any better. The door slid open and he heard voices. Habit had him keeping out of sight, even though with him being cloaked they wouldn't be able to see him if he stood right in front of them.

The voices grew louder as the people approaching got closer.

"I have planned something special for you."

Storm had heard his voice enough to know who was talking but it was strange to hear his voice come out of another man.

"Really?" Heather responded.

Hearing her voice thrilled him. Made him wish he could run in there and sweep her up in his arms. To know she was okay made his heart soar. Now he had to get her away from himself. Storm could hear the nervousness in her voice. She was worried about something.

"Heather, I promise I am just like your mate. Our intimacy will be the same." He led her to the small grassy area where he had placed a blanket and a basket earlier.

"But you're not my mate."

They came into view and Storm felt his heart leap. Heather looked wonderful. At least they weren't harming her. Not yet.

"Your mate is gone, but I'm here. You promised to go through with this. Are you going to back out?"

"No." Heather sighed as she wiped her palms on her skirt. A nervous habit she had when things weren't going her way.

"Perhaps we should walk a little more? Help relax you?" his clone offered.

Pumpkin leaped off Heather's shoulder and started to prowl. Great, now he was going to have to corral the cat as well before he could get Heather off the ship. She made a bee-line for him, rubbing her body against his leg. How did the stupid thing see him? Then he remembered the insert Bert put in it.

Storm needed to separate his clone from Heather in order to get her out. Bert gave him a sedative to use on his copy while they brought Heather's clone on board and switched them out. Something crashing to the ground jolted him out of his thoughts. He glared at the cat, who had knocked over a large plant vase. "You're not helping."

"Did you hear that?" S. C. said.

He looked to where the other Storm stood. Did he hear him talk to the cat? Storm thought he had kept his mike off but in his excitement to get Heather home, he could have forgotten.

"It was probably Pumpkin." Heather looked calm, but he could tell by the way she held herself she was frightened.

"I'm going to check it out anyway." He got up and headed in Storm's direction. The moment he got close enough Storm grabbed him and gave him the shot to knock him out.

We have a problem. Storm heard Skye's voice in his head. *I don't know if we tripped some sort of sensor, or if we missed one of their security sweeps, but I have to move. You're going to have to stay there until I can come back for you.*

Crap. Storm grinned. His mate used that word a lot and it fit the situation. *I have already given my clone the dose Kuarto gave me.*

I'll work on another dose, Storm. He heard Kuarto's voice in his head.

In the meantime, you're going to have to stay put. We're going to have to reevaluate our plans to make this work. I'll be back as soon as I can.

Storm looked down at the clone. He was only going to be out for an hour, maybe a little more. The medication was supposed to keep him out long enough for Heather to load her memories into her clone and for them to join Skye and Kuarto.

Now he had to come up with something to keep them all safe. He looked in Heather's direction. She was the answer.

TEN

"Heather, can you come here for a moment?"

What did S.C. want now? He kept trying to seduce her, doing things that he knew would excite her. She got up from the blanket and walked toward his voice. "What do you need, S.C.?"

"Your help."

With what? She went around a turn to see S.C. bending over something. The moment he saw her he came to her and wrapped his arms around her.

"Are you alright, my heart?"

"You haven't been gone that long." She pushed away from him. Something wasn't right here. "When did you change your clothes? And what is that?" She pointed to the lump on the grass behind him.

"Right." He wasn't happy she pushed him away, she could see it in his body language, but he kept his distance and pointed to the small mass. "I need to hide him."

"Him?" She looked and saw Storm. Another one? That didn't make sense. Did Reasta make a second clone? Heather took a step back. "I don't understand."

He reached out to touch her face, but she moved again so he couldn't make contact. What game was he playing now?

S.C. followed her and grabbed her by the shoulders. "I have been worried. Have they harmed you?"

"They killed my mate and want me to have sex with you. They have kept me here instead of letting me see my family." She pulled out of his embrace. Why was he acting like this? "How would you behave if you were in my situation?"

"Heather, I am your mate."

"And that is what you say every damn time you open your mouth." She jammed her hands on her hips. "I'm sick of it. I have tried, really, I have, to be nice, but not anymore. I refuse to give in. If Reasta wants to give me drugs to make me forget then so be it. I can't do this voluntarily."

He stepped toward her and reached for her again.

"Oh, hell no!" She went to strike him but found herself caught in a vise grip, which only made her fight harder.

"Heather! Stop struggling!" S.C. used his weight to wrestle her to the ground. "When did you become so strong?"

He had her hands pinned above her head and made sure he had her legs pinned with his. She could feel his erection resting against her. She wanted to cry. Heather squeezed her eyes shut because she knew if she looked up at him, she wouldn't see his eyes glow.

"You're safe, my heart."

"You promised me you wouldn't force me." A tear slipped from between her closed lids.

"I would never force you." He was quiet for a moment. "Heather, look at me."

"I can't." She turned her face away. Another tear

escaped. Then another one slid out when she felt his lips against her lashes.

"Heather, I need you to look at me." He had switched his hands so only one held hers while the other stroked her cheek.

She took that moment to try to pull free. They wrestled for a moment before S.C. had her pinned once again. She looked up at his face to beg for mercy and stopped moving. "Your eyes."

"What about them?" He smiled then, that wonderfully heart-stopping one that had her doing whatever he wanted.

They were glowing. How was that possible? She didn't understand any of this.

"I wish we were in the white room." His voice was soft. He kept watching her like he was looking for something.

The moment she heard those words it was like a veil lifted from her mind. The white room was their key word unlocking memories. Skye was supposed to save Storm, but what if he wasn't successful? If the clone knew the word they were in a lot of trouble, but if he knew the word why didn't he say it before?

"How do you know that phrase?" She had to be cautious. Not let her heart betray her. They had worked so hard to keep all this information protected and she needed to be sure before she let her guard down.

"Because I was there when we created this plan. I am your mate, Heather. You are my heart. I had planned on bringing you home and ended up being trapped."

"What are you talking about?" Could it be true? But how did he get here? With the way Reasta kept this place under lock and key, there was no way anyone could have snuck on, yet there was that glow of his arousal staring her in the face.

"I'm not the clone, Heather, he is. I'm Storm, your

Storm, your mate, and the father of your children. The twins, and Sam."

"I saw my mate blow up in that ship." It would be too easy to believe this only to have it turn into a nightmare, but how did the clone suddenly know about the twins, the white room, or have glowing eyes? She could feel her resolve start to slip.

"You did see the ship blow up, but I wasn't on it. Latimer did as you asked and pulled me out before it exploded. He and Bert used the time travel machine so he could be with you when it happened. He timed it perfectly so Reasta wouldn't detect it. He kept me safe."

"Storm?" Skye was successful? Her heart leaped in her chest. Please let it be true. "And how do I know that you're not another clone?"

"You promise not to fight me anymore?"

She nodded and he released her. Storm moved into a sitting position.

"Because you know me better than I know myself. You know all my secrets, including my ability to shapeshift." He shifted in front of her, taking on the form of the wolf he had perfected.

Heather was glad she was sitting as well because she was pretty sure her knees would have given out when she saw the beautiful wolf sitting in front of her. Grasping his fur, she ran her fingers through it to be sure she wasn't dreaming. Storm was alive! "Then what we did worked?"

"Almost," Storm replied once he shifted back. He didn't have the problem with speaking after shifting anymore. Working with Dian fixed that. "Once I get you back to the safety of Bert's ship we have stopped this plot. Using that cloak Fridon came up with, Skye came aboard the ship and overheard Reasta saying they couldn't try to alter the timeline again. Something to do with the energy it takes to run it."

"Then we need to see that machine and make sure she can't get the energy to use it again." Heather stood. The moment he stood she walked into his arms, sighing as she rested her head against his chest and heard his heart beating. She had missed this so much. "Thinking you were dead these past few weeks has been awful. I don't want to go through that again."

"One thing at a time, my heart." He wrapped his arms around her. She melted against him. "Your safety is first."

"Those times when I was meditating I thought I had created you."

"I was there, my heart. That was real and we will have time to talk about this later." He ran his hands up and down her back. "Right now, we have a little bit of a problem. I don't know when Skye and Kuarto can come back for us and I know we can't stay here for too long before it looks suspicious."

"What about S.C.?"

"He is my first concern. First, I need his clothes." Storm gestured to his state of dress after shifting. He still hadn't mastered that part of the shift. "Then we need to keep him out. The shot I gave him was only supposed to work for an hour maybe two. Can you use the prayer you used on Ialog?"

"Of course, but what if that is only for ancients?"

"Then we'll come up with something else." He touched her face with tenderness. "I also need his memories. If I have to interact with Reasta I need all the ammunition I can get."

The memories would be easy. Taking Storm's hand, she brought him close enough so she could touch both men at the same time. Heather rested her hand against each man's forehead then looked at her mate. "It might be a bit of a jolt. Like when you got your memories back on Earth."

"I'll be fine, my heart."

She closed her eyes to help her focus and started the process. The transference flowed between them so Storm would have the memories he needed. Then she altered it so the information only went one way. It took a second or two before she let go and smiled at him. "You should have everything you need now."

He grinned as the memories filled him.

"We need to remove his clothes before I try the prayer." They shifted and lifted the clone as needed to pull off his clothes. "What is that?"

"I don't know." Storm touched the metal piece resting on the clone's right pelvic bone. "But I don't have anything like that. It could be a sensor that gives him access to different parts of the ship."

"Considering its location, it could be a hormone boost to be sure I get pregnant." She looked at Storm. "Whatever it is we're going to have to figure out a way to remove that and put it on you if you want to replace him. Reasta would probably notice if it is missing."

"What I want is to get back to the safety of our friends, but we have to make do with the situation at hand." He retrieved a small pouch and a gadget from beside the clone's body. "This is all I brought with me, but it should do the trick. Your brother prepared me for returning with you. After our dealings with Ialog he was ready for you having some sort of insert as well."

"My brother, always thinking three steps ahead. Got to give him a big kiss for this." She got on her knees and ran her fingers around the edge. "It seems to be on top of the dermas. We might be able to pull it out."

"Before you do let's be sure we can replant it into me

without detection or damaging it." Storm pulled the small device out of the packet and ran it over the area then looked at the screen. "It looks like we can move it to my body without any trouble. There is a tube running down to his groin. There is also a chemical inside the device."

"That proves it is a fertility drug." Heather sat back on her heels. "Her desire for one of our children is an obsession that frightens me."

Storm hit two small buttons and the device came free. He pressed it against the same spot on his pelvic bone and felt it insert itself. His frown showed it hurt, but it only took a moment for the pain to pass because he started to put the clone's clothes on.

"You okay?" Heather felt her fear climb when she realized he would be masquerading as S.C. What if Reasta detected the change immediately?

"Yes, My heart." He touched her face. "Time to make sure he doesn't cause us trouble while we're here."

Heather moved onto the prayer. She closed her eyes and brought forth the words she had used to bind Ialog. A sigh of satisfaction came from her when she saw the binds appear on Storm's clone. Standing, she completed the prayer and spoke softly to the ivy plant nearby.

"What are you doing?"

"Something he showed me. It should be in the memories I gave you." She looked at her mate. "These plants actually move, and I have asked it to hide him and keep him safe until I return."

Storm was quiet. He must have been working his way through the data. He smiled when he hit the information. "He was trying hard to seduce you, wasn't he?"

"Only because Reasta wanted him too."

"My heart, he is my clone with my memories. He remembers our life together, minus a few things you blocked down to the DNA, which shows just how strong your ability is, by the way. The joy we feel in each other's arms is part of his memory."

She never looked at it that way. "Watching your ship blow up then being confronted with him hurt so much I only saw him as an imposter. He told me he had your memories, but I never thought he felt as though he had lived it."

"I felt the same way about your clone until now. It is very strange to see yourself walking around as another person." He pulled her into his arms. "I have missed you."

"Not as much as I have missed you." She snuggled against him. "I know you're going to hate this, but we're not supposed to leave this place until we're intimate."

"I never hate being with you." He touched her face. "I strive to be intimate with you as much as I can. Just the thought has my heart pounding."

"And your eyes glowing." A lump caught in her throat. All along she had feared she was being tricked, but there was that wonderful glow only she could put in his eyes. This was her mate.

"That is not a new thing."

"True, but his eyes don't glow." Then her eyes grew wide. "We're going to have to figure out how to hide that. What does that device do? We need to be sure you read as the clone not the original."

"And we will, but later." He pressed his lips against her throat. "First, I want to show you how much I missed you. See if I can make you scream in pleasure."

She removed the outfit he had just donned as he worked her dress free of her body. No words were spoken while they focused on what they wanted from each other. Storm eased her back onto the blanket his clone had spread for this purpose.

"My heart." Desire blazed in his eyes. No foreplay was needed as he drove into her.

"Wow." He had just shifted, and it always affected his size. She arched up against him when he filled her so completely.

Storm pulled her into a seated position. One of her favorites. She moved against him. Taking her time to enjoy their intimacy together. Muscles stretched and contracted inside as her body accepted him in again and again. Oh, how she missed this. To see the glow in his eyes get brighter and brighter as he got closer and closer to his release filled her with such joy.

Heat unfurled deep inside. Heather could feel the flames lick along her insides as it encompassed her. Her stomach muscles tightened as she felt her body flush with desire. Her breath hitched. "So close."

Storm slipped his hand between them and started to gently caress her core, heightening everything she felt. Her orgasm raced toward her, overtaking her and flinging her out to the stars. He held her close as she became boneless.

As her muscles continued to spasm Storm reached his release as well. He held her tight as they relaxed and regained their voices. "My heart."

"I wish we could stay here." She looked up at him, sadness filling her. "But I know Reasta is waiting for us."

"I don't want to leave either." He nibbled on her neck. "I want to bring you to ecstasy as many times as I can."

"Remember I have fought this. More than once will catch her attention."

"Even though she wants you to get pregnant? What if she wanted him to be intimate with you more than once?"

"Storm." She leaned back to regain his focus. "We still have a few things we need to take care of."

He sighed but let her get up.

Heather offered him her hand. "Your clone is S.C., that's what I call him. He communicates with Reasta all the time."

"So you think he wore a communication device?'

Heather held out her hand, having already removed it. "It goes right behind your left ear. I don't know how it will affect the one you already have."

"I'll deal with it." He pressed it against his ear and widened his eyes as it started transmitting. "I don't hear a thing."

"This place is supposed to be clean so that is a good thing. Once we walk out those doors it will reconnect with the system."

They made all the necessary adjustments.

"That little contraption of Kuarto's is very cool. Reminds me of Fridon's." She looked up at him. "Ready?"

"One more thing. We can't remember any of this."

"No. I refuse to go back to thinking you're dead."

"And what if she can read minds?"

Heather shook her head. "She can't."

"How do you know?"

"Because I planted information to see if she could read minds. I have never been confronted with the information and it was something she wouldn't have been able to pretend she never knew about."

"What did you plant?"

"That you and I have had other partners to try to have children."

"Heather."

"It had to be something she would use. When I refused to sleep with S.C., she could have brought that up to convince me to do as she asked."

"Anyone I know?"

"It's in his memories and you're not going to like it."

Storm was quiet for a moment before he growled his displeasure. "Latimer?"

"He made the most sense." She shrugged. "And you know it never happened. I have no desire to be intimate with him. I felt he was the right choice because he was a visitor. You could send him away whenever you or I grew tired of him."

"You also made me like him. When I was no longer under the control of the reality you created, I didn't know how to treat him. Part of me remembered the fake reality and part of me remembered the real one."

"He's a good man, Storm. Our daughter has good taste."

"Back to the subject at hand. Removing our memories so she can't figure out the truth."

"She won't know the truth. I can alter our minds so we behave the way we should without removing our memories." She touched his arm. "I didn't know what she was capable of and protected us against everything. Now that I've been here and been watching I know she has ancient technology but doesn't know how to use it. She can't add to it or repair it either. Reasta might have been able to take an ancient ship but she never got the ancients on it to show her how to use it."

"Have you seen any of the ancients?"

"No. If they're here I'm not allowed to see any of them."

"I worry about your safety, my heart. You know I can ignore what you want and use the safe phrase to make you forget."

"True, but you would still be yourself. My idea will protect us both." She held out her hands. Once he placed his hands in hers, she closed her eyes and spoke softly. It didn't take her long. "When we walk out those doors we will behave and act like nothing has changed. You might find yourself saying things you never would have because of it. Trust what I have done to keep us safe, and we should be fine. Every time we come in here the facade will drop and we'll be ourselves."

They dressed in silence.

Heather took a deep breath and after Pumpkin jumped back up on her shoulder, walked out the doors with Storm right behind her.

"Let me walk you to the medlab." He placed his hand on the small of her back.

"Reasta's asking for us already?" She knew his touch was to steer her and make her do as he asked.

"She wishes to see if you are pregnant."

Heather sighed. "And if I refuse?"

"She will send guards to make sure you comply."

"I have had enough of this." Heather marched into the medlab, Storm on her heels. Anger filled her when she saw Reasta. "I am tired of being a nice little puppet for you."

"Why, Heather. I see you're a little feisty after sex." She smiled at Heather before she nodded to the doctor.

The man moved toward her, revealing someone on the bed he stood next to.

"No." She grabbed the doctor's arm before he could touch her. Heather stopped when she saw herself sitting on the bed. "Another clone, Reasta? Really?"

"You've met her."

That quieted Heather. This was the clone that went back in time. The one that was sitting in a ship with Skye and her brother waiting for the switch. Was this when she was created? Somehow, she needed to touch her to transmit the data she absorbed that helped her prepare for all of this. "This is the future me I met? She was nothing but a clone?"

Reasta smiled. "Would you like to meet her?"

A guard came up behind her and she stepped forward

before he could touch her. Approaching the clone slowly she gathered what she had gotten from the clone originally and prepared her mind to transmit it.

"You are Heather?" The clone offered her hand and Heather, after hesitating for a moment, took it.

"Yes." Sure everything she needed to send had been given to the clone Heather broke the hold. "If you can clone us why not just do that to get this child you want so badly?"

"Unfortunately, Heather, I can't get what I want with a clone of you."

"So you have tried."

Reasta didn't respond. "Time to let the doctor check you."

"No."

"Heather, you really don't have a choice right now."

The doctor moved toward her. "I said no." She moved away from her clone and the doctor. "My mate is dead, and I want to grieve, but you have other plans. You bring this thing and flaunt him in front of me when all I want is to go home to the comfort of my family so we can move on from this tragedy. Then you say I can go home once I become pregnant. You don't care that my heart is breaking. I just broke my vows with your clone because no matter how much you say he is Storm he isn't. Not to me."

"Nice speech."

Heather glared at her. "I'm done with your demands and promises, Reasta. He will never touch me again."

"Oh, but Heather, he will. Even if I have to drug you to make you have sex with him until you conceive."

"I can't conceive. I'm barren."

"Then how did Sam come along?"

"You know the answer to that."

"Ialog."

"He wanted the same thing." Heather brushed a strand of hair out of her face. "Tell me, Reasta, was he working for you? Or are you working for him?"

"Work for Ialog?" She laughed. "I am the one in charge of an ancient ship. If he was in charge, wouldn't he be the one standing here?"

"That doesn't mean anything. He wields a lot of power."

"He is nothing but a puppet." She smiled then. "Like I said the doctor needs to examine you."

"No." Heather moved so no one could get close to her. "I refuse to let your doctors touch me again."

"Now Heather. I thought you wanted to go home. See your family."

"Not at the cost of an innocent life." She crossed her arms over her chest. "You haven't explained why you want this child so bad."

"To help repopulate the galaxy."

"You don't need to hold me hostage to do that. I want to help the dying birthrate."

"Yes, but you'd give the cure to anyone who asked for it, wouldn't you?" Reasta shook her head. "Before your arrival, I don't think the Vespians would have been so giving either, they might have done the opposite thing and kept it to themselves. Neither way works for me, so I needed to take control."

"You want to only give it to your allies."

"And anyone who can afford it."

"And how does my child fix this problem?"

"You haven't figured it out?"

"You haven't given me enough information. I know what I would do if I found out a child had the ability to cure the low birthrate, but you haven't explained your plan. Why? Afraid I won't go along with it?"

"I have been at war with the Ancients for years."

Heather grinned. So she was a bit delusional. "You're kidding, right? Except for Ialog, there aren't any."

"There were never that many in the first place." Reasta moved closer to Heather who took a few steps back. "They were the all-mighty Ancients. The ones who controlled this sector and they refused me. Ha! Where are they now?"

"I have the same question. This ship is ancient in design. I recognize a lot of the markings from the ones I have seen in the great hall. What did you do with all of the ones from this ship? Kill them?"

"Of course not. They have too much knowledge to lose like that. But I couldn't keep them underfoot, so they are in a safe place."

"Safe? I don't think you understand what that word means." What did that mean? Did she put them on a remote planet? And what about the fake ones she tried to pawn off in the beginning? As much as she wanted to ask about them, she knew she would show her hand if she did.

"Oh, I do, Heather. If you take your injection, I'll even think about showing you how safe they are."

"Injection? What for?"

"To help you become pregnant, if you aren't already. Allow the doctor to give it to you and I'll show you the ancients."

"Your offer is very tempting, but how do I know you will keep your word?" That meant they were on the ship.

"You have to trust me."

Right, Heather didn't trust the woman. That was the problem. She also had no way off the ship so no matter how hard she fought she'd still get the injection. If she went along, she might gain a little more info on what happened to the Ancients. "Fine."

The doctor stepped up to her and gave her the injection then went back to working on her clone.

"I have allowed him to inject me. What do you have to show me?"

Reasta smiled. "You love to push, don't you?"

"So do you." Heather glared at her. "Show me or I won't go back to the hydroponics lab with him."

"I allow you to go to the lab. It isn't needed for you to conceive."

"Then you'll have to replace your clone because I will kill him before he touches me again."

"I don't know how your mate put up with you." She looked at the two guards who had accompanied Heather and Storm to the lab. "Clear the halls so we can visit the science section."

Heather wondered why the halls had to be cleared. Would she see something she shouldn't if they didn't? What was Reasta up to? She rubbed her forehead. Too many questions with no answers.

Pumpkin shifted on her shoulder.

"The cat stays here." Reasta went to reach for her but Pumpkin hissed and scratched at the outstretched hand.

"Pumpkin goes where I go. You agreed to that when she came aboard the ship."

A hard edge entered her eyes as she stared at the cat. "Fine."

Heather relaxed a little as she petted her feline friend. "Show the way."

Storm, posing as S.C., walked beside her, his hand on the small of her back. She moved just enough so he couldn't be in contact with her as she walked. As much as she wanted to allow it she knew if she suddenly did Reasta could become suspicious.

They traversed several corridors before Reasta stopped

in front of a set of non-descript doors. Heather noted the slight inscription on the wall near the door. Ancient words telling her where the doors led. They were heading into the science section of the ship. As they passed other doors she found more inscriptions, engineering, another said medical lab, which made her wonder if the one she just left was something Reasta created. Several others read science labs. Did Reasta know what they said? Did she know Heather could understand what the symbols meant?

The door opened at Reasta's prompting, but Heather noticed a keypad was installed next to the touchpad that would normally trigger the door. Either she didn't know how to use it, or the ancients keyed it for their DNA only.

Heather saw rows and rows of the same type of containers Ialog had been kept in. Lights flashed on different ones. The ancients were alive, just kept in cryostasis. So Reasta had them close for when she needed them but kept them under when she didn't. What would Reasta do if she touched the controls to open the pods? She could free them all, but would they be able to help? She didn't want to show her hand. Not yet. Not until they had a way off the ship just in case things didn't go her way.

Weird cables ran from each of the units to one central panel. Readings showed full power, but what was it powering? Heather looked at Reasta, knowing she would be too proud of what she'd done not to brag.

"Your ancient friends were very ingenious. They learned how to harness power from anywhere, even their own bodies to power the ship."

"Like giant batteries?" Heather felt chills at the thought of these people trapped inside the units powering the ship that held them captive.

"Yes. So even though they aren't here, sharing their knowledge with us they are still helping us."

"How many must you have in stasis in order to keep the ship running?" Reasta might not know how to run the ship but she did figure out the things that allowed her to control it.

"Now, Heather, why would I tell you that?"

"Because I'm your prisoner with no way to escape?" Heather shrugged. "I'm just curious. Always have been. I drove Storm crazy with the questions I'd ask."

"Yes, well, the tour is over. Time to go back to your room, and we've made a few changes to help you acclimate to being with this Storm."

What did she do now? Heather walked back with Storm to their room. Wondering what Reasta did to help her adjust to her new life.

"Do you wish to eat, Heather?"

She looked at Storm. Could see the pain in his eyes over what they just saw, but they continued to play the roles they had to.

ELEVEN

Bert had watched as Reasta revealed what happened to his people on the ship. He had feared she had killed them all, but this fate wasn't much better. How were they going to get them out of there? The faint glow from the second screen that Kuarto's face floated on made him realize they were still connected.

"What are you thinking?" asked Kuarto. "Making more clones to replace them too?"

"I have their DNA in the computer so we could, but we need to get Heather and Storm out of there first. As much as I'd like to free my people, we need to stay focused on the task at hand. But this will allow me to test if it will work. If they don't detect their clones, then we might be able to get my people out the same way."

"I think what we have perfected should keep that hidden, unless her technology is more advanced than yours. What will we do if they can see through Heather and Storm's clones quickly?"

"We will have Heather and Storm back. I know they will agree with me about my brothers and sisters needing to be freed. If this doesn't work, we will come up with something else." Bert looked at Kuarto. "The next window to retrieve them will happen again in a few hours. I have downloaded the details to your system."

"I have another dose for Storm's clone and the time will give me a chance to work on Heather's clone again. She's has been getting injections and I need to be able to dupli-cate whatever Reasta is doing. I'm going through the data from Pumpkin so I can make the right adjustments. Storm should be a quick update before we can release his clone."

"Bring them home, Kuarto. Everything we need to do hinges on them coming home."

"I will."

Bert sat back in his chair. This was one of the visions he had seen over and over but with three different scenarios. One showed Heather coming home without Reasta know-ing. That was the one they wanted. The second was where they escaped but got caught, causing a long war that Vespia ultimately lost. The third was the ship Heather and Storm escape on got destroyed, taking Skye and Kuarto with them and Reasta took control of the planet without a fight. That couldn't happen.

If they didn't stop her she would take over the galaxy and watch as all the wonderful races he had lived among died off.

———

Storm watched his mate move about the room when Skye contacted him. *You alone?*

I'm with Heather. What do you need?

We want to try to extract you two in the next half hour.

We're under constant surveillance and have been told to remain in our room for the rest of the evening. I can't go against my normal behavior or Reasta will become suspicious. You'll have to wait until the morning. Storm hoped he didn't show any reaction as he answered Skye.

And how is the morning going to be any different? It's not easy to time this.

Because I will push Heather to a point that will make Reasta do something rash. I have learned that Heather is so intricate to her plan that she wants to keep her as happy as she can.

All right. I'll contact you when I have my next window.

———

Heather opened the drawer where she kept her nightgown to find it gone. "Odd."

"Something wrong?" Storm came up behind her.

"I'm missing my nightgown."

"Reasta wishes to remove any blocks you might use to keep us apart."

She turned around to look at him. "She also knows I refuse to have sex with you in this room."

"She had hoped since we have been intimate, you'd reconsider."

"So she can watch? I don't think so." Heather moved around him. Taking a few spare pillows, she started to line them up down the middle of the bed.

"What are you doing?" He pulled a few of the pillows off only to have Heather yank them out of his hands and replace them where she had placed them.

"Setting up a barrier between us."

"Have you thought about what Reasta will do if you continue to fight her?"

"What do you mean?" She clutched one of the pillows to her chest.

"Think about what she has already done. She took your

gown because you used it as a shield. What would she do with pillows, blankets or sheets if you did the same thing?"

As much as she hated it he was right. She pulled the pillows off and threw them on the floor before crossing her arms over her chest.

"I can speak to her about allowing us to have a section in the lab if that would make you more comfortable?"

"Nothing is going to make me more comfortable here, but if it means I can get out of her ever-watchful eye I'd like to see what she says."

Storm nodded. He stood there for a few moments. "She wishes to have a little time to think about this request. We will have an answer in the morning."

Great. They had to sleep together. This was her mate, not the clone she kept turning away. Would Storm be able to keep his hands to himself? Could she turn him down if he couldn't? "Fine but remember your promise."

———

Heather woke up to the warmth of Storm's body against hers. His breath fanned against her throat. She wanted to snuggle into his strength but knew they were being watched.

"Good morning." He slid a hand across her hip.

"Morning." She went to sit up but found herself pinned under her mate's leg.

He smiled down at her. "Did you sleep well?"

"Yes." She so badly wanted to touch his face the way she had every morning since they mated, to accept him into her body and feel the joy only he could bring her. "Have you heard from Reasta yet?"

"She hasn't gotten back to me." He touched her face

with gentle fingers. "You are still going to be stubborn about this?"

"Wouldn't you if you were in my place?" Her last words were soft. "My mate would understand. I refuse to let Reasta turn something so beautiful into some sort of experiment. If I let you touch me, she will be in here seconds after we're done, running tests and adjusting the injections to make me pregnant. She doesn't understand that there is so much more to sex than the act. That emotions get involved. Without them, we wouldn't care who we were with."

"But that is the Vespian way."

"For those who are unmated, yes, but Storm and I talked about how mated couples handled having other partners and it was done with respect and care to their mate's feelings."

"True." He pressed a kiss against her throat. "But it is hard for me to not want to touch you when we are like this."

"Only in the garden."

"Are you sure?" He closed his mouth over one of her nipples.

"Yes." Her voice came out breathless. His tongue flipped against the tip and she felt it to her toes. "Please don't do this."

Her words seemed to penetrate Storm's desire because he sighed as he placed another kiss against the tip of her breast. "Then I shall see if we can go now."

Heather felt her heart flutter at the thought of being with her mate again. She looked up at him with so much desire she hoped the security system didn't pick it up. "Can I get up in the meantime?"

"Afraid I'll convince you to change your mind?" He rolled off her and let her go.

She just looked at him. Was he forgetting where they

were? He gave her one of his bone-melting smiles. She sure hoped he knew what he was doing. Not knowing how to answer that she got up and dressed. Having clothing on gave her the boost of confidence she needed. "I have explained before. Vespians mate for life and I am Vespian. My heart belongs to my mate. So does my body. I need time to mourn him before I can even think about taking another partner and that partner would never replace my mate."

"I am your mate, Heather." He pulled her into his arms. "In essence, I am the same man with the same memories."

"No, you're not." Tears sprang into her eyes.

"I am pushing you too hard, aren't I?" He rubbed his hands up and down her spine. She noticed a pattern against her back. They had done this before when they worked with the team on missions.

"More than I want." She wiped her eyes. Skye was going to try to extract them? How?

"Perhaps we should go for a walk. Let you calm down." He shifted his hold until his hands were around her waist, still drawing the small patterns on her hip.

"Thank you." With Pumpkin perched on her shoulder, she allowed him to walk her out into the hallway. Several guards followed them for a few minutes, but slowly they dropped off until it was just the two of them again. "I see our entourage has disappeared."

"Reasta has pulled them back to a discreet distance. She has agreed to let us go to the hydroponics lab."

"So she expects me to be intimate with you again?"

"No." He looked down at her upturned face. "I know how much you enjoy the plants, and I thought it would allow you to relax for a few moments. Maybe you can find a spot and meditate. Being intimate will be up to you."

"Thank you." She looked away from him, afraid she'd

give something away. They came up to the doors which opened at his touch.

The moment the doors closed they both let out a pent-up breath. They looked at each other and laughed.

"I'm so glad this is almost over." She touched his face, something she had wanted to do since they had been in bed together.

Storm wrapped his arms around her. "They should be docking in about fifteen minutes, and we'll have a very short window. They are bringing a clone for Pumpkin as well. Kuarto needs a scan of you to see what he needs to do to your clone."

"How short a window?"

"A couple of minutes."

"How do they expect to get all this done in a few minutes." That was too short a time to get everything done.

Storm brought her to the spot where his clone was hidden. "The scanner Kuarto sent with me will give them what they need. They are close enough now for him to get the information. Hopefully, we'll have just enough time to switch everyone out."

He picked up the scanner and ran it over her. "Okay. Kuarto has received the information. Now we have to wait."

She slid a hand up his chest. "So what shall we do in the meantime?"

"What did you have in mind?" One of his hands captured her roaming one while the other pulled her against him. "There are no walls nearby."

She laughed. He loved hearing the sound. It wasn't something she had done since he had arrived and knew she probably hadn't done it since she saw that ship blow up.

"We don't need walls." She looked up at him with so much desire.

"No, we don't, but I want time." He ran his hands up and down her back. Her need spiked his, making him want to forget about everything but the two of them. He pressed soft kisses along her jaw and down her throat to her mark. "Time to show you how much you mean to me. How happy I am to have you back in my arms, safe and sound and I don't want to be interrupted."

"That has never stopped you before." She tilted her head to give him better access.

The soft skin called to him. His mouth covered the velvet flesh, gently tugging on it. Heather's hand brushed across his mark, drawing a growl from him. She wasn't fighting fair, having opened his outfit so she could touch him. Need poured into him. Storm claimed her lips with his. Her mouth opened for him to intensify the kiss. His tongue searched for hers. Wanting to feel her skin against his, he worked on the seals of her dress, breaking the kiss when he exposed more of her. He blazed a trail down her neck to capture one pert nipple in his mouth.

Storm? Are you in the lab?

He sighed. It figured that they'd be early, but it meant getting his mate to safety and that was the goal. *Yes.*

We're docking now. Kuarto will be coming in with Heather's clone. You have less than two minutes to make the changes and get on this ship.

I know what to do, Skye. He pulled back and looked at his mate. "They are here."

Heather tried to hide the disappointment on her face, but he caught it. He felt the same way.

"We shall continue this when we're safe, my heart."

Heather nodded and closed the seals of her dress. He did the same for his uniform as he went to the door to let Kuarto in. Heather's clone followed along.

"Here." He handed him a uniform before going to

Heather's side. "I have made all the alterations for her to read as you. You need to put your memories into her, so she'll believe she is you. Once you have the two clones done we go."

"And it's good to see you too, Kuarto."

"Hugs and kisses are going to happen, but every second counts right now." He went to Storm's side and examined the device he took from the clone. "You were lucky this didn't have a sensor on it or she would have known."

"Just get it off me." Storm stood still as Kuarto extracted the small piece of equipment then went to his clone. Heather had already spoken to the plants to reveal his body so Kuarto could work on him.

"Do you know if she scanned you?"

"I'm assuming because of that thing. She knew we had been intimate and needed to reload it."

"And she didn't notice anything out of the ordinary?"

"Not that I'm aware of. Heather and I did our best to make sure I read as the clone. I don't think I raised any suspicions." Storm pressed the nodule behind his ear and extracted the link he had to Reasta. "But she believes I'm dead so wouldn't expect me to replace her clone."

"I sure hope so." He took the nodule from Storm. Placed it on a pad he had pulled out and watched as a second appeared on the surface. "Okay, place the first one behind his ear."

Heather came to their side. "She is ready. I have told her to lie down and wait for S.C. to come back." Kneeling beside the clone she gestured for Storm to join her. It took only seconds for her to transfer the memories so he believed he was the one who was intimate with Heather. "Done."

"Then let's go."

"Wait, I have to get Pumpkin." Heather called the cat to

her. Kuarto was already through the door when she called again.

"We might need to leave her behind," said Storm.

"And have two cats here? No." Heather breathed a sigh of relief when she saw her. Scooping up the cat, she entered the ship waiting with Storm right behind her.

"Seal the door." Skye sounded agitated. "Now!"

Heather looked and saw why. A scout ship filled their viewscreen.

"Crap."

Storm sealed the door and turned to see the ship coming at them fast. He jumped to a seat to help. "Can you evade?"

"First we have to get shields up then turn the cloaking device on."

"Shields are up."

"Too late. They're signaling to board." Kuarto looked at Heather then Storm. "We have to hide you two."

"Hide? Where? The ship was too small."

Kuarto moved to the center of the ship. "Floorboards. It's the only place."

Storm helped him pull the panels up then helped his mate climb in. He stepped in right behind her. Pulling the first panel down he lay beside Heather as Kuarto dropped the second one down on them sealing them in.

"And no loud noises."

———

The guards, who had boarded the ship about fifteen minutes later, looked at the chip Skye gave him.

"Your ship ran out of power?"

"As stupid as that sounds, yes." Skye hoped they wouldn't do too much research on his fake ID. If they did, he and his family could be in trouble. "The doctor here was on a mercy run. We, well, there was a miscalculation done and we ran out of power and started to drift."

"Right into Reasta's command ship?"

"Does the damn thing have magnets on it? Our trajectory should have allowed us to drift to the space dock, not here." Skye showed him what he was talking about.

The guard looked at the data and made a few notes on the pad he held in his hands. The screen gave off a white glow for a few seconds before it turned green. "We'll tow you to the dock so you can refuel, but before you leave, we'll scan this ship."

"Of course." Skye climbed into his seat and snapped on his safety strap. "You better buckle up, doctor. This could get quite bumpy."

———

Heather felt the ship lurch.

"What the hell?" Storm growled.

"I think we're being towed."

"Is Skye out of his mind? They'll search the ship and find us."

"It depends on where we're being towed. If it is to Reasta's ship we're in trouble."

———

Skye stood outside the ship as it was fueled. Kuarto stood beside him. Relief filled him when his credentials held up.

"How did you dump the fuel?" Kuarto asked quietly.

"I'll explain later."

"And the scan?"

"We wouldn't be here if it wasn't clean."

"Why didn't you just have them tow us back to Vespia?" Kuarto asked, trying to act normal.

"It's one thing to ask to be towed to the nearest space-port, but another to ask to go to the planet that big ship orbited, even though we were in Vespian space. We have the proper credentials, but I didn't want to be forced to dock in that large command ship because we asked to go to Vespia."

Kuarto didn't ask anything else as guards swarmed the ship. They did a thorough search. At one point they heard the head guard tell his security to pull up the floor panels.

"They're searching the floor panels too?"

"Standard procedure, doctor. The sooner they finish the sooner we can get back to Vespia." He turned to look at him, this time his voice was nice and loud. "This is also my last assignment for you people. My commander from the Conglomerate told me I could ship home once you did your little rescue mission and I'm looking forward to it."

"Thought you didn't have a home."

Skye gave him a glare.

"Sorry to break this up," said the main guard. He handed Skye a screen to sign. "Your ship has been refueled and cleared for flight."

"Thank you." Skye signed then looked at Kuarto. "Ready, Doctor?"

He nodded.

They climbed on board and sealed the door. Kuarto started for the panels when Skye stopped him. "Strap in."

Kuarto was confused but did as he asked. Skye received the all-clear and took off. They cleared the space dock and headed for Vespia. "Kuarto, can you hand me that scanner? I'm getting some irregular blips."

"Sure." He leaned over and picked up the item Skye asked for. "Want me to do it?"

"That's okay." He held the scanner up and showed Kuarto where the cameras had been planted. "The system will purge itself in a few moments. You might want to cover your ears."

A loud screeching noise filled the air. Sparks flew from the areas where the cameras were hidden.

"Was that necessary?"

"Every space dock tries that, and they don't get too far without being detected, but they do catch a smuggler or two before the system is destroyed."

"Then you knew they would plant the equipment?"

"Had an idea." Skye hit a few buttons and brought up the border of Vespian space. Four ships waited for them. "Some security systems are even sneakier where they have a few that can survive a purge."

"Thought that went against Vespian air space." Kuarto looked at Skye, realizing why Skye stopped him from allowing Heather and Storm out. They had a long way to go before they were safe enough to release them.

"Once we cross into it, we might be searched again if they detect any sort of unauthorized scanners." He programmed the ship to head toward the other ships. "They'll scan us before we get close and if they find anything they shouldn't we'll be boarded."

———

Storm held Heather's hand as they lay beneath the floors. They could hear every word Skye and Kuarto spoke.

You have enough energy to block us from view again if we're scanned?

Not sure. Blocking scans is a little different than hiding us from view. Do you have enough space to move if they pull the floor again?

If I did, I wouldn't be worried about scans, my heart. We'd be too busy to care.

He felt her laugh in his head. His heart stopped when someone pulled the panels up and more guards looked right at them, but Heather worked her magic and kept them concealed from prying eyes and scans. Her ability amazed him.

Ha! You can shapeshift. Think about that, you could have done the same thing just by changing the way you look.

She was right. He had kept to the wolf shape because it was easy, but now he would have to push himself. So would she. They would soon learn if their abilities had limits.

————

The ship went around the planet and started its approach. Skye pressed a key and sat back. "You might want to grab a hold of something."

Kuarto grabbed the dashboard in front of him just before the ship stretched and winked out of sight. "I hate that."

"I know, but it is the only way to make sure our true destination remains hidden." He watched the screen as the massive ship Bert owned grew larger and larger.

"And you're sure there are no more cameras or listening devices?"

"We're clean, doctor." He shut down the engines and allowed the main ship to bring them in. "Our first purge was done by Bert's equipment. Nothing could withstand that."

"Can we let them out now?"

"Yeah, it should be safe." Skye got up and helped

Kuarto pull the panels back so Heather and Storm could sit up.

"That was fun." Heather took the hand her brother offered her so she could climb out of the hole.

"It's not Vespia, but we're going someplace safe." Skye offered Storm a hand as well.

"Bert's ship?" Heather looked at the screen by leaning on Skye's chair.

"Yes." Skye went back to his seat. He looked up when Storm wrapped his arms around Heather and pulled her back. What was that all about?

Kuarto ran scans to make sure they weren't hurt while in the cramped space. "Sorry you had to stay in there so long, but it felt like everybody in this quadrant was on this ship at one time or another."

"This way no one could accuse you of smuggling anything anywhere." Heather brushed her hands against her skirt. "My heart stopped when I saw that cruiser coming at us when we were next to Reasta's ship. I thought we were caught before we could escape."

"I knew we didn't have a big enough window to get everything done so I was ready for them. I used a controlled drift to get to the ship and used a shifting pattern I created to make it look like we were drifting the whole time. I'm grateful the ruse worked." The ship floated into the hanger bay of Bert's ship. Skye looked back at her and Storm. "Glad to have you two back."

"Thank you."

The doors opened to reveal Bert, Toki and a few chosen others. Fridon was the first to grab her and hug her before doing the same to Storm. "I thought we lost both of you."

"It is good to see you too, my friend." Heather returned his hug. "I thought you were now in control of Security. Reasta did let me see newsfeeds from time to time."

"I never did any feeds."

"Then everything I saw was for me and she has clones of some of the most powerful people on Vespia." She leaned into Storm when he came up behind her and wrapped his arms around her.

"Who did you see? Besides Storm?"

She looked up at her mate. "Just about everybody, either in videos or in person."

"What about me?" asked Kuarto. "How many times did you see me?"

"Once."

"And that was me, but they could have gotten my DNA at that time."

Bert gestured for them to follow him. "The question is who you didn't see, Heather."

"You, of course, because she doesn't know you exist, Ed or Dian. I didn't see Toki or Iresna, either."

"Toki went into hiding early, and I sent Iresna after something of Ed's right after she landed so their interaction was minimal." Bert led them into his main lab.

"But he was at the dinner when she first arrived so was Toki."

"True, but she didn't see them as a threat at that point. We also put a small implant in Iresna so she wouldn't recognize him from being Ialog's slave. I thought it could be something we can use in the future."

Heather nodded and with Storm's urging started toward his room.

Bert stopped them. "I know you have been through a lot and want to be alone with each other, but I need to run scans before I can let you do that. For your protection as well as ours."

"Of course." Heather walked to the spot where Bert gestured.

Skye stepped up to Storm's side. "What was that all about?"

"What?" Storm watched Bert as he scanned her.

"You pulled your mate away from me."

"Oh, I just missed her."

"Don't think so."

"Latimer, you worry too much."

Skye wasn't sure, but he knew Storm wasn't going to tell him anything.

Bert arched a brow when he saw her readings. "She really wanted you to get pregnant, didn't she?"

"A little too much." Heather pressed her hand to her stomach. "I'm just glad she wasn't successful. If and when Storm and I are to have more children, it should happen naturally."

"I can flush the chemical she pumped into your body out, but you realize whatever she did wouldn't have worked anyway, don't you?"

"Are you talking about that odd comment my parents said to me once? That it takes more than the physical act to create life?"

"I am." He grinned when Heather knew what he was talking about.

"I asked them about it and never got an answer. Can you explain it?"

"That is because they had that thought planted. Dian planted it."

"So either of you going to explain it?"

"Because of your mental strength, you can control your body like no one else. If you wanted to get pregnant you can will it."

"What?" Heather shook her head. "How can that be?"

"You don't realize just how powerful your mind is or will be." He opened the seal above her right collar and gave her an injection. "That should flush your system within the next twenty-four hours."

"Thanks." She resealed her dress. "I practice what I have learned from the books you have given us."

"Yet you keep pushing back when it tries to expand, but no matter how much you try to ignore what you are capable of it is getting stronger every day. You are ancient more than Vespian and you need to face that fact."

"I know that."

"Yes, but you haven't embraced it." He turned to Storm and scanned him as well. "Wow, as much as she dosed you both I'm surprised it didn't happen."

"Does that mean our clones could have children? Will have children if she gives them the doses she gave us?"

"It is highly possible, but they can't have the children you two are destined to have. They are your clones, and they will have the same limitations. Neither clone has any ancient blood, so your special abilities never developed."

"Which is why she never knew about them."

"I know. It actually saved you. If she had known, you never would have been able to escape. She would have come up with something to block it."

"Just like Ialog did."

"Yes."

Heather rubbed her head. "Let's get back to the conversation you started. About children? My ability to make myself conceive?"

"Ah, another tactic of yours. You love to change the subject when you don't want to talk about the subject at hand."

"Bert."

"It is something that needs to be addressed, but it can wait. Something will make you realize that fighting the strength of your mind did you no good. So let's talk about how you can get pregnant. I guess I didn't explain it right. Your mind, your emotions need to be as involved in the conception as your body."

"But isn't that true for anyone?"

"They don't have the mental power you do." Bert looked at her. "You haven't learned to manipulate your body yet, but you will. You can will the sperm to connect with the egg and cause conception. As your mind gets stronger, you'll be able to do this to other people."

"Wait. What?"

"When Ialog created you, he took the strongest part of each of us and put that in your DNA. It makes you unique even as an ancient."

"Great." She crossed her arms over her chest. "Just what I wanted to hear."

"I know you don't like that, but it is the truth. Your mind is the key to all of this, Heather."

"I find that a little farfetched." Heather reached for Storm's hand. She needed his support.

"I know, and I would have rather allowed you to develop and discover these different talents on your own with Storm at your side, but Reasta's presence forbids that."

Heather's mind would get even stronger? How did anyone think this was a good idea? Skye knew he had to stay now, keep an eye on her, keep her in check.

"And what if you're wrong?"

"I'm not." Bert got close enough to place a hand on her shoulder. "After all you have learned about yourself? Have been through? You still refuse to believe in your own abilities?"

"Why me?"

"Heather needs to rest." Storm interrupted. "Give her some time to process the information you have given her, us."

"I'm sorry." Bert smiled apologetically. "You're right. I forget sometimes that I push a little too hard. It is a lot to process and you two do need to have a little time alone. We can continue this later after you had some time to think about what I said."

Storm nodded once and steered Heather toward the room he had occupied while he was waiting to rescue her. He relaxed against them once the doors closed. "Are you alright, my heart?"

She sat on the bed in the room. "I don't want this, Storm. I want the life we started, not some sort of crazy mind monster."

"You're not a crazy mind monster." He sat beside her and took her hand in his. "You have a talent, a very unique one, just like I do. You're a mother, my mate, and have the biggest heart I have seen."

"Yeah, and someday I'll become as crazy as Ialog and someone will have to put me down."

"My heart, you are nothing like Ialog and you know it. That is nothing but fear talking." He rubbed his knuckles against her hand. "And I know how to get your mind off everything but us."

"Yes, you do." She smiled and shifted on the bed so she faced him. "I want Skye to be my bodyguard, for real, not part of some fantasy I made up."

"Heather."

"I know what you did, pulling me away from him because of that fake memory I gave your clone. No matter what you say, you are bothered by it, but he's not my type. You are. I trust Skye. His suspicious nature is what I need as I push my mind. If I go crazy he'd stop me." She touched Storm's face. "He's in love with our daughter. I see him as a son, not a potential lover. That's a bit of an eew for me."

"I can protect you."

"I'm not saying you can't, but could you pull the trigger if you had to? On me?" He didn't answer her. "I didn't think so. I know Skye would. He'd never kill me, but he would make sure I was out of commission."

"It won't come to that, but if that is what you want." He touched her face. "I know it will make you feel better."

"It will."

She leaned her head against his chest, listening to the steady beat of his heart. "Do you think I could really become pregnant with just a thought?"

"Bert has always been honest with us." He ran his hands up and down her back. "There is no reason for us to not trust him with this information. Is that what you want?"

"Wouldn't it be wonderful?" She lifted her head and looked at him. "If we weren't on the verge of war I would love to see if we could."

"You could try something else. Something safer."

"Like what?"

"Bert said you could get someone else pregnant. It would have to be someone who would never be in harm's way."

"Oh, I don't know about that." She shook her head. "If I'm successful that would scare me, if I'm not then I'll fear I'm not where I should be to face this war I brought to your people."

"You didn't bring a war to my people. They are our people. What has happened was inevitable. Your presence hasn't changed that outcome."

"She wouldn't be here if it wasn't for me." Bert made her think. What if her mind created all this up and it would disappear when she had pushed her mind too hard.

"My heart, stop." He pulled her toward him and covered her mouth with his. The gentle pressure he started with increased when she opened for him, his tongue drawing hers to dance with his. Slowly she relaxed against him. When he broke the kiss, she sighed.

"Liked that, didn't you."

"Of course, but it doesn't change—"

He captured her lips again, keeping her from saying what she was thinking. "No more pity for yourself. If I have to kiss you senseless I will."

"You are so good for my ego." What if all this disappeared after she and Storm were intimate?

"Good, now let's change the subject." He brushed a few strands of hair out of her face. "And I just know how to help you forget everything but us."

Storm pulled her to her feet then broke open the seals on her dress. Heather did the same for him. They undressed each other quietly.

Storm brushed his fingers along her hip. His touch reverent, loving. "I missed you so much."

"My heart, thinking you were dead was heartbreaking." She looked up at him. "And having a mirror image of you around made it even harder."

"You are here now, safe and with me." He wrapped his arms around her, gently moving her back to the bed. "I'll make sure the last few weeks are a distant memory as quickly as I can."

"They are already fading with your touch." She felt her knees bump up against the foot of the bed. "I'll be glad when you wipe them away completely."

He eased her down on the bed, continuing to gently caress her in the areas he knew heightened her desire. Once she was lying down, his lips followed the trail his hands had blazed across her body.

She wanted to touch him, needed to touch him but he angled himself so she couldn't reach him. "Storm, don't hold yourself way from me right now. After all I've been through, I need to prove this isn't a dream or something I conjured in my mind."

"My heart. I promise you this is real." He shifted his body so she could touch him once again. Centering himself he drove into her, taking her breath away. "What we have is real. Our children, our intimacy."

She clung to him as he set a rhythm that had her panting. Her body shook as he kept hitting one particular spot. She didn't want this to happen so fast. She wanted to prolong their time together, just in case.

"My heart, relax and enjoy this." His lips pressed soft kisses to her mark. "We have all night."

And that was what was driving her. Each time, when they were intimate in her mind her orgasm forced her to lose the hold on the world she created. The only time he didn't disappear was in the hydroponics lab. Part of her told her this was real, and she was now safe, but there was still that little voice whispering it was all a dream and this would all disappear once she had her orgasm. If this was a dream, she didn't want it to end. It would destroy her.

TWELVE

Storm sensed something in her that he had never noticed before. A fear that had power over her. She had been afraid in the past, but nothing like this. Why was she so afraid? Their mindmeld didn't always tell him her deepest emotions.

Touching her face, he thought about what she said earlier. Then he figured it out. Her fear was that this would all disappear when she reached her climax.

He smiled.

She watched him. Her eyes filled with curiosity. "Why are you smiling that bone-melting smile of yours?"

"Because you know how much I like a challenge and proving to you that this moment is very real is something I promise to do. I also want to make it one of our best so when you look back at this moment you react the same way I do when I see that beautiful picture."

"That picture arouses you."

"I know." He pressed his mouth to her mark. "But I remember how I got that picture, and the memory is one of my favorites."

"Sex is one of your favorites."

"Is my favorite. Especially with you." He slipped his arms under her and pulled her into a sitting position. Desire swirled in her eyes once she settled on him. "What we have is special. Nothing can destroy it, not people who wish to come between us and not time. We have proven that."

"We have, haven't we?"

One hand slipped between them, inching its way down until he found her delicate folds. Soft gentle caresses relaxed her. Storm was glad he still had one arm around her as she allowed her body to enjoy the strokes he used.

She started to move, sliding up and down his length. He helped her tilt back, so each stroke hit a very sensitive spot inside her. Her muscles clamped down on him, making each glide exquisite.

"My heart." His fingers continued to stroke her, feather-like caresses that had her shaking at the intensity.

She arched against him. Her body vibrated as she reached her climax.

Storm pulled her close and drew the delicate tissue of her mark into his mouth. He was gifted with a moan. Her head dropped back as her release gripped her and flung her out of her body. Holding her against his, he allowed her time to come back to him.

She smiled up at him as she touched his face. "You're still here."

"Told you this was real and I'm more than ready to prove it to you over and over again." Her muscles contracted around him, letting him know she was willing to let him. "Just know you won't be getting very much sleep."

"I don't need sleep when I'm with you."

"Good answer." His mouth dipped to her mark once

more. "I want to hear you scream for me and that could take a while."

———

Heather opened her eyes and stretched. Storm had kept his word about not letting her get much sleep and she loved it. She had missed him so much that she needed what they had shared.

"Morning, my heart." He pressed a kiss to the nape of her neck. "I would love to keep you in this bed a little longer, but Bert has asked that we go see him first thing. He has also promised not to keep us for too long."

"Can you wait? Mornings are one of your favorite sessions."

I know." He laughed as his lips made their way down her spine. "My thought is we go and see what he wants then I can have you all to myself. Our mid-morning sessions are wonderful too."

"One track mind."

"At least I'm consistent."

She laughed as she climbed out of bed. They dressed and walked into Bert's computer room. They were greeted with bad news.

"Reasta knows." Bert brought up a communiqué sent to the security office.

She looked out like she could see them. "I know what you have done. You may have won for the moment, Heather, but I will regain the upper hand."

"That is all she said?" asked Storm.

"It is enough." Another message loaded. This one from the council. Storm's mother was the one talking. "Reasta has come to our planet as a friend and is willing to share her people's technology with us. So, I have allowed her and her people to intermingle with our race. Welcome them with open arms. They have so much to teach us."

"That is not Mother. She would never do that."

"That has to be the clone. I saw her several times through communiqués on Reasta's ship, telling me the planet felt my pain, only to learn later the planet didn't even know about your death." Heather touched Storm's arm. "This gives her free rein. We won't be able to declare an all-out war on her, we'll have to go underground."

"I thought once we came home it would be easy to cut her off, send her away, but not now." Storm rubbed his face. "We need to find out what she has done with the real council. Find them and free them. Take that power away from her."

"We also need to free those ancients we saw on her ship. Bert, why hasn't she cloned them?"

"Because of their ancient blood. I studied your clone and the data on Storm's clone. Neither had ancient DNA. That's why I sent your father to Ed's old place. That piece of equipment he brought back not only cured your clone, but it was able to answer why she left out the ancient blood when she cloned you."

"And what did you find?"

"Not something I like. She worked hard to manipulate that part of your DNA out. Ed made a few comments about her wanting our blood, but we don't know why." He showed them the data they had gathered. "Everything she needs is on that ship. She has ancients to help her use the technology, yet she decided to piecemeal equipment to get what she wanted instead of learning to use the ancient technology."

"None of this makes sense."

"I know. All she had to do was clone one ancient and she would have freed the power to run that ship. She has the ability to manipulate DNA to work for her, why didn't she do that with one of the original crew members? Did she try and fail? Is that why the clones are basic shells? No ancient blood because she doesn't have the power to clone properly?"

"But the Storm clone had his memories. She did do more with that clone than she did with some of the others."

"But did he have his abilities?"

"No." Heather shook her head. "At least not that I'm aware of."

"Your clone wasn't a complete copy either. She was made to come back and convince you to not fight Reasta when she arrived and that was all. That was why she doesn't have any of your abilities either." Bert turned the screen off. "If Reasta can't make one hundred percent copies, then the clones we've seen make more sense."

"What do you mean?"

"If she had the proper power and up-to-date equipment you wouldn't have been able to tell the clone wasn't Storm."

"What about our mind-meld."

"That would have been part of the clone's creation."

"But I would have known about his creation if I had a connection to both of them, wouldn't I?" Heather shivered at the thought.

"I believe so. At least until she had killed Storm off."

"Then the outcome would still be the same."

"Possibly." Bert touched her arm. "That could be another reason why she cloned them the way she did. Perhaps the other times she did a full clone and you figured out what she was up to too soon. All that really matters now is everything is the way it should be, and she can't try again."

"The way you saw it in your vision?"

Bert nodded.

"I just wonder how many times we have been through this?"

"We might not ever figure that out. We don't know how big the time bubble she created is."

"Oh, my God, the twins."

"It might not be as bad as you think. You need to talk to your friend first. He should tell you how long your children have been with him. They could be inside the bubble as well."

"I altered his mind too, remember? He believes they are his sister's children and he's watching them while she's in space. Everything I did is still unraveling in my head. I have no clue what sort of timeline I put in there for him yet."

"Then talking to him is your first priority. One I will try to make happen as soon as I can. I just want to be sure Reasta can't detect any of my transmissions."

"I doubt she can. She had special pads on the rooms she was using so her people could access them and the one for the communication section didn't have one. Whenever I spoke to anyone off ship it was through what she called her command center."

"I noticed that from the video we got from Pumpkin. It does reinforce my thoughts about the clones. But she knew how to use the cryopods. I find that interesting. I never got a good angle of the ones in use. How many ancients did you see?"

"Out of all those Pods? Wow." Heather thought about what she saw. "She didn't give us a long time there so I couldn't tell if all the pods were full, but the ones I did get a good look at were occupied. They reminded me of the one Ialog was in so I knew what it looked like turned on. I saw at least two dozen there if not more activated, but those were only the ones I was close to. There were a lot more I couldn't see."

"That sounds about right. Our science ships were designed to travel far distances with a small working crew. Most of the members would be put in stasis. Those who weren't needed to run the ship would remain that way until the ship reached its destination. Those pods would have been the ones you saw in a distance. The rotating skeleton crew manning the controls would have been a total of thirty-six if they were all awake at the same time. The rest would stay in stasis until they reached their destination."

Heather nodded, that was close to what she saw. "She had said something about the people actually giving their energy to power the ship."

"That is true. Some of the areas we travel into might not have an energy source so the ships were designed to use our energy when there was no other source. Reasta and her people might not have learned how to power the ship properly, but she learned enough to keep it running."

"That is the impression I got. The extra keypads to rooms she learned to use, not wanting me to see anything she didn't approve of. Her command center didn't have any ancient equipment." Heather sat in a chair next to Bert. "So, if we can get your friends off the ship then we should be able to cripple her and retake the ship."

"Don't think she'll be that easy to get rid of. She has been planning her revenge for a long time."

"You never explained why she is after your people, Bert. I think it's time you did." Heather hated confronting him, but they needed to know.

"You mean our people."

Heather nodded. She wasn't about to argue with him.

"Ialog spent time on the planet she came from. I don't know all the details but at times we found people we felt were inquisitive and brilliant enough to understand what we were doing on their planet. Those people we befriended. We never kept our knowledge from anyone who was smart enough to figure it out. But Reasta fooled Ialog, her race turned out to be darker than he realized. He found out too late that they were known for being conquerors. We don't know what happened to cause her to want to wipe out our race, but she is bent on eliminating any ancient she can find. That's why Ed didn't want to come back here at first. He had been hiding from her for a long time." Bert looked at Heather. "Her reaction to you surprised me. Her desire for you is an obsession that is a little frightening. I would think she'd want Storm as well since he is the catalyst. She saw you as the savior I saw but her goals were darker, to build an army from your children. Somehow, she knows about the prophesy, but I don't know how."

"Ialog must have told her."

"He didn't know that part of the prophecy. We had put him in stasis before I had that vision."

"And Reasta doesn't have all the information," added Storm. "She believes it is a child from Heather, not my mate herself. Could she have gotten that information from him?"

"But how did he get it? Ialog told me about the prophecy when I went back in time to bring Storm home. He laughed at me when I confronted him. Ialog told me it was never me he wanted but my children. Somehow someone must have told him. Unless it was left behind in the computer or written on the walls somewhere."

"I don't believe my visions are on any of the walls. Most

of what is in the main halls of Vespia is history lessons. Unless he spoke to another ancient after the Vespian council woke him up. "Ed?"

"Anything is possible."

Heather sat back. "I'm going to have to talk to him, aren't I?"

"I think so."

"No!" Storm stood. "That man has been hell-bent on taking my mate from me. I won't allow him to get another chance with the new threat. No."

"I'm not going to go to him." Heather stood and pressed her hand against his heart. "Skye will go and retrieve him. You will both be at my side when I interrogate him."

"The man won't care if we have him captured, he will still try to take you from me." Storm wrapped his arms around her and held her tight.

"Storm, I'm not freeing his mind. I just need to ask him a few questions. He won't remember a thing."

"I still don't like it."

"I know, but it needs to be done."

———

Storm stood in the background with his arms crossed over his chest when Skye brought in Ialog. The man looked scared as he entered the room and he found so many people staring at him.

"Have I done something wrong?" he asked as he sat in the chair Skye gestured for him to take.

"No." Heather moved into his line of sight. "We just have a few questions."

"And who are you?" He looked at her curiously.

"A friend and you haven't done anything wrong." She looked at Storm before she focused on Ialog. "First though,

252

I want you to relax. Breathe in, breathe out. We are not your enemy. Every muscle in your body is relaxing, you are safe here. Protected here. I want you to remember. Remember me and my family."

Heather's voice came out soft, a simple methodic cadence that affected Ialog. His chin dropped to his chest. She gave it three beats before she spoke again. "Hello Ialog."

"Heather, I see you need my help." His eyes were closed but the tone of his voice made Storm's skin crawl.

"Yes, I do. I need to know about Reasta."

"Reasta? Is she here?" His body stiffened.

Was that fear in his voice?

"Yes, and she seems to have the same goal you do when it comes to me." Heather kept her voice soft and melodic to keep him under. "Why?"

"I had hoped she wouldn't find you. That I could give her what she wants without harming anyone."

"What are you saying?" Storm didn't mean to interrupt his mate, but he didn't like his answer.

"She tricked me. I thought she cared, but she only wanted information. Once she had what she wanted from me she threatened my people. If I didn't help her then she would wipe out my race."

Heather looked at Storm. What was the man saying that he did everything to protect the ancients? That didn't make sense.

"How?"

"She befriends races that have something of value to her then takes what she wants before anyone can stop her. That is how she got my ship. My goal was to perfect the race. Make it stronger." His voice held so much sadness. "You were to be my shining moment. The first true ancient, with all the perfection the rest of us didn't have. At least I was able to make you perfect, but she knew. Somehow, she figured out what you were. What you meant to all of us."

"Perfection?" What was he talking about? She wasn't perfect. Her mistakes throughout her life proved it. "I'm not perfect."

"Genetically you are. I corrected all of the DNA sequences in you so none of our flaws would be there. I took the best from those around me to give you the perfect combination. I was so proud of you." Ialog's head remained against his chest, but Storm could hear the pride in his voice. "I wanted to make you years ago. Had almost completed you too, but Bert started having those damn visions. He kept saying that it was wrong for me to create you. He kept telling others that I wanted to create an army. I knew none of it was true so ignored him. At least I did until I met Reasta. Then it all started to make sense. It was because of her the visions showed me as a traitor."

"And you were stopped and put in stasis."

"Yes, but then the council found me and released me. I began my work once again. I knew Reasta was still out there, waiting. I don't know what happened to all my brethren who had been on the planet when I went into stasis, but I knew I needed to get the people I left on the ship free."

"How old is Reasta?" She had been part of Ialog's life before he went into stasis? That was before any of the ancients had left the planet.

"Thousands of years old. She learned how to use our blood to keep herself from aging."

"Is that why she's hunting the ancients?" Use their blood? That was what Bert had said a few times. If Ialog knew why maybe they could figure a way to stop her.

"Yes." He sighed. "She learned that I built the longevity gene into you and wanted it for herself."

"What?" Heather didn't want to believe what he said. Longevity gene? What about her mate? "You need to explain this."

"My heart, we don't have time for this," Storm whispered in her ear. "You need to stay focused."

"But I need to know," she said it softly, but Ialog heard her.

"There is a file with all your information on the ancient computer," said Ialog. "Ask Cim to show you. I give permission."

Heather took a deep breath. That file would be the first thing she would pull up. Storm was right, she needed to focus. "You said that she needed blood from the ancients, why?"

"Longevity is something natural in our systems. She knows how to extract the chemical from our systems and inject it into hers."

"Is that what all this is about? She wants to live forever and she can only do it through ancient blood?"

"She learned to draw it from other races, but she needed a lot of people on a steady basis. With our blood, she only needs one every few hundred years."

"What about the ancients on the ship? She has them in stasis. Can she draw just enough to keep her going if she has a large group?"

"I don't know. If she has them in stasis, then I don't think so. Our blood reacts differently when in those pods. Goes dormant. She'd have to wake them to use their blood."

"And if she did that, they would have the chance to escape."

He nodded, his head bobbing against his chest.

"So she must wake one at a time to get what she needs." Heather looked at Bert, this couldn't be what he wanted to hear. "How did I become part of this equation? Why does she want a child from me?"

"My calculations show that you will have a child who will have this gene and a natural ability to reproduce it. She would be able to siphon off the gene and it would naturally reproduce itself. If I could get you to produce that child, then she would leave the rest of us alone. My goal was to get you to maturity, have that child she wanted so badly, and then let you live your life."

"But the elders got in the way," Storm said. "Then she met me before you could intervene."

"Yes, Heather was not supposed to meet you until after I gave Reasta what she wanted. But your family interfered. They sent her away where I couldn't find her. I had to manipulate your council to get them to go looking for her."

"And this is why you have been after my mate this whole time? To help the people trapped on the ship?"

"Yes. I knew once you two met there would be no way I could get a child from you. Even if I explained my dilemma. You would be too attached. My goal the first time was to make Heather believe the dream world was real, finding out she was already pregnant worked beautifully with my plan and then when it was time for the birth Heather would believe she had lost it. Once I had the child, I would have let her go. I know that sounds cruel, but I was desperate."

"How did she find out about me in the first place? She couldn't have known about the visions. Ialog, think. We need this information to face her."

"Reasta showed no interest in my desire to create you at first, but she did ask the right questions as I worked on my formulas. I told her about everything, thinking she was just curious. When she first took over the ship, I thought she only wanted the ship's technology, but she learned quickly she couldn't control the ship alone. She locked us out of the bridge only to have to relinquish control when the ship refused any of her commands. Only an ancient can work the ship and once we realized we couldn't trust her everyone refused to help her."

"Then how did she regain control?"

"Reasta is very resourceful. We had isolated her in her room, but I didn't think allowing her access to the computer system would cause any harm. I went off ship to investigate a planet and she found a way to get out of her room and lock my crew in those pods. I never taught her to read ancient, but she must have studied while we had her locked in her room because she was able to override the system to take total control of the ship. She had a crew and technicians standing by to bypass whatever she couldn't use. She is almost as brilliant as you are, Heather."

"I don't understand. You're an ancient, why didn't you just go back on the ship? Wouldn't it obey your command over hers?" Storm found his explanation sketchy.

"Don't you think I tried that?" His voice held such sadness. "Once she got me off the ship, she was able to keep me from gaining access. Any command I tried to give it wouldn't work. I don't know how."

"So now we're back to me." Heather had already figured out most of this information, Bert never told her it was Ialog's ship, but it at least confirmed what they had been guessing.

"All my information was on that ship. Reasta had to have read through my files while we had her isolated and found the details of your DNA. She was quite complacent when we first incarcerated her. We explained that we would take her back to her planet after she tried to take the ship the first time. It wasn't until she started accessing files that she plotted to take the ship again."

"And all that is in my files?"

"I will give you access to that information as well."

Heather nodded. "Alright. Let's talk about Reasta some more. If she can read ancient, then why did she ignore so many sections of your ship? If she has had it that long, I would think she would have found a way to access more of it."

"You have been on the ship?"

"Unfortunately, yes." Heather wasn't sure what she should tell him. "She has rigged most of the ship she is using."

"Then any ancient can take command of the ship, including you."

"How?" Heather had tried when S.C. wasn't around her but hadn't been successful.

"You need to get into the command center, the true command center, and touch the main console. Then in ancient, you give it my password then a new one for you." Ialog spoke quietly. "You will have to disconnect her over-rides before you have total control."

"And your password?"

"Perfection."

"Is there a way to get on the ship undetected?" asked Storm.

"No, or I would have been able to do it myself. The only thing I was able to do was access the ship's computer so I downloaded what I could of my research to the ancient computer on Vespia. That was when my fellow ancients put me in stasis the first time. They didn't understand what I was trying to do."

"You never told them the truth. They thought you wanted to build a perfect race. One that would replace all of them."

"I also led Reasta right to them. She now knew where

258

our home was. She started hunting them and they had no idea why. I wanted to create a powerful upgrade for my people, but I also created a killer."

"Upgrade?" Heather didn't like the sound of that. Now she sounded like some sort of computer program.

"You are ancient. Your perfect DNA could reverse the tragedy plaguing my people. That's why I kept running different computations. I needed to be sure." He sighed. "I didn't listen to enough of the visions to know who you were destined to mate with, but at that time it didn't matter. All I worried about was that your children had the same DNA. As your DNA enters our gene pool it would repair the damage we did to ourselves and make us stronger."

"And she wants it for an entirely different reason."

"No wonder why she wanted to get you pregnant so quickly," commented Storm. "The sooner you had the child she wanted the sooner she could use their blood to keep her alive."

The whole idea made her cold.

"When the elders opened my pod, I knew I had to continue my work. I found a message from Reasta on the main computer. She had found my research and was on her way to Vespia. For you. She threatened to attack if I didn't give her you."

"But you had been stopped in creating me." Heather started to pace. "And you felt my creation would keep her from attacking? Since when has giving in ever stopped a megalomaniac."

"Bert's vision showed you as a savior for the races. That meant Reasta would be stopped. His visions hinted that you would be the one to stop her. I had to make sure that happened. I just never expected my own people to misunderstand why I had to create you. I couldn't tell them about

Reasta or how she bested me. That was my mistake. One I needed to correct."

"How was she your mistake?"

He sighed. "I trusted her. I found her people interesting, even though I knew they were the type that would conquer instead of building a treaty. I didn't understand how deep that desire to conquer went into their DNA. Up until I ran into her race all other races found the desire for knowledge dominated the need to conquer. Most learned that knowledge kills fear and fear is what drives war."

"And that makes you feel responsible?" Storm didn't believe him.

"I didn't believe she could be that bad. I didn't believe the visions until it was too late." He sighed again. "I wish I had listened. My pride got in the way."

"Does she have any weaknesses?" growled Storm.

"Does it really matter?"

"It might help us figure out a way to stop her."

"You stopped me each time. You should have no problem stopping her. She thinks the same way I do. If I had paid attention and not been so focused on creating your mate, Storm, I would have seen the pattern and stopped her." He took a breath. "My computer has all the data you need, your file, and all the communiqués I had with Reasta. My theories might seem child-like now that you know the truth of what happened, but I couldn't believe I had made such a massive mistake."

"And where is that computer?" asked Heather.

"The ancients took control of it when they locked me away in the stasis field. I had the data on a chip that I used on Vespia, but they have that information as well. I don't know where they hid it, or I wouldn't have had to recreate everything when I woke up from stasis."

Heather smiled. Hopefully, Bert would know what he

was talking about. "Thank you. I want you to relax now. You are a good man, Al. Well liked in your society. You work hard and help all who need it. When I walk out of this room you will feel very tired and fall asleep. When you wake up you will be back in your house, in your bed and you will not remember any of this. The only thing you will know is that you had a wonderful dream where you were the hero."

———

Heather sat next to Storm after Skye had taken Ialog back where he belonged. She felt totally drained and wanted to rest but knew they had to find the data. "Bert, have you seen any of these files he was talking about?"

"When we locked him in stasis we went through and purged his system. There were a few files that I believe were kept, but most of it was wiped. I dismantled his computer after that and used part of it to create the system under the elder's hall."

"And somehow he knew that. He tried to access data when I first ran into him. Cim?"

"Yes, Heather?" The android stepped up to her when he was addressed.

"What do you have in your system?"

"Searching."

"There are several files created by Ialog but only one hasn't been wiped. That file doesn't have what you are looking for. I will need time to recreate the other files."

"Do it," said Storm. "In the meantime, Heather should rest. Controlling Ialog the way she did drained her."

"I'm fine, my heart."

"Then explain that little crease on your forehead." His fingers brushed against it. "That only appears when you haven't meditated in a while and your mind is feeling overloaded."

"You worry too much."

"I know you better than you know yourself." He offered her his hand and urged her to her feet.

"Rest, Heather. Cim will let you know when he has anything."

She nodded.

Storm steered her back to their room. His hands on her gown, opening the seals before the door had a chance to close. He sure wanted her out of her clothes fast.

"Are you alright?"

"Yes." He pressed his lips against her throat as he backed her against the wall. "I can't seem to help myself."

His hands were everywhere, heightening her desire for him, but he still managed to remove his clothes before he drove into her. A sigh escaped him when he felt her heat surround him. "So much better."

He shook as her muscles clamped down on him. Slipping one hand between them he worked his fingers into her folds, caressing her, sending a warmth racing through her blood. Storm started to move, setting a quick pace that took her breath away. Over and over he slid in and out, while his fingers worked their magic, overpowering her with his need. His mouth worked on the delicate tissue of her mark, making her lose control.

She met him thrust of thrust, wanting more. Her body quaked when one stroke hit a sensitive area. A moan escaped her. "My heart."

"It feels so good. You feel so good." He quickened the pace and groaned himself. "I don't know what caused this."

"Oh!" She closed her eyes as excitement filled her. She could feel the beginning of her orgasm start to unfurl. "I'm not complaining."

He pounded into her, inching her closer and closer to her release. Sex was always wonderful, but she loved it when he lost control. It gave her power to know she could still drive him to this.

Her body clenched around him, tightening as her release exploded around her. She dropped her head against his shoulder as he reached his climax, her body so relaxed she felt like she had no bones. Storm disengaged from her and carried her to the bed.

"You never cease to amaze me." He brushed a few strands of hair out of her face once he had laid her on the bed and joined her.

"You really became overpowered. I can't say I've seen that happen before."

"You know what I find interesting is that you didn't have one of your orgasmic episodes. I know you taxed your mind to keep him from regaining total control yet answer your questions." He pressed a kiss to her mark. "You think using my mind to help you maintain control also allowed you to dump your need into me?"

"You think that came from me expanding my mind? But instead of it affecting me it affected you?" Her fingers traced the defined planes of the muscles on his chest. "I didn't know I could do that."

"Something new to watch for." He pressed a kiss against her collarbone. His hand slid up her right thigh then over her hip. "You want to try again to see if it worked?"

"I don't think I need to." Her hand slid down to his already hardened member. "You don't seem to be having any trouble responding to being with me. I know you. You'll want to say that it is because of your desire for me, that it's part of your natural libido."

"We'll have to see how many times we're intimate to see if my libido has been enhanced by your powerful mind."

———

"I have the file rebuilt. There are a few sections that are still blank, but you should be able to get the information you need from what I have recreated." Cim pulled up the data on the computer everyone sat in front of.

"Show us." Bert watched with everyone else as the files loaded and data filled the screen.

Ialog had kept a journal of his time with Reasta's people. Most of it was mundane information.

"Cim, can you narrow down the information to what we're looking for?" Heather asked.

"What are we looking for?" asked Bert.

"Weaknesses in the race, in Reasta. How did she take the ship from Ialog? The data on me that she got her grand plan from." Heather looked at him. "Maybe why she hasn't tried to access any part of the ship she doesn't control. We also need an up-to-date set of schematics on the ship. We need to find a way to rescue the people on the ship and stop her from taking over the planet."

"I can only extrapolate from what you and Pumpkin saw while you were on the ship, Heather. You saw what she had converted. I can also mark areas of the ship she might have tried to access because of what having control of those rooms would do for her, but I won't have up-to-date schematics if that is what you need."

"Thank you," said Heather. "Now what about what Ialog talked about? Do you know what file he spoke about?"

"There was a file he created that had all your information on it, but the file is now gone."

"How?"

"I was dormant for thousands of years. The file was in

my system when I was shut down. I don't know what happened to it after that."

"You also want to know what is in that file, don't you?" asked Storm.

"Yes." Heather folded her hands and placed them in her lap. Storm wrapped an arm around her shoulders. She looked up at him with a smile. "Ialog made it sound like I'm some sort of god and I want to know why."

"The file I recreated is a very large file and has some of that data." Cim loaded the data on the screen. "I'm not sure what it is you want to look at."

"Let's start with the gene she wants so badly. How can she pull it from someone's body and insert it into hers?"

"Ialog's research is focused on one chemical, based on what he did tell you this should be the one Reasta is after. The ancient DNA that affects aging is a very complicated formula. The only way to remove it is to remove the blood and separate the chemical manually."

"Then she has to kill in order to get it?"

"Yes."

"Once the chemical is removed. It needs to be processed." Cim brought up a section of the file to show the strand of DNA he was talking about. "The extraction takes several weeks, but one ancient would have enough for several injections."

"Vespian blood has some ancient in it. How different is it from a pure ancient?"

"This is your mate and your brother's blood. That particular gene is diluted."

"But it's there. And she can steal it from their blood as well."

"Yes, but it would take the blood of ten Vespians to make the same amount that is in one ounce in one ancient."

"She'd wipe out the whole race."

"Only if she wins."

———

Storm landed the ship Bert lent them inside the main compound of their penal colony. Knowing that Reasta could come here and try to use their blood had Heather and Storm racing to the planet. They needed their people right now, all their people. There was no way she would use any Vespian against them.

The ship landed in the large ground opening near the main building. Storm chose this ship out of the three Bert had because it was large enough to hold every person there. It took only seconds before alarms went off, alerting the convicts and well as security that there was an intruder. Good. He wanted everyone's attention. Heather stepped out of the ship after him. She was going to deliver the message they all needed to hear. He felt they would under-stand the seriousness of their situation if she told them. He was the next leader, and they would follow him because he told them to. They would question his mate and he knew those questions would make them understand what they were facing. That message would be carried to the rest of Vespia without Reasta's knowledge.

Guards ran into the area then skidded to a stop when they saw him standing there. He knew they didn't know what to think.

"What have you heard?"

"That you had been killed."

"The rumors of my demise are false, as you can see, but you seeing me is top secret." Storm looked around at the people gathering. "It will be explained once we speak to everyone."

One of the guards contacted the staff in the building.

Storm looked at the prisoners. "I need all your people as well. We're going to war."

It didn't take long before there was a sea of people waiting.

He took Heather's hand and brought her forward. "My mate."

None of the people there had seen her before. They knew of her and had heard the rumors that she was the daughter of an elder and had been sent to Earth to keep her safe, but none had ever seen any of the newsfeeds about her or her life with Storm.

Heather looked out at all the faces in front of her. "Vespia has a new enemy. She tried to take my mate from me and has captured the elder council. Each of you is here because your aggression wasn't allowed during peacetime. But now we're at war and need your particular skill sets. I know each of you can say no because Vespian society turned its back on you, but I was hoping the Vespian loyalty I have seen time and time again is still stronger than any anger you might have toward the council. We need you to help defeat this threat to our way of life."

"We've heard the rumors, but how do we know you care about Vespia. You were raised on Earth."

"I might have been raised on Earth, but my heart is Vespian." She looked at the man questioning her. "That makes me one."

"And what about your Earth?"

"Where is home to you?"

"Here."

"Why not Vespia? Wasn't that where you were born and raised?"

"This is home now."

Heather smiled as she crossed her arms over her chest. "So you understand."

"I do." He smiled back. "So why should we fight for you?"

"You're not fighting for me. You're fighting for your parents, your brothers and sisters, your children." She looked at the faces watching her. Storm might have thought it would be best if she spoke to them and not him, but she didn't agree. They didn't see her as a Vespian. She turned to him, uncertain. "Storm."

"Tell them, my heart."

"Are you sure?" The council had released some information about her family ties but not her true heritage, yet Storm wanted her to tell them the truth. She didn't understand why. "I don't see how this is important."

"They need to know why she is here and the danger we are in. But we can't just broadcast this information. Not yet, not until we're ready. You tell them and discreetly, throughout our people, they will learn the truth."

"We could..." Heather didn't finish. She could never ask Storm to leave Vespia. He was the next ruler. They needed him. "I'll leave. She'll follow me and leave all of you alone."

"That is not an option, my heart. She will never leave you alone and I don't want to live my life without you." He pressed his hand against her heart.

Although they spoke to each other enough of their conversation was overheard by those close enough to ask questions. "Who is this 'she'?"

Heather turned to face the one asking questions. "Reasta. I don't know what you have seen here. She wants to destroy Vespia."

"Why?"

"Because of me." She took a deep breath. "She has learned how to take our blood and extend her life. She believes I will have a child that will be able to reproduce this gene naturally. If she can get that child, she believes she could live forever."

"You keep saying she believes, why?"

"We don't have enough information on how she would be able to do this. She is the reason there are no more ancients among us. She has used their blood to extend her life. If she can do that to them, what could she do to us? I fear that she won't stop with a child of ancient blood. Each of us has ancient blood in us."

"A child of ancient blood?"

Heather looked at Storm. It was time to tell them the truth of her heritage. "I thought I was human until I came here, but I have learned that I'm genetically engineered. I have more ancient blood in me."

"You're an ancient?"

"A genetically engineered one." She felt Storm wrap an arm around her, his silent support giving her what she needed so badly right now. How many times in her life had her uniqueness alienated her?

"And you think that makes you special?"

Heather laughed. "No."

"You think once she's done with you, she'll take our blood too?"

She nodded. "That is what I fear. She has been hunting ancients for years. If she can't get the child she wants from me all of Vespia would be her next target."

"And Storm? I would think she would want him to help you get pregnant. Why did she try to kill him?"

"He wasn't part of her picture which is why she thought she could remove him. She has tried this before. While I was in her care I learned she was using a machine to travel back in time to try to make sure the future she wanted happened. From what I learned she only had so much power to run her machine and this timeline was her last shot. Stopping Storm's death should allow the timeline to continue on now, I hope, but until we're sure we must remain in hiding." She took Storm's hand for support. "She will come here the moment she knows Storm is alive to press you into her military, thinking you hate Vespia for putting you here. I'm hoping you still love your planet since even though a lot of you could have gone home a while ago you decided to stay here instead."

"What are you proposing?"

"You come with us now, before she can get to you."

"All of us?"

"Almost."

"You mean Lewmard." The man talking laughed. "You sure that is wise? We have taught him to respect the Vespian Way."

"His hatred for me would keep him underfoot while we're dealing with Reasta. Let her have him. He can annoy her instead."

"And if she doesn't come here because she figures out you had already been here?"

"Then I will leave that to you, but you will be responsible for him," said Heather.

———

Heather stood in front of the screen, clinching her skirt as she waited for the connection. Reasta appeared on the surface, shock on her face for a second before she smiled and hid any thought she might have expressed. "Heather. Good to see you are well."

"Much better now that I'm away from you." She smiled, the one she learned while in Earth's security. Not real, not for her.

"And why have you contacted me? Decided to come back?" She returned the smile.

"No. That will never happen. I'm here to ask you to leave our planet in peace. If you do not, you will have war."

"Heather, you know as well as I do that you can't fight a war without your leader. Who will these Vespians follow? You?"

"Fridon has been a wonderful leader since you took Storm away from us." Heather sat back, her smile turning cat-like.

"But he's not from the royal family, is he? The people might think that he is trying to take over the planet."

"True, if he didn't have family backup."

"I have the elder council."

"You might have, but the Vespian people know this now. I'm transmitting this conversation to the entire planet, so they now know you're trying to take control of the planet, not help us." She watched as Reasta gave orders to cut her feed.

"Sorry, that won't work. There is a new shield protecting our airwaves. So you can't stop me from revealing what you are. Or what you want."

"Very smart, Heather, but it won't help you."

"Actually, it will. The people of Vespia need to know you're here to conquer. That you have the elders captured and the people we're seeing are nothing but clones. Just like the clone you made of my mate."

"They won't follow you. You're an outsider."

"You might think I am, but there are a lot of people here who would disagree with you." Heather leaned forward and widened the camera so Storm, who had been standing behind her, unseen the whole time, was now visible. "Including my mate. You've lost before you have begun, Reasta. I know you can't go back and try to change the

271

timeline again. We're going to fight for our planet and our people."

Reasta's face lost the fake smile. "How? I made sure he was gone! His death meant my success."

The outburst let Heather know she hit a nerve. Good. That was her goal. "Now are you going to leave before we have to show you what it is like to go to war with Vespia? We don't lose."

"You might have won this battle, Heather, but I will win in the end. I will have my army from you no matter what I have to do to get it."

"So be it." Heather killed the feed. Pressing her hand against her rapidly beating heart, she stood and turned to look at Storm. "Are you sure that was wise?"

"Yes, my heart. Did you see the fear in her eyes when she saw me? We know she can't go back and change the timeline again. Now she's going to have to scramble to try to make her plan work." He wrapped his arms around her in support. "We will defeat her."

———

Reasta turned from the screen. "How? How did this happen?"

People all around cowered in her presence. Only one was brave enough to answer her. "It shouldn't have happened. Perhaps she has a clone of her own, trying to trick you."

"You better run your data again. Now!"

———

Heather stood on the observation deck of Bert's ship,

wondering about the future. How were they going to defeat this woman? She wished she had the answer.

Storm came up behind her and wrapped his arms around her. "Why so deep in thought?"

"I brought war to your planet."

"Our planet, my heart and this is not your fault."

"I know." The words slipped out, but she knew better. Deep down inside she was blaming herself. She couldn't help but think if she had left, the people and the planet would be safe. Reasta wasn't going to stop until she either recaptured her or destroyed the planet in the process.

"I spent several years on your planet when I lost my memory and learned that humans tend to question themselves. Mike felt like he didn't do enough to save his wife from cancer even though there was nothing he could do. That is what you are feeling right now."

"I feel I have caused so much harm to your people since we met. Fridon was almost killed. Ialog keeps taking me and you keep bringing me back, and now we have a woman bent on war all because of me."

"So you think if we hadn't mated this would have never happened?"

Yes. No. I don't know." She rested her head against his chest. "Why should your people fight for me? They don't even know me."

"That's not true. You have been on the council for several years now. Think about how many lives you have changed being there. Mother told me that you are now the one who most people request to hear their complaints because of the way you make both sides accountable. Without even knowing it you have become the head of the council."

"I have not."

"My heart, you have. You might not be sitting in my

mother's chair yet or lead the meetings, but your opinion is what everyone looks to." He rubbed her back when she stiffened in his arms. "This is a good thing. Mother and the council love you and trust you to carry on when it is time for them to step down. Each elder must find their own replacement and Mother is proud to have chosen you. She knows when the time comes it will be an easy transition."

"I'm still an outsider."

"You are part of this world, whether you want to face it or not. Our people don't see you as an outsider anymore, no matter what you think. You heard the prisoners, even they had heard the rumor about you being born here and sent away for your protection. They want you here and will do everything to protect you."

"I don't want people to die for me."

"When you worked for Earth Security did you think about the lives of other members of security? How you might have to put your life on the line to protect them?"

"That was my job. I always knew that every mission I went on could have been my last."

"Our people feel the same way. They will do every-thing in their power to protect you. Not because you're my mate but because they see you as an important a member of this society and losing you would be a great loss." He could tell by her face she didn't believe him. Her human training was hard for her to step away from at times. Storm had hoped she would have seen how their people felt about her when she spoke to the colony. They had questioned her loyalty and she had shown them that she cared, but it didn't prove to her that she was part of his world now.

"Come with me."

She took his hand and they walked to the main computer room where they were converting it for the war they knew was coming. "How many have volunteered for this so far?"

Fridon tapped a few items on his screen so he could pull up the recruitment information for Storm. "More than half the population, sir. And your message hasn't reached the entire planet yet. Some of the more remote areas have yet to check in."

"More than half the planet in the few minutes since we went live? Good. Was it the overall reason for joining?"

"To protect what is ours."

Storm turned to look at Heather. She didn't say anything, but he could tell by the set of her jaw that she still didn't believe people saw her as a member of their society. "Any specifics on my mate being mentioned as the reason?"

"Yes, sir." He brought up several interviews and played the feed. Each of them said pretty much the same thing. They were angry that this woman wanted to take Heather from them, and they were willing to put their life on the line for her. There were a few who had met her or had her judge on one of their complaints and they found her honest and caring. They loved her.

He watched her as she heard the comments. Watched as her eyes filled with tears as she heard how they felt about her. "Soft heart."

She laughed then. "You don't fight fair."

"You wanted to leave to take the danger away. Do you realize what would happen if you did that?"

She shook her head.

"We'd bring the fight to Reasta. She might follow you to the ends of the universe and we would be there to stop her."

Heather wrapped her arms around Storm. "I am humbled by everyone's loyalty."

"Why do you think you don't deserve it?"

"It's going to sound silly."

"My heart, nothing you say is silly. You rarely talk about your past. Why?"

"I had no parents growing up. No one stepped forward to adopt me. I was nothing to my planet, not worthy of a family, not worthy of love." She dashed the tears spilling from her eyes. "Then I come here hoping to fit in. I never thought anyone would be willing to die for me and I wasn't willing to force them to."

"And now?"

"I want to fight. For our future and our world's future."

The End

Don't miss out on your next favorite book!

———

THANK YOU FOR READING

———

Did you enjoy this book?

ABOUT THE AUTHOR

Writing for Barbara Donlon Bradley started innocently enough, like most she kept diaries, journals, and wrote an occasional letter but she also had a vivid imagination and wrote scenes and short stories adding characters to her favorite shows and comic books.

As time went on, she found the passion for writing to be a strong drive for her. Humor is also very strong in her life. No matter how hard she tries to write something deep and dark, it will never happen. That humor bleeds into her writing. Since she can't beat it, she has learned to use it to her advantage.

Now she lives in Tidewater Virginia with a cat who thinks he owns everything, her husband and daughter.

www.barbaradonlonbradley.com

ALSO BY BARBARA DONLON BRADLEY

Novels
Love Is…

A Portrait in Time

Love on the Run

Love's Quest Series
A Quest For Love

Magical Quest

Desire Series
Dominated by Desire

Passionate Desire

Animal Desire

Unwanted Desire

Hesitant Desire

Forgotten Desire

Stolen Desire

www.ingramcontent.com/pod-product-compliance
Lightning Source LLC
Chambersburg PA
CBHW020606260626
47157CB00003B/891